his
REVERIE

his REVERIE

Monica Murphy

everafter ROMANCE

Prologue

The future

I'm not good enough for her.
And I know it.
But it doesn't seem to matter to her.
So it doesn't matter to me.
The only thing that matters *is* her.
She is my everything.
My heart.
My soul.
They found out who I am.
What happened to me.
Where I've been.
Even though they don't know the truth.
They tell me we can't be together.
They try their best to keep us apart.
But when she's not by my side.
It's like a piece of me is missing.
I'm numb until I see her face.
Catch her smile.
Kiss her lips.
Hold her in my arms.
I come alive.
She loves me.
I love her.

No one can keep us apart.
We won't let them.
I sometimes wonder if she's a dream.
A figment of my imagination.
But then I touch her.
Feel her skin against mine.
Her lips on mine.
Her tongue on my...
You know.
And I realize that this dream.
Is my reality.
My Reverie.

Chapter
ONE

The past

I'M a new man. Reborn on this late spring morning as I walk out of the county jail, breathing deep the fresh, warm air.

When had I last inhaled air that wasn't tainted by the scent of sweat, illegal cigarettes and that always-present hint of desperation? Eleven long, agonizing months ago, that's when.

Finally I'm out. Finally a judge listened to me and my county appointed lawyer and realized the evidence against me couldn't stand. Yes, I'm the dude in the jailhouse yard proclaiming to anyone who'd listen that I was innocent. They all say that but I'm telling the truth.

I didn't do it. I never even saw that guy that night. I was seventeen and dumb and my friend was dumber and the next thing I know, he's making statements against me, claiming I murdered someone and he helped me.

Murdered.

"Nick!"

I turn at the sound of Mom's voice and see her standing in the public parking lot across the street, her hands clasped together as she beams at me. I can see that familiar smile even with the distance between us and I instantly feel young again. Ten years old and insecure and desperately needing my mama's love. Tears prick the corners of my eyes and I fight them off, blinking like I got something in my eye. I will not fucking cry.

Spending nearly a year in jail forces you to man up. I have seen things I can't unsee. Had things happen to me that I can't…

Nope. Won't go there.

Pasting a smile on my face, I jog along the crosswalk toward Mom. She's leaning against her faded gold 2000 Camry, wearing beat up jeans and a bright green T-shirt, looking so familiar, so much like the mom I know and love and missed so damn much that the tears threaten again.

I pull her to me the second I stop in front of her, her face smashed against my chest as she quietly falls apart, her shoulders shaking with her silent sobs as she holds me tight. But these aren't sad tears. I can tell the difference, since I've seen her cry enough to last me a lifetime.

"You look so good Nicky," she says, her voice muffled, her breath hot against my shirt. "It feels so good to hug my baby again."

I'm all she has. We're all each other has ever had. That I was taken away from her hurts me still. She put on a brave face every time she visited me. Told me everything was fine, she was fine, she had enough money, she missed me but hey, she had to get used to me leaving sometime. We just didn't plan on it happening like this though, did we?

Ha, ha funny joke. Easy to say when she's not the one behind bars but I don't hold that against her. She didn't know how to cope with her only child in jail. She did the best she could.

"Mom." I grab hold of her skinny arms and pull her away from me so I can look at her. Really look at her. "Are you okay?"

The smile hasn't left her face, though her cheeks are beet red and tears are streaming down them. "I'm wonderful now that you're standing here in front of me."

My stomach growls so loud she hears it and bursts out laughing. "Some things don't change, do they Nicky? Always led by your gut. Come on, let's get you fed."

We get into the Camry, the lingering scent of her familiar perfume hitting me the minute I shut the door. The same crystal dangles from her rearview mirror, and when she cranks the engine, her favorite radio station blasts out of the tinny speakers. I feel at home. Comforted by the normalcy of the situation compared to my completely abnormal existence this last year. It feels good.

You never realize how much you miss normal until it's gone.

"Where we going?" I ask as she turns onto the main drag of our small coastal town. I grew up here. She grew up here too and when Dad told her he hated this Godforsaken town (direct quote) and he wanted the hell out, she told him he could go on ahead and leave then. Since she didn't fight him, he did, moving up to Washington, where I visited him for one Thanksgiving, one spring break and one month of summer before he got into a motorcycle accident and died that following fall.

I was ten and wailed like a wounded beast when Mom broke the news to me. She explained, gentle and firm, that I was the man in the family now. Not only the man of the house, which she declared me to be after Dad left, but the man of the entire *family*. Our family of two.

This meant I not only took care of me, but I needed to take care of her. Talk about pressure. So we've never left, never had an inclination to. She has a decent job. And she had to stick around when I got tossed into jail. Oh, she wanted to make bail for me but we had nothing. No collateral.

"You'll find out where I'm taking you soon enough," she says with that smug smile she wears when she's got something good up her sleeve. I lean back in my chair and breathe deep, taking in the perfume, the slightly musty smell that lingers because of the ocean, the faint scent of cigarettes. She quit smoking a couple of years ago after I harassed her one too many times. I already lost one parent. Really couldn't afford to let that happen again.

She takes me to my favorite breakfast place and I utter a mock "thank the lord Jesus" under my breath as she parks the car. I order the biggest meal they've got on the menu, and when they set the plate in front of me I dive in, not even bothering to act polite. I flat out devour the food like my mouth is a vacuum. Like I'm eating the best meal I've ever had in my life.

Which isn't too far from the truth, considering what I've been living on.

"Your hair is long," Mom says as she watches me, amusement lighting her eyes that are the same color as mine, dark, dark blue.

I flick my head, the hair that falls over my forehead flipping to the side. "Yeah. Didn't bother much with haircuts in there."

She hadn't come to see me much the last couple months I was locked up. She was at her job most of the time and needed the money since I was not there to help. She's a LVN nurse and works at a senior care center, AKA a rest home. She loves it, tells me she finds it rewarding. To me it's like she's always losing someone there. That's where the old folks go to die. I don't know how she can stand it. Liking someone, caring for someone, then losing them.

Witnessing her cry over one of her patient's death, combined with how I lost Dad...I don't let myself get close to anyone. It's easier that way. Less chance to get hurt.

I've been hurt enough. By my best friend, who I still refuse to talk to and will until the day I die if I can help it. By my ex-girlfriend, who told me she loved me and banged my best friend all in the same day. By the system that failed me.

The only person who's ever been there for me with unconditional love is sitting across the table, her eyes going wider every time I shovel more food in my mouth.

I can't help it. I'm fucking starving. Jail food is shit.

"You act like you haven't ate for days," she says, wonder in her voice.

Pausing in my shoveling act, I stare at her for a moment before grabbing the glass of ice-cold chocolate milk in front of me. "Feels like I haven't," I say just before I chug half the glass down.

The cold liquid hits my gut and makes me grimace. I ate way too fast and I need to slow down before I puke. Leaning back against the booth seat, I watch Mom as she eats a far more civilized meal, but she doesn't bother putting the fork in her mouth. Just pushes her food around with her silverware, streaking syrup from her French toast all over the plate.

She's barely touched it.

"Mom." She glances up, guilt and worry written all over her face and I know something's wrong. Alarm races through me, buzzing through my veins and I try to stuff it down. "Why aren't you eating?"

"I don't have much of an appetite lately." She shrugs, her eyes skittering away from mine.

As if she's guilty of something.

My gaze roams over her, noticing for the first time the gauntness in her cheeks, the pale color of her skin. Her hair is long and curly, dyed blonde to hide all the gray, she told me that long ago. She has it pulled into a ponytail and it looks...

Thin.

She looks thin. Tired.

Too tired.

"You've been working too much," I state, not bothering to ask if that's the case. I know it's the truth.

"Not so much lately." She pushes her plate away and rests her arms on the edge of the table. "I didn't want to do this now, not with you just being released, but I can't hide it forever…I need to talk to you, Nicky."

Fear slithers down my spine like the coldest, deadliest snake. This isn't good. It can't be good. "What's up?" I try for nonchalant. Casual. But I'm just deluding myself.

I can feel the bad news she's about to deliver, creeping over me like the thick, damp fog that can settle in around here, even in the summer. Especially the summer. What she has to say is going to devastate me. I know it.

"Honey. Nicky. I…" She pauses and the tears form again, welling up in her eyes and I shake my head, push my own plate away with such force it bumps into my glass of chocolate milk and it spills all over my remaining breakfast. Mom's eyes widen in horror. "Call the waitress," she urges. "We need to get this cleaned up."

"Forget it." I shake my head, not giving a shit if the rest of my bacon is swimming in chocolate. "Tell me what's wrong."

"But your food…"

"Fucking tell me what's wrong!" I slam my hand on the table, and the plates, glasses and silverware rattle enough to cause the couple sitting across from us to turn and stare. I glare at them back. My meanest, hardest stare until they finally look away.

Guess I learned something useful when I was locked up.

"I have cancer," she says, the words rushing out of her, like she said one word instead of three. *Ihavecancer.*

I blink once. Twice. The waitress approaches our table with white rags clutched in each hand but I wave her away. She doesn't hesitate, scurrying away from our table like her shoes are on fire. "Cancer?" The word comes out a croak, my throat sandpaper dry.

Mom nods, her expression resolute. "Terminal, Nicky. I'm…I'm filled with tumors. They're all too risky to remove."

"What?" I blink again. Terminal. Tumors. Too risky. It's all a jumble and makes no sense. "Can't you do some sort of treatment? Chemo or whatever?" Isn't that normal? How bad can it be? Did this happen because she smoked? God, she should've stopped sooner. Here I am, thinking all about myself, and Mom is sitting there with fucking cancer.

"No. It's no use. The cancer has spread into my organs and my lymph nodes. The doctors are afraid it's too late. So I've decided whatever happens, I'm going to live. And when I die, I want to do it on my terms." She smiles, the sight of it like an arrow to my already breaking heart. "And I *am* dying. I-I don't know how much longer I might have."

I say nothing, just sit there as my brain tries to compute what she's saying, the spilled chocolate milk still swimming in my plate, the food settling in my gut like a hard, ugly reminder.

Nothing in this world is perfect. I learned that long ago. But this? This was just…wrong.

Scary.

"We'll make the best of it," I vow to her, my voice quiet, my thoughts scattered all over the place. "However long you have is going to be the best time of your life. I promise."

She reaches across the table and grabs my hand, giving it a squeeze. "Such a good boy, Nicky. You always try and take care of me."

Not good enough. Not while I've been in jail for almost a year.

"I'm gonna take care of you. Now and forever." I pull her hand to my mouth and give her knuckles a kiss. "I figure you have at least a few years right?"

She doesn't answer.

Mom had less than two months. I got out of jail April 26th. She died June 6th. It was like once she told me she had cancer, her body shut down methodically. One day after the next, she just broke down. Like the lights shutting off in a giant skyscraper, one floor at a time, until finally she was just…dark. Empty.

Gone.

Chapter
TWO

Believe: to have faith in.
June 23rd

From the moment I got out of jail, life has delivered me nothing but endless shit. Mom has cancer. I can't find a job. Mom dies. None of my old friends will talk to me. The only friend who wants to talk to me is the one who almost ruined my life so forget that fucker.

No matter how much it hurts, I have to forget him.

Finally though, it's looking up. Just when I thought I'd have to give up the apartment Mom and I lived in because I couldn't make rent, I get a job.

Working for a crazy man.

Yeah, he's not really crazy. He's actually pretty smart since he has all these people snowed. They believe every word he says, listening to him with rapt attention. They open up their wallets and give him a crap ton of money too. I guess I should admire the guy for being so convincing.

But it all feels fake. What he says. How he looks. The way he acts. The convict that still lingers in me recognizes a smooth liar when I see one and I've met plenty. Some might even say I'm one of them.

I'm not though. Not really.

The Reverend Harold Hale is my boss. He of the Flock of the Lambs cable network, the current most influential televangelist around. The guy is freaking famous and rich as…sin. Yeah, I said it. So sue me.

Actually I better watch what I think and say because I had to sign a huge privacy disclosure where I'm not allowed to breathe a word of what I see and hear while working for Reverend Hale or else he'll bring litigation against my ass so fast I won't even see it coming.

Why would he hire an ex-convict like me? I'm officially not a convict at all but we all know that's what people see when they look at me. When they hear my name. I have a reputation that was blasted all over the local media and it follows me everywhere I go in this town.

It will for the rest of my life. I'm innocent but I may as well have done it, what with the way people treat me. I need to escape. Get out of this place and never look back. But I have no money. That's why I need the job. I save up enough I can leave this town.

That's my plan. I'm determined to follow through.

Lucky for me, Reverend Hale is on a current crusade to save lost souls. That's what the guy who initially interviewed me said. When I protested that I'm not a lost soul, that I never committed the crime I'd been accused of, the dude just nodded and closed his eyes for a brief moment, like he was saying a prayer for me or something.

He probably was. Kinda tripped me out but I let it slide. I need the job. I need the income. I probably needed the prayers too.

I'm working at the Hales' summer home. Yeah, the guy is so rich he has multiple houses. And this house I'm working at is freaking amazing, there's no other word for it. First day on the job and I'm being trained by Michael, a cool dude that's worked for the Hales the last three summers. He's a little older than me, I'd figure around twenty or twenty-one, and a college student home for the summer.

According to Michael, we'll be cleaning up around the estate, doing mostly yard work, various odd jobs and setting up for the multiple parties and social events the family hosts throughout the summer.

And from what Michael's told me, they party a lot.

Weird.

"It's all about the social connections for the Hales," Michael explains as we're walking out toward the very edge of the property. He's showing me everything he can today before we have to go back to the pool area and clean it up for the dinner event they're having tonight.

You know, just forty of their closest friends are coming over.

I don't even have *four* friends, but whatever.

"Social connections?" I ask because I pretend I care.

"Sure. The more people he knows and makes direct connections with, the more money he can get out of their pockets." Michael rolls his eyes. I like this guy. He's tall with bright red hair and bright blue eyes, his face covered with freckles. "They have these sort of get-togethers here all the time."

We're out walking along the fence line, a thick grove of pine trees on the other side and I can smell the salt of the ocean in the air mingle with the forest scent. The house isn't that far from the Pacific but it's not what I would call beachfront. Still a badass house though. "This place is awesome. I can see why they'd want to show it off."

"Yeah well, I think it's kinda stupid if you ask me. Why use this place to brag about how much money they're making? Won't their donators wonder if it's their money financing the parties and the out-of-control house?" Valid point. One I didn't consider, but I'm too dazzled by the wealth I'm seeing. "Okay, see that?" Michael points toward a building not too far from where we stand. He's already moving on to the next subject. I notice he does that a lot. "Over there are the horse stalls. We'll need to clean 'em up, not too often though, thank God."

Gross. "You gotta be kidding me."

"Wish I was, bro. They have stable staff but not full time. And the kids love riding horses, especially Hale's daughter."

Huh. Didn't know Hale had kids, not that I know anything about this guy beyond what I've learned since they hired me. Probably spoiled, demanding brats who get whatever they want whenever they want it.

Lucky little bastards.

Michael takes me on a quick tour around the stables, which has four horses bordered inside.

He showed me what needs to be done and where the cleaning supplies were. Then the smug jerk left me there with the instructions I needed to clean the place from top to bottom.

"As the new guy, this is your job until you can prove to me you know what you're doing. Consider it a sort of initiation." Michael grinned at me then strode off whistling like he hadn't a care in the world.

Muttering a few curses under my breath, I gather the supplies I need. It stank like hell and was damn hot in the mostly enclosed structure so I went to work, wanting to get it over with. Within ten minutes of hard-ass manual labor, I'm stripping off my shirt since I'm sweating like crazy. I leave it hanging over one of the stall's doors then start digging into the pile of horseshit at the farthest corner of the stall.

What a freaking disgusting job. Not that I can't hack it but man. The things I'd do for some cash in my pocket. I'm that desperate, something I can admit to myself but not anyone else. Michael told me the stable cleaning would only be about once a week since we mainly had to do it on the weekends. He also mentioned this was the worst part of the job. Otherwise, he reassured me, it was easy street. Like working at a country club or something, as if I have any idea what that's like.

Country clubs are things I see on TV. I have no idea how that side of life really lives. I'm a broke joke, not a rich boy with money to waste. The building I'm in now is nicer than my apartment and this place houses the *horses*. I can't imagine what the main house is like. I know what it looks like from the outside and it's impressive. The house is huge, two stories and with giant windows. From what I can tell at least. Not that I've been inside or anything, but it looks pretty damn nice.

Almost too nice. I had no idea televangelists make so much money.

I work for a solid hour until the stables are practically gleaming they're so clean. Working this hard, concentrating on doing a good job so they won't fire me helps keep my mind off the heavy crap. The stuff that has been weighing on me since pretty much the moment I got out of jail.

I just want to forget, to lose myself in something mindless and push all the worry and the stress out of my head and my heart. I'm sick of it.

Pausing, I lean the shovel against the wall and glance around, one hand on my hip as I wipe at my damp-with-sweat forehead with the wrist of my other hand since I have gloves on. My throat feels like a desert, I'm so thirsty and the horses all watch me carefully, nodding their heads as if they like what I've done with the place.

Glad at least someone approves.

There's nothing to drink and I forgot to bring my bottle of water out here with me so I shed my work gloves and exit the stables, thankful when I catch sight of a faucet and hose right outside the doorway. I crank on the water and grab the hose, let it run for a while so all the hot water gets out before I bend over and start slurping the running water. It's cold and feels good going down my throat and I close my eyes, feeling like I'm six and drinking from the hose like I did when I was little and didn't want to bother going inside.

I can still hear Mom yelling at me not to put my lips on the hose. Just remembering her puts a catch in my throat, making it hard to swallow...

"Thirsty?"

I jump at the sound of a soft female voice, my hand jerking so the hose splashes me right in the face. Muttering a curse, I drop the hose and reach out blindly, wrenching the faucet off with one hand as I swipe at my eyes with the back of the other. I hear the girl laugh and I whirl around, fully prepared to find some bratty preteen Hale daughter mocking me.

But she's not a preteen. Not even close. More like around my age. She's tall and slender, her long blonde hair falling far past bared tan shoulders. She's wearing some sort of sundress or whatever you call it and she's pretty much covered since it hits just above her knees, though her arms are exposed since the dress is sleeveless. The sun catches her just right though, shining through the thin fabric of her skirt so I can see through it.

My gaze drops and all I can see is long, long legs through the shadowy fabric. Damn. Those sexy legs are endless. She clears her throat, like she knows exactly where I'm looking and what I'm thinking and I jerk my gaze up guiltily to meet hers, feeling like a jackass.

That's when I notice her eyes are blue. As blue as the sky above us, and she's so damn pretty, with delicate features and pink, pink lips, that I can't seem to form words.

"Who are you?" she asks curiously. Her voice washes over me, sweet and melodic and now it's my turn to clear my throat to get the lump out so I can freaking speak.

"Who are you?" I ask back like an idiot.

She smiles shyly and my entire body reacts, a bolt of electricity seeming to go through me. "I asked first."

"Are you Hale's daughter?" If she is, that sucks because holy hell she's hot but yeah.

She's completely untouchable if she's a Hale.

"What if I am?" She kicks at the ground with her sandaled foot, her cheeks coloring the faintest pink. Innocence radiates from her. She looks like a damn angel and seems a little uncomfortable with me.

Despite her seeming discomfort, I think she might be trying to flirt with me.

"Well, I'd make sure and be extra polite to you since I work for your dad." I go with the truth because I don't want any problems from this girl. I probably shouldn't even be alone with her. She could say anything, accuse me of something terrible and I'd have no defense. Her word against mine.

And her word would win every single time.

Another laugh escapes her and she slowly shakes her head. "I like your honesty."

I like everything about her so far but I keep my lips clamped shut. I've already said enough to make myself look like a total loser. "So I'm guessing you're definitely Hale's daughter?"

She nods. "I'm Rev."

Rev? What kind of name is that? "Like reverend?" That's the only logical conclusion. Though she looks my age so there's no way she could be a reverend or whatever right? I wasn't raised religious. I've never been to church. I believe in God but I've never read the bible.

Admitting anything like that would probably shock this preacher's daughter. Reverend's daughter, whatever.

She stops laughing and rolls her eyes. "Sorry. I can see why you'd think that because of my dad and stuff." She pauses and takes a step closer, her gaze dropping to my chest for a too-long-moment, her eyes going wide before they meet mine once more. I totally forgot I'm not wearing a shirt and I scratch between my pecs, self-conscious. This looks really bad. Like majorly bad.

I'll probably lose my job first day in if she runs and tells daddy the bad boy half-naked ex-con talked to her.

"My name is Reverie," she explains, confusing me further. What the hell kind of name is that?

"Reverie," I repeat. "Uh, that sounds unique."

"You're just being polite. It's weird, right? Not really a name for a person, you know?" She shrugs those slim, pretty shoulders again. Her skin is smooth and golden from the sun and I bet it's soft to the touch too. Like I'll ever get a chance to touch her.

Not.

"What does it mean?" When she frowns I continue. "Reverie."

"Oh! Daydreaming. Lost in thought." She smiles, a little more timidly now and that show of uncertainty fuels me.

Makes me feel a little braver. If she didn't want to talk to me she would've jammed by now, right? That's what I'm going with. "So why didn't they name you daydream?"

"Well, that would've been even weirder. Don't you think?" She tilts her head, studying me. "You never did tell me your name."

"Nick," I offer, flicking my chin at her like she's my homeboy or something stupid. God, what the hell is wrong with me?

"As in Nicholas?"

"Just Nick."

"As in a cut or a dent?" She's smiling again, her voice light. She's teasing me about my name like I teased her.

This girl is definitely flirting. And I'm flirting right back.

"I guess so, Daydream," I drawl, making her blush.

"I'd rather call you Nicholas," she says, taking yet another step toward me. I catch her scent, light and sweet and I inhale as discreetly as I can. Like I'm trying to imprint her smell on me.

"Only my mom called me that. And only when I was in trouble." Which was a lot of the time.

It hurts. How much I disappointed her. Right till the very end.

"Really? It's such a nice name." She pauses, sinks her teeth into her plump lower lip. I don't think she's wearing gloss or lipstick or anything so that deep, pink color is all natural. Damn. She's not even trying to be sexy but she just...is. "Nicholas."

I like the way it sounds when she says it. "Well, you're definitely not a Rev to me. So I think I'm gonna call you Daydream every time I see you." Which probably won't be often because come on. She's the owner's daughter, a rich girl who probably has a packed summer schedule and a hundred guys chasing after her and I'm the hired hand.

Yet she beams at me like I said something amazing. "I like it."

From far away I hear someone call her name. It's a guy. He sounds younger but maybe it's her dad? A rush of panic steals through me and I back away, glance over my shoulder quick so I don't fall on my ass. "I gotta go finish cleaning the stables. Nice meeting you Daydream."

I turn and practically run through the stable doorway, my heart racing. I hear her voice, rising above the roar in my ears.

"Bye Nicholas."

The door slams as I pull it shut, cutting off whatever else she might've said to me.

Chapter
THREE

Dear Diary,

(June 23rd, 10:17 p.m.) I met a boy today. Well, I shouldn't call him a boy since he was tall and broad and had a man's body. He wasn't wearing a shirt. I didn't mean to look. It felt wrong to look and I should probably say some extra prayers tonight but...

I looked. A lot. And he was all muscle and skin, covered in little droplets of water that ran down his bare chest. I scared him. He was drinking out of the hose in front of the stables, his sun-kissed hair kind of stuck up all over his head like he'd run his hands through it a lot and his jeans riding low on his hips. All I saw at first was the muscles of his back and the width of his shoulders before I said something to him. I can't even remember what I said.

Okay I'm lying. I totally remember what I said. I asked if he was thirsty.

He literally jumped when I spoke, the water from the hose going everywhere. He didn't know I was standing there. He turned to face me and it was like I swallowed my tongue. I couldn't speak.

He was just so...beautiful.

Can a boy be beautiful? I never thought so before. I mean, I've seen handsome men but I try not to pay attention because Daddy says vanity is a sin. And he's right. Focusing too much on your looks, worrying about brand names and stuff...it all gets you in trouble. I'm not allowed to wear makeup. I'm not allowed to wear cute bras or panties or low-cut shirts or too-short skirts, dresses, shorts. I'm modest. I have to be.

I have an image to uphold. And I don't want to disappoint my parents.

But the boy...Nicholas...he stared at me like he thought I was beautiful too. I tried to flirt with him. I have never flirted with a boy in my life so I didn't know what I was doing, not really. The things I said, my voice, all of it changed. I sounded like a different person. I acted different too.

I liked it. So did he. I think.

He teased me and called me Daydream. I'm usually so self-conscious of my stupid name. I hate it. He didn't seem to mind though. Oh, he stumbled over it and I could tell he thought it was a little odd but then he made me feel special.

Boys don't really talk to me and I can never work up the nerve to talk to them. I go to an all-girls' school and never get a chance to talk to boys anyway so I have zero experience. I wish I did talk to them more so I could've sounded confident. I wanted to say more but then Evan called me and Nicholas seemed to get a little panicked. Like we were about to get caught or something. He took off so fast but I know it wasn't because he didn't like me. He just didn't want us to be seen together since he works for Daddy.

So he's my little secret. Nicholas. I'm going to the stables to see him again soon. Or maybe...he'll be around the pool or on the yard or something. He might work with Michael and that would be perfect because I always see Michael every summer. He ignores me though. He always has which is fine with me. I usually don't want to be noticed.

I liked it when Nicholas noticed me. When he called me Daydream. That was sweet. He seemed sweet. And he wore no shirt.

I kind of can't get over the fact that I stood there talking to a guy like no big deal and he wasn't wearing a shirt. Can your fingers itch? Because mine felt like they wanted to reach out and touch him. Just...stroke my hands and fingers all over his firm, naked skin...

It's nice, having a secret. I've never really had one before beyond intangible ones. Bad thoughts or secret desires. Desires are bad. It means we want something we're not supposed to have. Daddy says that all the time. I try to keep my thoughts as pure and clean as possible. I swear Daddy can read my mind. It's best to keep it blank...or full of God.

Right now though, locked away in my room, my thoughts are anything but blank. They are full of the boy I met today. The boy I talked to. The boy who talked to me.

I can't help but wonder what Nicholas' lips feel like. They were full and looked soft. I've never been kissed and I want to be so bad. I read a lot. Scandalous romance books Daddy would flip out over if he ever found out. I watch as many romantic movies as Daddy approves of because I want that. A special love, a boy who will want me and love me above all else, who will do anything for me. Do anything to have me...

Chapter
FOUR

Reverie: a daydream.
June 27th

I'VE worked at Hale House for four days. I've cleaned out stalls, I've mowed the back lawn—which felt like a billion acres but whatever—I've moved rocks from one pile to another, I've weeded the garden, I've cleaned out the pool house, I blew up all the toys with an air compressor for the pool party they were having yesterday afternoon for a bunch of screaming brats and I trimmed all the bushes in the rose garden. My arms are now covered in scratches from the thorns and my entire body aches in a way I don't think I've ever experienced. Not even in jail. Not even when I was on the football team my freshman year in high school, which feels like another lifetime.

But the one thing I haven't done at Hale House is seen my little daydream. Not one glimpse, not a mention of her name, nothing. I've seen Harold Hale. I've even spoken to him though I have no idea how to address the guy. Reverend Hale? Minister Hale? Preacher Man Hale?

I just call him sir. I figure that's gotta work best.

I'm starting to wonder if I imagined her. Reverie. Fitting right?

Considering the meaning of her name. I don't wanna ask Michael about her because next thing I know, he's giving me grief. And that guy loves to dish out the grief, trust me. I've learned that quick.

So I keep my mouth shut and my head down for the most part. Only occasionally looking up in the hopes I see Rev.

Reverie.

She's still not a Rev to me. The nickname feels edgy, tough and it doesn't fit her. She looked like some sort of fairy princess when I first saw her. The sunlight in her hair, shining through the skirt of her dress and highlighting those endless legs…she was gorgeous. She comes to me in my dreams. Pretty and smiling and laughing. I haven't dreamed about anything in weeks. Months. My mind is…void. After I lost Mom, I felt like I had nothing. Thought nothing. No emotions. No family. No friends.

I have a job. That's it. A place to sleep at night and a car to drive. Mom's old car. I don't have anything else. I don't need anything else. That's what I believed.

Until I met her and suddenly, she's all I can think about.

"Get to movin', Fairfield," Michael says, nudging the center of my back and nearly sending me sprawling. I save myself from falling and send him a dirty look over my shoulder, making him laugh.

"What are we in for today?" I ask as we start walking toward the giant barn that's behind the equally giant garage. It's not really a barn, though I guess it was one once and that's what everyone still calls it. The Hales converted it into a cavernous room where they can entertain people. Like a reception hall or something, with a full kitchen built right in the center. I've seen these sorts of things like the VFW hall in town but never on someone's property.

"They have a ton of Fourth of July stuff they want taken out of storage," Michael says as he pushes open one of the double doors to the barn. I follow him inside, my gaze snagging on all the art lining the walls. I never noticed it before, but then the last time I came in here, I ran into the kitchen to pick up some extra silverware for Mrs. Hale and then left, too focused on grabbing what I needed versus lingering around checking the place out.

Every single painting is of God, an angel, or Jesus, or some other biblical looking character. They look really old fashioned and I stop and study one of them. It's of a scary looking Jesus hanging on the cross with a crown of thorns around his head, blood dripping down his face.

His eyes are looking upward, thick nails through each of his palms and I can't help but stare, horror running through me.

Freaking creepy. I thought religion was supposed to give you hope and purpose, not scare the crap out of you.

"Come on dude, help me out over here. We have to carry out all this patriotic crap," Michael calls.

I find him standing in front of a closet full of clear plastic storage bins on the shelves, every bin stuffed with red, white and blue decorations. We each brought a hand truck with us so I go to the closet and start grabbing boxes, handing them to Michael so he can stack them and we can wheel them out of here.

"So I'm guessing they throw a huge party for the Fourth?" I ask, trying to make conversation. Not that it's hard to talk to Michael. The guy always has something to say.

Plus, I'm trying to find out information about the Hales. Specifically, Reverie.

"Massive," Michael says. "Family, friends, their parishioners, and lots of little kids running around and always falling into the pool. My first summer working here, a kid almost drowned. They've hired special lifeguards just for the day ever since."

"Crazy." I shake my head and lean on the tall stack of boxes I was supposed to take out. "Lots of hot girls show up or what?"

Michael burst out laughing. "Are you kidding? No way. Hale's a man of God, remember? Not a bikini in sight unfortunately. Everyone's good and covered up. You'll appreciate that, bro. Most of the people who attend these parties are around the Hales' age. You don't want to see those women in bikinis." He mock shivers.

"But the Hales have kids," I point out. "Don't the kids have friends?"

"Not really. The Hale kids are pretty sheltered. They don't mingle much around here in the summer so they don't have many local friends that I know of. No one really knows them, though I've heard the boy has come out of his shell and been seen driving around town lately." Michael pulls out the last patriotic-filled box and shuts the closet door before he turns to face me. "The daughter goes to a private girls' school and every time I see her she's either riding her horse or reading a book. And Evan just graduated so I'm guessing he's off to college in the fall. I don't know. I don't pay them much attention."

I don't say anything else. If I start asking more questions, Michael will suspect I'm fishing for info and he'd be guessing right. I don't want him to know I'm curious. And I especially don't want him to know I've talked to Reverie.

That's my secret. One I don't want to share with anyone.

"We'll take the boxes over to the main house," Michael says as we exit the barn. "Mrs. Hale will want to go through it all and pick out what she wants to use. She does this every year. And then she'll run into town and buy more crap. It's the same routine each summer."

I remain silent, letting Michael chatter on. The guy has a mouth that won't stop once he gets going but I don't mind. Listening to him helps pass the time.

Besides, I'm nervous. This is the first time I've been in the Hale's house. Even when I was hired, it was at a youth center where they were having a job fair. I'd been forced to go in and put in applications by my high school counselor. I hadn't expected anything to come of it. Next thing I knew this guy was telling me he could make a difference in my life and wanted to hire me on the spot.

Whatever. I ran with it. I didn't need to be saved. I just wanted a job.

We approach the French doors at the back of the house and Michael knocks on the wood frame, tapping his foot as we wait for someone to answer.

Imagine my freaking shock when it's Reverie I see opening the door to us.

"Hey Michael," she greets, her gaze going to mine, her eyes widening subtly. "Hi," she breathes.

I nod, trying for cool, probably failing. I don't want her to acknowledge anything in front of Michael.

"Rev, this is Nick. He'll be working with me this summer," Michael says, flicking his head in my direction. "We have stuff for your mom."

"Um, nice to meet you," she says, her sweet voice washing over me, her gaze never leaving mine.

"Yeah," I say. "Same." I tear my gaze from hers, looking anywhere but at her. Though I'd rather look at *her* than anywhere else. I can't though. I refuse to make eyes at her in front of Michael.

"Where should we put the boxes?" Michael says, sounding impatient.

"Oh. You can put them in the study." Reverie opens the door wider and Michael walks past her, pushing his hand truck in front of him. I fall in behind him, my eyes going to hers once again, seeing the hurt swimming in the pretty blue depths.

I feel like a dick.

As I walk through the door, I catch a hint of her intoxicating scent. Sweet and light, I can't peg what it is exactly but I know I want more of it. She's wearing denim shorts that hit just above her knee but fit her skintight and a pale pink T-shirt. Her long hair is pulled into a high ponytail and it's damp. Like she just got out of the shower or the pool.

My mind instantly goes to naked and I banish the thought.

"Looking good Daydream," I murmur under my breath as I pass by her, needing to say something to her to let her know that I'm not a total ass.

She doesn't acknowledge me, just shuts the door and strides past me so she can lead us to the study. Her head is held high, her ponytail swinging to and fro and I have the sudden urge to wrap all that long hair around my fist. Give it a gentle tug. Test just how soft her hair is just as I test the texture of her lips…

"Watch it," Michael mutters as I run into him with my stack of plastic boxes. They almost topple over and I reach around, slapping my hand on top of the highest box, holding the stack steady.

Reverie pauses and turns around, her delicate golden brows furrowed in concern. "You okay?" she asks, looking directly at me.

Aw, she cares. I feel pinned in place by her intense gaze and her question makes my heart leap, which is freaking stupid. "I'm fine."

"I'm the one he ran into," Michael points out, jerking his thumb toward his chest and making Reverie laugh.

I immediately frown. I don't want him making her laugh. I think that should be my privilege.

And mine alone.

We wheel our respective stack of boxes into the study and set them up for Mrs. Hale to go through. Reverie stands at the open doorway, watching us the entire time though I swear her eyes are only on me. I can feel her tracking my every move and it makes me self-conscious. Makes me wonder what she sees.

If she even likes what she sees.

We finish up pretty quickly and then we're leaving the house, Rev trailing behind us the entire way. Michael shoots me a strange look, flicking his head in Reverie's direction in a, *what gives with her* way but I just shrug in answer. I don't know why she's following us.

But I can hope she's doing it because of me.

"Thanks for your help, Rev," Michael says as we're walking out the back door. We left the hand trucks in the study since we'll be coming back in a day or two to retrieve the boxes. I feel sort of lost without it, like I need something to hold onto, or I should be doing something with Reverie standing so close to me.

I feel edgy. My hands are tingling, like they want to reach out on their own and touch her.

"You're welcome," she says cheerily before her gaze settles on me and her expression goes somber. "Nice meeting you Nicholas."

Michael frowns. He introduced me as Nick. "Likewise," I tell her and her eyes narrow.

She didn't like my one word response. But what am I supposed to do? Fall at her feet and tell her I think she's hot? It would be the truth but I can't react in front of Michael. No way.

A brand new BMW pulls into the driveway, its engine purring as it comes to a stop right in front of the open garage. The driver cuts the engine and a young guy gets out, his expression impatient. He looks about my age, tall with light brown hair but I don't recognize him. He props one arm on top of the car, shoving his glasses up and off his eyes to the top of his head with the other. "Come on, Rev. You ready to go?"

"You're early," she says, her gaze skittering to mine quick before it darts away.

Who the hell is this guy? He's wearing a white Polo shirt and khaki shorts, an expensive looking watch on his wrist, looking every inch the perfect preppy rich boy. I can't fucking compete with that. "Well, it's now or never, sweetheart. You coming or what?" he asks, sounding impatient.

She rolls her eyes and doesn't bother to grab a purse, a cell phone, nothing. Just walks over to the car, throws open the passenger side door and slides inside, pulling the door shut behind her. Her arms are crossed in front of her chest and she keeps her head bent.

Like she doesn't want to look at me.

Preppy boy shakes his head, offers Michael and me a quick salute and then jumps back in the car. He starts the engine and throws it into reverse, then drives away in a big ass hurry, kicking up dust from the gravel driveway.

"What a jackass," Michael mutters.

"Who was that?"

"Evan."

I don't know who Evan is but Michael says it like I should. "Evan…"

"Hale. Rev's big brother." Michael turns to look at me. I hope the epic relief I feel isn't written all over my face. "Why did she call you Nicholas anyway? That was weird."

I shrug, immediately defensive. "I don't know."

But I do. I know why I call her Daydream too. I hate how indifferent I treated her but she can't act so familiar with me in front of Michael. No way would I ever tell him I met her and flirted with her a few days ago. Alone.

No way.

Chapter
FIVE

Dear Diary,

(June 27th, 9:56 p.m.) I don't understand boys. I was so excited to see Nicholas standing at the door with Michael today. My heart felt like it was going to beat out of my chest. He looked surprised to see me too but when I said hi to him, he barely reacted. He hardly talked the entire time he was in the house with me and he even pretended that he'd never seen me before.

I didn't like that. But I guess it makes sense if he didn't want Michael to know that we'd talked once already. I don't think Michael would say anything or even care. He's never paid attention to me and this is his third summer working at the house so why would he now?

Nicholas did call me Daydream and that was sweet. He said I looked good when I know I looked lame. I'd just gotten out of the shower and was waiting for Evan to show up. I didn't even do my hair, just threw it in a ponytail because I was feeling rushed.

I hate that I can't look pretty for him like other girls can. I want to wear makeup and stylish clothes like what I see in magazines. I talked to Mama about it last night. I told her I was almost seventeen so why couldn't I at least wear mascara and lipstick or something but she said no. Blinked her thick with mascara eyelashes at me and told me I was to remain pure. I'm just a young girl. I don't need any makeup or sexy clothes to make me look like something I'm not.

I didn't protest. What could I say? I'll be seventeen in three weeks and a senior in high school but that doesn't matter to my parents. I'm still a child in their eyes. I still have an image to uphold as a Hale. At least he doesn't parade Evan and me around on his television show anymore. The best thing that ever happened was when Evan put his foot down almost two years ago and said we weren't Daddy's pets to show off for his followers. I still remember how Mama cried. How Daddy and Evan fought.

But Evan won. And his win was a victory for me too. We were taken off the show. Daddy mentions us casually here and there, mostly to say he's proud of us. That's it though.

The second Evan didn't have to deal with the show anymore he changed. I follow the rules but he doesn't. He drives the fancy car that costs almost as much as a house. He wears a Rolex. Designer clothes. Daddy lets him do whatever he wants but he won't let me.

It's so unfair. Evan's the boy that's why he doesn't get in trouble. I'm the girl. I have something to offer, Mama has told me more than once. I'm sweet and innocent and I need to remain that way.

Maybe I don't want to. Maybe I want to know what it's like to be wild and free. Maybe I want to ask Nicholas if he'd take me out on a date. Maybe I want him to kiss me…

He looked mad when Evan picked me up. I thought he knew I had a brother but maybe he hadn't met Evan yet. We went into town and bought Mama a birthday present and Evan let me sneak in a special dress for me to wear at her party. She's a Fourth of July baby. I came two weeks after and she likes to call me her late birthday present. When I was little we would have joint birthday parties but now she wants one all to herself.

I think she likes all the attention. She says the fireworks are just for her and Daddy agrees. I think he says that to keep her happy. Not much else does lately.

I love fireworks. The bright lights and the way they sparkle.

his REVERIE

The colors and the loud boom that rattles through my chest, throughout my entire body...

A book I read a few months ago said that the perfect kiss felt like fireworks. I want to know what that's like.

With Nick.

Chapter
SIX

Weak: not strong.
June 30th

I'M at home alone, hiding out in the living room with the lights off, the TV off, everything dark. Except for my phone. I'm curled up on the couch with an old quilt my grandma made when I was little, Google becoming my best friend as I do a search for Reverend Harold Hale.

There's so much on the guy it's unbelievable. He has an entire channel on YouTube. He has a dedicated website, numerous magazine articles about his ministry, television features, his TV show...the works. He's everywhere. I had no idea how popular he was.

I remember that disclosure statement they had me sign when I first started working for him. That I wouldn't release any sort of information to the media, not even the color of the guy's socks, or else I'd put myself at risk for being fired.

Now I totally get why. He's a media sensation. Everyone wants a piece of him.

So then I decided to Google Reverie Hale.

There's not nearly as much information about her and most of it is old. Seems like the Hale kids fell out of the spotlight a few years ago. Reverie and her brother Evander don't even make appearances on the television show anymore but there's a lot of old footage out there. And pictures. Tons of pictures. My favorite is of a cute little Reverie in a white dress, her hair pulled back and topped with a snowy white bow, a shy smile on her face as she stood with her family.

She was adorable. And on such blatant public display for most of her life along with her brother...then they weren't. I wonder what happened. What changed that? Why were they taken out of the public eye so fast?

I can't ask her. It's none of my business.

There's a knock at my door but I ignore it. It's late, past eleven at night and I'm definitely not expecting any guests. I keep it low key because I'm living on my own since Mom died and I'm still underage though I don't feel it. Child Protective Services would probably try and throw me into foster care until I turn eighteen or something stupid like that and that is the last thing I need. I don't know why they haven't come sniffing around already but whatever.

CPS isn't knocking on my door this late at night though. Who the hell could it be? And why are they so persistent? The knocks just keep on coming, getting fiercer with every attempt.

"Nick! I know you're in there," a voice yells from the other side of the door and I sit up straight, surprise and irritation coursing through me.

I recognize that voice. It's my neighbor, Krista. She's my age. We've known each other forever, since elementary school. She was my first kiss. My first real girlfriend. The first girl I had sex with. I had sex with her right after I got out of jail too.

She called it my welcome home present.

"Nick! Open the damn door. I can see the glow from your phone through the window, asshole. Why are you avoiding me?"

Krista is super classy too. Though I really shouldn't bag on her. We're the same, Krista and I. We grew up in the same neighborhood and our moms were acquaintances. It's a natural progression, Krista and I ending up together. I broke up with her in the middle of sophomore year and she got so pissed at me. I blew her chances to go to prom, she accused. I didn't really care. I got sick of her neediness. And her disloyalty to me.

Monica Murphy

Two months later, I'm accused of a crime I didn't commit. By my very best friend—the same guy she screwed around with that eventually led to our breakup. My life changed completely.

And she wasn't there for me. She was before. She definitely was after. But during the hard stuff, when I struggled and I needed a friend to stand by my side? Nope. Krista disappeared.

She knocks again, rattling the cheap-ass door so bad I'm afraid she's gonna punch a hole through it. I climb off the couch and go to answer it, wrenching the door open to find Krista standing on my doorstep, looking practically naked in a red string bikini top that barely covers her tits and the tiniest white shorts I've ever seen.

I immediately think of Reverie. What would she look like in an outfit like Krista's? Fucking hot, is what.

"There you are." She reaches out, plants her hand in the center of my chest and shoves me as she walks inside, slamming the door behind her. "You're looking good, Fairfield. Where ya been?"

"Krista. Wassup." I grab hold of her bare upper arms, telling myself I need to stay immune to her charms. Because she's got them. The girl is sexy and she knows it. All that wavy brown hair, the pretty, sometimes overly made-up face and the tempting curves. She is stacked. And her ass is pretty damn tight.

She's fucked a lot of the guys at school, including David. That was the reason I dumped her. I can't be with a girl who'd screw around with my best friend behind my back.

But I'd been weak and horny when I got out of jail and she knew it. We'd fooled around in the backseat of her Dad's beat up old car and I'd immediately regretted it after. Then I got wrapped up in Mom's illness. Wrapped up in the shit that became my new life. Death and sadness and wondering how I was going to survive.

Getting lost with Krista… was a way to forget. At least for a little while.

"I've missed you. Haven't seen you around much the last few days." She somehow breaks free of my hold and steps in close to me, curling her arms around my neck, her hands in my hair.

"I got a new job. It's keeping me busy." I reach behind me, trying to disengage her hold on my neck but she presses even closer, her huge tits smashed against my chest. I can feel the heat of her skin through my T-shirt.

I know what she's doing. And I hate to admit it but it's working.

31

"Too busy for me?" she asks, blinking her heavily mascara-ed eyes at me. She tugs on my hair, pulling my face close to hers. "You don't want me anymore, Nick? Don't bother lying. I can feel that you do."

I close my eyes, trying to fight this. She's persistent. Greedy. And so am I. I can't help it. When you have nothing, you grasp at any pleasure you can find, no matter how fleeting. No matter how empty. "We can't keep doing this," I say as I rest my hands lightly on her hips. I mean to set her away but instead I pull her even closer. So close, not even a piece of paper could fit between us.

"Who says? I don't have a boyfriend and you don't have a girlfriend. I'm bored, Nick. Nothing's the same anymore. None of our friends are around this summer and David's still in jail. They didn't let him out quick like they did you, since he lied and all. So let's have some fun." She drags her lips down my neck, her hand slipping from my hair to touch my chest. And lower.

I hate that she mentioned David but it doesn't kill the sexual buzz running through me. Not with the way she's boldly touching me. And I don't want to think about David. How he wronged me. How he's still in jail and I'm not.

So I keep my eyes closed and think of Reverie instead. I don't deserve her. I'm not a good person. I'm letting some girl use me to get her kicks because I want to get off too. Reverie would never do that. I bet she's never been touched. Never been kissed. I'm used up goods and she's virginal perfection.

Tonight…this very moment, it almost feels like I'm being unfaithful to Reverie, being with Krista. I can't believe I'm thinking like this but there it is. And I don't know how to deal with it.

So I don't.

We're kissing now. Or at least Krista is trying to kiss me and I keep avoiding her lips so she dives for my neck. We're stripping off each other's clothes, falling onto the couch, hands everywhere. I'm trying to lose myself like I'm so good at doing but all I can envision is Reverie.

Earlier today she was out by the pool, shooting me shy glances whenever she thought I wasn't looking. But I've become quite adept at looking at her all the time, as slyly as possible. She passed by me and I called her Daydream, making her smile and blush. That smile made my heart swell, the scent of her made something else want to swell and I could hardly contain myself.

It seemed she felt the same way because she tripped somehow and nearly fell into the pool but I rescued her. Slipped my arm right around her tiny waist, making her breath hitch when I tugged her close to prevent her from falling right into the water. I held her to me for one too-long second, savoring the feel of her nestled close to me.

She was a perfect fit. And it was a struggle to let her go.

Krista is tugging on my T-shirt and I pull away so she can yank it off me. I'm like a robot, going through the motions, intent on finding my satisfaction. Drowning out the sounds of Krista moaning against my neck, how she seems to get her lessons from porn stars in how she should act when she's having sex.

All the while I can imagine Reverie's disappointment if she knew what I was doing. How much I'd rather be doing it *with* Reverie.

"Come on, Nicky. Act like you want it at least," Krista mutters, her fingers curling around my dick and giving it an almost too firm squeeze.

Leaning back, I study Krista, the way she's rubbing against me like a cat in heat, her lids lowered, her lips pursed. Deciding the hell with it, I grab hold of her hand and drag her back to my bedroom where I can close the door, shut off the lights and pretend I'm with someone else.

Someone else I absolutely one hundred percent do not deserve.

Feeling like this is ridiculous. Pointless. I mean nothing to that girl. She might flirt with me, smile at me but it's meaningless for her. I'm not the type of guy she'd ever be involved with. If she knew what I've done, what I've been accused of, she would freak out. She *should* freak out. I have secrets I can never tell her. She wouldn't understand.

I know it.

Chapter
SEVEN

Dear Diary,

(June 30th, 10:43 p.m.) I spied on Nick today. I know, I know, I feel silly for even writing it, but I want to remember every detail of what I saw. He's so incredibly good looking. I know I shouldn't care. It's about the integrity of a person that counts. Not how someone looks on the outside, but who they are on the inside.

I believe Nicholas Fairfield (I love his name!) is a beautiful person both inside and out.

How do I know this you ask? Because I watched him, first from my secret spot in the living room, in Daddy's old chair that sits close to the window. The back of the chair is so high I can peek around it and see the backyard without anyone noticing me.

Nick definitely didn't notice me. He was outside working around the pool. Taking the net and picking out every single leaf and bug floating at the top of the water, his dark brows wrinkled in concentration, his mouth scrunched. His mouth...I think about his mouth all the time. I have an unhealthy fixation on it. I can't help but wonder what it would feel like on mine.

Anyway. He was wearing khaki shorts that hit him just above his knees and a plain white polo shirt that was wrinkled. No little navy blue jockey on his chest, like what Evan wears and the rest of his friends. Only my brother can get away with being so completely materialistic while Mom insists I shop at Old Navy or Target or Walmart and nowhere else. She wears brand name stuff too, which makes me so incredibly mad. It's unfair. I don't know why they treat me this way. Why I can't have the same privileges everyone else has.

Sigh. I need to stay on topic. So I spied on Nick cleaning the pool, my eyes constantly dropping to his legs. He has really nice ones. They're kind of hairy but not in a gross way. No, more in a, I wish I knew what they felt like when they rub against mine sort of way.

(Oh my God if my parents ever threaten to search my room again like they used to all the time when I was fourteen and boy crazy, I must burn this book forever!)

Michael was with him and I know he likes to joke a lot. I couldn't hear what they were saying but Nick smiled and laughed. And shook his head constantly, which I totally get because Michael can say crazy stuff. I've heard him before. Anyway.

Nick's smile is the most beautiful thing I've ever seen. He has nice teeth. And cheekbones. And jaw. I don't think he shaved this morning. The sunlight would hit him just right and would highlight the golden stubble on his jaw and chin. Every time I thought about his stubble-covered cheek against mine a shiver went through me...

I have it so bad. This crush on him is...crazy. After about an hour of me playing spy, I finally worked up the nerve to go outside in my swimsuit cover-up with plans to take it off and lay on one of the lounge chairs, but I chickened out at the last minute. I skipped right by them like I was five years old, my sandal catching on a lone piece of bark on the concrete and I nearly went sprawling. Like, almost into the pool.

But Nick caught me. His strong fingers curled around my waist, stopping me from falling into the water. I was pressed against him and my skin sizzled where our bodies connected. I felt my face go hot with embarrassment. Then he said to me, his voice all low and deep,

"Better watch it, Daydream."

I wanted to swoon. Seriously, just fall into a heap on the ground and hope like crazy he'd pick me up again. When he calls me Daydream, I just melt a little inside. It's the way he looks at me too. As if he likes me. As if he thinks I'm pretty and not some idiot girl who trips over her own feet and can't even manage to take off her cover-up to show off her boring, ugly, black one-piece swimsuit. The only suit her parents will let her wear.

I couldn't say anything back to him. Not really. Michael was watching us with this amused look on his face. Nick slowly let go of me, his fingers sliding against my skin in an almost caress. I rocked on my feet when he did that, a little shaky breath escaping me.

Then I said thanks and practically ran away from him. I worked up the nerve to look over my shoulder real quick to see if he was still watching me.

And he was.

I wanted to die.

Instead I jumped up and down in victory once I got out of his sight behind the house, punching the air with my fist. Mama caught me, the frown on her face marring her Botoxed forehead as she asked what in the world was wrong with me, direct quote.

She took all the wind out of my sails. She has a way of doing that so easily. I feel like sometimes she doesn't like me much and I don't know why. What did I ever do to her? I always follow the rules. I'm a good girl. I'm downright boring, just like they want me to be.

But it's not enough. It's never enough.

I want to be enough for someone. For Nick. Nicholas Fairfield. I want to be more than enough because I think he could be enough for me.

I know he could.

So there it is. On June 30th, somewhere around 10 a.m. on the most perfect summer morning ever, Nick Fairfield touched me. Smiled at me. Called me Daydream.

I want to remember this moment forever.

Chapter
EIGHT

Faith: confidence and trust in a person or thing.
July 3rd

I'M tired and the blowout for the Fourth hasn't even happened yet. Well, the big one. Tonight is a small party for just the family and a few close friends, which in the Hales' interpretation, that means about fifty people. It's Mrs. Hale's birthday. She's turning forty so it's kind of a big deal. I think she wants it to be a big deal but then again…

She doesn't like it. It upsets her. Makes her feel old.

I only know this because Michael told me. He's confessed a lot more to me lately. Crazy stuff that I find hard to believe sometimes but he says it so earnestly I kinda have to believe him. I mean…why would he make up shit like that?

And I like that he tells me so much even though I like to give him grief for the way he always talks. I feel like I actually have a friend again.

It's nice.

He's regaling me with his latest story at this very second as we're moving the outdoor furniture around yet again. I swear Mrs. Hale makes us do it just to watch us lift stuff. I think she gets off on being difficult, but she's not around right now. She's still getting ready for her party.

I haven't seen Reverie at all today. I remember how a few days ago she'd walked by the pool, almost tripped and fell in but I saved her. I remember the sensation of her soft skin under my palm nearly doing me in.

I had to act like it didn't matter. That she doesn't matter. But she does. I don't even know her so it's crazy that I react to her this way.

That was the same day Krista and I did it. Haven't seen her since either. I kicked her out the minute we finished, which made her mad. I really didn't care. I was already mad at myself for letting it happen again.

I didn't see Reverie at all today and I missed her. Missed seeing her smiling face, hearing her voice, catching a glimpse of that sweet as hell body. Though I shouldn't miss her because she's not for me. I need to remember my place. And it's not with Reverie.

Not even close.

"So yeah," Michael says, warming up with his new story. "It's Labor Day and that's when the Hales have their big end of summer party and we're invited as guests instead of employees, you know? The sun is out, not a cloud in the sky and I'm swimming. We're all having fun. There's a barbecue going and the food smells amazing. I'm sneaking in some booze in a flask someone else brought to the party so I'm feeling good. I'm buzzin.'"

"Yeah?" I urge when he stops. He likes it when I encourage him to keep talking. Plus, I can tell this story is gonna be a good one. His talking helps make the time go by fast.

"Uh huh. So I climb out of the pool and I'm dripping water everywhere. I grab my towel off a lounge chair that's in the farthest corner, right next to the pool room, you know where I'm talking about? Anyway, I'm over there, drying myself off when I feel someone touch my lower back, then fingers curl around the waistband of my trunks and those fingers are practically touching my ass." His voice lowers and I lean into him, waiting for the big reveal. "I thought it was Brenda, this hot chick who worked here last summer, but it wasn't. Dude, I was shocked as hell when I turned around " Michael pauses again, his eyes going wide. He loves the dramatic effect. He's damn good at it too. "It was Valerie."

I frown. "Who?"

Michael thumps me on the chest, making me stumble backwards. Asshole. "Valerie Hale, dumbass! The reverend's *wife*." He shakes his head. "She ran her nails up and down my back and said I'd filled out over the summer. I mean what the eff? I about leaped out of my skin when she did that. Ran away like a scared little boy with my dick shriveling up faster than you can say cougar on the prowl."

"Are you saying she hit on you?"

"No, I'm saying she gave me a simple back scratch." Michael rolls his eyes. "Yes, she was hitting on me! I couldn't freaking believe it, dude."

I can't believe it either. I've seen Valerie Hale in action, buzzing around the house and grounds, clapping her hands at us while she yells commands like we're all her servants. It's annoying as hell. "Did she ever try and touch you again?"

"Naw, dude. It was my last day of work for the season. I was gone the next day."

"I'm talking about now. Since you've come back this summer," I say, curious. I keep glancing toward the back of the house. The windows are huge, all of them uncovered and they run the full length of the living and dining room. I saw Mrs. Hale pass by a few times earlier and I want to make sure she doesn't catch us standing around.

Gossiping about her.

"No, she hasn't tried anything weird." Michael smirks. "Caught her checking you out once though."

Gross. She's older than Mom. "No way," I mutter as I lean over and grab the end of a wooden lounge chair. I start dragging it over to the others, not caring that I'm scraping the wood up on the concrete. I'm sick and freaking tired of moving furniture. It's pointless. She's just going to make us move it again anyway.

"Dude, let me help you." Michael runs over to grab the other end of the lounger and helps me heft it over to where Mrs. Hale wants all of them clustered together. "You're not into cougars, huh?"

"Hell no." I rest my hands on my hips and glance around, making sure we've rearranged everything she asked us to. I want to change the subject. I don't like the idea of Reverie's mom hitting on me or whatever. "Don't tell me we have to stay for the party."

"Nah. Tomorrow though, we have to. We're working it till the bitter end so it's gonna be a long day. No independence for us." Michael laughs and scratches the back of his head then flicks his chin at me. "You can go. See you tomorrow at eight? Bright and early?"

"Yeah. See ya." I wave and wander off toward my car. Mom's car. I want to get rid of it. I'd rather have a truck. Once I get a few more paychecks in my bank account, I think I could sell or trade in Mom's and buy me a little used truck. Something I can throw all my crap in and use to get the hell out of here at the end of summer. Unless I decide to take some courses at the local community college, but I'm not sure what I'm going to do yet.

I'm going somewhere though. I need to. Not sure where but I don't want to stay here anymore. I need a fresh start.

I need a new life.

The Hales have designated parking for employees and I walk along the graveled driveway toward the small lot. My car and Michael's is still there, along with a few others, including Heather's. She just graduated high school and she works inside the house, as assistant to Mrs. Hale's assistant, which we all think is hilarious. Michael loves to give her grief for being the assistant to the assistant.

I think Michael is hot for Heather and I can't blame him. She's all long limbs and straight dark hair with exotic features. She feeds him snippets of information about the Hales, specifically Valerie Hale. What Heather sees in Michael I don't know but those two are always flirting. She's way out of his league.

Just like Reverie Hale is out of mine.

I'm about to turn into the lot when I hear a noise come from the other side of the driveway. Turning, I catch a flash of red, then blonde. My entire body goes still as I watch someone run into the thick pine trees that line that side of the property.

It's Reverie.

Without thought I take off, hoping to catch up with her. The sun is low, casting beams of saturated gold light through the thick pine trees and if I look toward my left, I'm blinded. There are so many trails here I don't know which one she took and so I head down the middle one that goes straight through the trees.

She's fast. I don't see her anywhere and I run for a while then stop, looking all around me. I try to calm my breathing, my racing heart. I'm worried that I can't find her. My gut tells me she's upset and I want to know why.

I want to be the one who reassures her.

A breeze rustles through the pines, the branches swaying to and fro and I glance to my right. I see her, her long hair trailing behind her as she jogs through the trees. I follow her, thankful I can keep her in sight, slowing down when I see she is as well. The trees give way to an open spot and I watch as she drops to the ground, disappearing from view.

Holy shit. Did she faint? Hurt herself? I increase my pace, coming to a stop at the edge of the clearing to find her sitting on a fallen log, her body bent forward, her forehead pressed against her knees. She's covering her face with her hands and her shoulders are gently shaking.

She's crying. Should I stay? Ask her if she's all right? I should probably go. I don't know her, not really, and I'm clearly infringing on a private moment.

Backing up, I start to turn and leave but I step on a branch, the crack loud in the otherwise quiet forest. I pause, my back to her as I close my eyes and hang my head. I'm caught and I know it.

"Go away," she says with a sniff.

I slowly turn to face her and her eyes widen when she spots me. Who did she think I really was? "Are you okay?"

She wipes at her eyes with the back of her hand, another loud sniff escaping her. Her nose is red, her eyes are glittering with unshed tears. She looks…beautiful despite the pain emanating from her. "I'm fine. I just…I want some privacy please."

Always polite, even when she should tell me to get the hell away from her. "I don't feel right leaving you out here all alone."

Reverie drops her hands into her lap and makes an exasperated noise. "I'm out here alone all the time. Don't worry about me."

"Are you sure?" I don't want to leave her. She looks so sad, so lost.

"Fine. You want to stay? Stay. I don't care." She throws her hands up, then flicks her hair over her shoulder. I'm staring at her, I can't help it because she's wearing this red strapless dress that exposes all sorts of skin and she looks….

Freaking amazing.

"You hate it too, huh?" She stands and gestures at the dress. "Do I look trashy? Like a prostitute? That's what my mom said. She told me I couldn't come to her stupid party looking like this. She said I looked like…like…"

I stand there, scared out of my mind as a sob escapes her and she slaps her hand over her mouth, trying to stop it. But there's no use. She's full on ugly crying now as she reaches for the hem of her skirt with both hands and starts to yank it up. "I hate her," she cries. "I just wanted to look pretty for once and she never lets me. I want to burn this stupid dress. Burn it!"

There's a flash of slender thighs and then—holy God—the palest pink panties I've ever seen. I lunge toward her, my hands batting her skirt down, holding hers to keep them from lifting her skirt again and she glares up at me, her tear-stained face making my heart ache as I stare at her. "Calm down," I murmur as I grip her trembling hands. "It's okay."

"Oh no," she whispers, her face crumpling again. "Y-you must think I'm s-so dumb."

Crying girls. I just...I don't know how to deal with them. Yeah, I had a girlfriend before jail but nothing serious. That's how I look at my life. Before jail and after jail.

I hate it.

"You're not dumb," I say, keeping my voice soft so I don't scare her. She's shaking and I pull her toward me, wishing I could console her. "I just think you're really upset."

Reverie dips her head, her hair falling forward, concealing her from me. Her hands are small, her fingers slender as they curl around mine. Warmth spreads through my body at her touch, at her nearness. We're standing toe to toe and her chest is so close to mine we're almost touching. "You should probably go back home," I suggest, knowing it's the right thing to say, though it's the last thing I want.

She shakes her head, her fingers tightly gripping my hands. "I don't want to go home," she whispers. "I don't want to go to that stupid party. She said I couldn't if I wore the dress. We got in a huge fight and Daddy yelled at me for making my mom mad. They think I'm still locked up in my room pouting."

Her words put all sorts of crazy ideas in my head. Ideas I have no business suggesting. "They won't worry about you?"

"They don't even know I'm gone." She lifts her head, her damp eyes meeting mine. Her nose is red and so are her cheeks. She's beautiful despite the lingering sadness that clings to her.

I want to be the one who wipes it away and helps her forget.

"So. You want to get out of here then?" I ask, my voice hoarse. What am I doing? I should take her back home. Deposit her in front of her house where she'll be safe with her mommy and daddy and then I can drive away with my dirty thoughts. I shouldn't even be touching her right now. This girl screams off limits.

I wonder if that's what makes me want her more.

Her eyes light up. "With you?"

I nod quietly. Worried I'll ruin the moment by saying something stupid. I've never been great with words. And I won't lie. Reverie Hale intimidates the hell out of me.

A tremulous smile curves her lips and I feel like I've been punched in the gut. "Yes, please."

Chapter
NINE

Rebel: to resist or rise against authority, control or tradition.
July 3rd, later that night

REVERIE Hale is sitting in the passenger seat of my car and I'm not sure what I'm supposed to do with her. How I'm supposed to act. This is crazy, what I'm doing. Her parents could accuse me of kidnapping their daughter and they'd probably be right. I could get tossed right back in jail for taking Reverie away from her house.

But here I am, turning onto the highway and heading toward town.

"Where do you want to go?" I ask, keeping my voice nonchalant. I don't want her to know I'm nervous.

"The beach maybe?"

I glance at her and catch her watching me. Her long hair covers most of her chest and the red skirt of her dress hits high, stopping about mid-thigh. I remember seeing all of her thighs. Her panties. My breath comes a little shallower at the memory and my skin tightens.

"Are you hungry?" I ask.

"Yes. Um. Sort of." When I look at her again she shrugs. "Probably not," she says weakly.

If she's saying that sort of thing because she thinks I don't like it when girls eat, she's wrong. "I'm starving," I say pointedly. "We could go to the shit shack if you want."

Her brows rise so far they look like they're gonna disappear in her hairline. "The what?"

I grimace, feeling like an idiot. "Sorry." I shouldn't have said that in front of her. That's what we used to call the burger place at the public beach when I was younger. I bet they still call it that. Not that I have any friends to hang out with anymore. "The Snack Shack, down by the pier."

"I've never been there," she admits, then glances away from me so she can stare out the passenger side window.

I'm surprised. I know she doesn't live here year round but most everyone who comes around for the summer has been to the shit shack at least once in their lives. "You like hamburgers?"

She turns to look at me once more. "Maybe?"

I hate how unsure she looks. And sad. I want to cheer her up. Make her forget why she's so upset in the first place. "They have good ones. But their fries are killer." I wince the moment the word falls out of my mouth. *Killer.* If she knew what I'd been accused of, she'd run back to her house screaming. I shouldn't even joke around and use a word like that. At one point, most everyone thought I was a killer.

"Killer as in good or killer as in bad?" she asks.

"Good," I say, pushing my grim thoughts out of my head. "Really good."

"I am a little hungry," she admits and I smile at her.

"Then I'm taking you to the Snack Shack."

We're pretty quiet as we pull into the pier parking lot, not too far from the restaurant. The place is packed. There are a lot of people waiting outside and there's a line at the take out window. I put the car in park and cut the engine, reaching for the door handle when her voice stops me.

"Can I just...wait here? In your car?"

I let go of the handle. Dread makes my movements slow as I turn toward her, my gaze meeting hers. "You want to go home?"

"No!" She shakes her head, her eyes wide. The skin around them is still pink and puffy. It's pretty obvious she's been crying a lot. "That's the last thing I want to do. It's just...I look terrible."

45

"You don't look that bad," I say, wanting to reassure her.

"Please." She rolls her eyes and I appreciate the show of sass. "My head hurts. And my eyes sting from all the crying, which is so *stupid.*" She whispers the last word, her frustration clear. "I just…I don't want people to see me like this. And in this dress." She tugs at the skirt, her fingers pinching the fabric tight before letting it go.

"What's wrong with the dress?" The color looks good against her golden skin and blonde hair. Really, good doesn't even cut it. She looks fucking amazing.

"It's too short. Too sexy. My mom says—"

"Forget what your mom says," I say, cutting her off.

Her eyes go even wider. "But…"

"Do *you* like it?"

She bends her head down, her wavy hair falling across her face and obscuring her from view. I wish I could reach out and tuck all that pretty hair behind her ear but I keep myself in check. She seems too fragile right now and I don't want to push my luck. "Yes. I bought it when I went shopping for her birthday present. My brother encouraged me but he's always looking for a way to rebel against our parents." She lifts her head, panic written all over her face. "Oh no. I never gave my mom her gift."

"You can give it to her later." I give in to my urges and reach out, tuck a few strands of silky soft hair behind her ear, my finger tracing the gentle curve before my hand drops away. I don't dare touch her anywhere else. Once I start I might not be able to stop. "I can go stand in line and order at the pickup window."

A shuddery breath escapes her. "You'd do that for me?"

"Yeah. Sure. We can eat in the car. Or if you're feeling more comfortable by the time I've got the food, we could eat at one of the tables over there." I gesture toward the group of picnic tables that are in the back of the tiny restaurant, facing the ocean. A few of them are occupied.

She glances down, presses her lips together, as if she was trying to suppress a smile. "Maybe. We'll see."

Her words are like a victory.

And I feel like I just won the grand prize.

I order our food to go and the chick behind the counter flirts with me as she bags it up. She has no idea I have the most beautiful girl I've ever met sitting in my car, waiting for me. *I can hardly believe it.*

"Hot date?" she asks as she hands over the bag of burgers and fries. I already took Reverie's drink to her and she accepted it gratefully, taking a big sip of her Sprite, those pretty lips pursed tight around the straw.

She's so good she doesn't even drink caffeine. Realizing that reminds me yet again I could never measure up.

I take the bag from the cashier, not wanting to encourage her. "Yeah."

"Does she know she's a lucky girl?" She flashes me a smile, obviously flirting with me despite my saying I'm on a date. Which I guess I am. Sort of.

I don't know what to call what I'm doing with Reverie Hale but I don't want to question it.

Saying nothing, I turn and leave, knowing I probably pissed her off but not really caring. I stride toward my car, notice that the picnic tables are fast filling up, mostly with families coming off the ocean after a day in the sun and sand. I go and knock on the passenger side window. Reverie rolls the window down, smiling at me.

"Dinner?" She nods toward the bag.

"Yeah." I hold it up. "So have you decided?"

She frowns. "Decided what?"

"Car or picnic table? Your choice," I offer, tilting my head toward the tables, indicating my preference without saying a word. The weather has cooled down and there's the usual breeze coming off the ocean. It's a beautiful night and I want her to forget all her troubles and enjoy it.

"Oh." She chews on her lower lip with her teeth, dropping her gaze so she can study her lap. I try my best to be patient, but my stomach is growling and I'm hopping from one foot to the other like I'm eight and ready to run.

"If you'd prefer sitting in the car—"

"No." Reverie cuts me off, her gaze meeting mine, direct and sure. "Let's go sit outside at one of the tables," she says, her voice firm.

"Let's do it," I agree, opening her door.

She steps out, my drink and hers gripped in her hands as she walks by me with a small smile. I slam the door behind her and lock the car, then follow her as she makes her way to the tables. Her scent trails after her, bathing me in her sugary sweet fragrance and I inhale as discreetly as I can so I don't look like some sort of crazed junkie.

But I am. A junkie. Addicted to Reverie.

"It's so nice out here," she says as she settles at a table, setting both drinks on top.

"It is. Really cooled down since it was so hot earlier." I slide onto the bench seat across from her and open the bag, the scent of the freshly cooked food making my stomach growl. Loud.

Reverie stifles a laugh behind her hand before she asks, "Hungry?"

"Hell yeah," I say as I hand over her burger and fries.

She blushes. Again. She is definitely not used to bad language. I really need to learn how to control my mouth around her. "Smells good," she murmurs as she unwraps her burger.

"Tastes even better." I glance up to see her cheeks look like they're on fire so I decide to leave her alone and attack my burger instead.

We're quiet for a while as we eat, which allows me to check her out more closely. She's devouring that sloppy burger and pile of fries like they're the best meal she's ever had. I wonder what sort of food they eat at the Hale house. Probably healthy food, no junk allowed. Definitely no greasy burgers and fries from the Shit Shack. Her dad—and especially her stick-up-her-butt mom—would probably have a heart attack if they saw their precious little girl right now. Eating fast food all alone with the summer hire that just got out of jail a few months ago.

I didn't commit the crime but they wouldn't care. They'd hear the word *jail* and their daughter in the same sentence and my ass would be out the door. No one can know about us spending time together.

Nobody.

"I like it here," she says, her soft voice breaking through my thoughts. "Thank you for bringing me."

"You're welcome." I take a sip of my drink. "You don't come to the ocean much?"

"Not really." She shrugs.

"Why? You're so close. Like ten minutes away." I grew up here and I still love coming to the beach, especially in the summer when the weather is perfect and the girls in bikinis are out in force.

"I don't know. I don't leave the house much when we're here. Everything I want is there, you know?"

I didn't know. I would go stir crazy if I had to stay at that house for days and days on end with no escape. It's weird. Almost like she's Rapunzel or whichever princess I'm thinking of, trapped in her castle.

"You should come to the ocean more often," I suggest.

"Maybe you should bring me here more often." Her eyes light up with hope.

"Your parents would probably freak out."

"They would never have to know," she says, her voice soft and suggestive.

Shit. They would know. Parents always find out, especially diligent ones like hers. From everything I've seen and heard, it's like they keep her under lock and key.

I decide to change the subject. I can't confront this right now. "You feel better?" I see her burger is almost gone and there are only a few fries left. "You're not upset anymore, are you?"

"No." She slowly shakes her head, a shy smile tipping up her lips. I'm sure I disappointed her by basically denying that I'll ever take her to the ocean again like she suggested but what can I say? "I'm good."

"Good." I pause. Ah, I'm going for it. I want to know more about her and sitting around here talking about the weather and how much food we just ate isn't going to cut it. "So how long have you been coming out here for the summer?"

"Oh." She sits up straight and flips her hair over her shoulder. "Well, since I was twelve. My parents bought the house that year."

"And you're...how old?" I'm trying to find out information about her without looking like an obvious asshole.

"Almost seventeen. My birthday is in less than two weeks."

So she's younger than me. Almost an entire year. "So you'll be a senior?"

"Yes. Finally." She nods. "You?"

"Uh, I graduated early." Got my GED in jail. One of the best things I could've done while I was in there. Now I don't need to go back to that hellhole known as my high school. The minute I returned, everyone would've questioned what happened. It wouldn't matter if all charges were dropped, I know most of them would believe I did it or think I was somehow involved. Krista would expect to be my girlfriend again, I'm sure.

All of that shit, I wanted to avoid. So I did.

"Wow, you must be really smart," she breathes, her eyes wide, like I've impressed her.

Huh. I impress no one. If she only knew where I got my diploma. She'd be changing her tune quick. "Not really. I had to do it," I say, my brain scrambling for a reason. "Um, I knew I would be on my own because my mom had cancer."

"Oh, no," she whispers, her forehead crinkling in seeming concern. "How terrible. Is she okay? Or…" Her voice trails off, as if she can't bear to say the next question.

"Yeah, she died a few months ago." It hurt to think about it, let alone say it. I don't know if it's necessarily hit me yet, that Mom is gone forever.

"I'm sorry. I can't imagine." Her voice is so soft I can barely hear her. She seems to feel so much so quick. Her face crumples up a little, like she's going to cry and I immediately reach out and settle my hand over where hers rests on the table.

"It's okay. Really." Her hand is slender and warm and I stroke my thumb over the top of it once. Slowly sweeping over her skin as if I'm testing it. More like savoring it.

"I don't always get along with my mom but I don't know what I would do if she…died." She stumbles over the last word and her emotional reaction is making me feel all emotional too so rather than fall apart and cry in front of some girl I barely know, I snatch my hand back from hers and clear my throat. Silently demand the tears that threaten at thinking about Mom to get the hell back and stay away.

"I miss her, but life goes on right?" I ask, my voice sharper than I intended and the look Reverie gives me says she heard it. She winces, her eyes full of hurt and I immediately feel like an ass. "So I got my GED, got this job and I'm trying to save money."

She goes along with my change of subject thank God. "Do you plan on going to college?"

I shrug. "Not right now. Can't afford it. Maybe someday." Who knows if that maybe someday will ever come though.

"That's too bad." She sounds let down by my answer and I hate myself for saying it. I disappointed her and I don't get it. Why does it matter? Why do I matter? Yeah, there's an attraction between us. I feel it. She must feel it too. For whatever stupid reason I want to pursue it, pursue her though I know this is going to end in disaster.

So what is it with me and this girl? Why do I want to impress her so bad? Not that I can. Besides, she doesn't know me. She doesn't know what I've done.

And that's for the best I guess. I should throw up my usual walls and not let her in. Take her home right now and ignore her for the rest of the summer.

But I don't want to.

"How about you? You want to go to college?" I ask, but I already know the answer. She's a good girl. Good girls want to go to school, get their degrees, find a nice guy to marry and live in a pretty house with a white picket fence and pop out a couple of kids.

Must be nice, to have your future so firmly in sight.

"Oh yes." She nods eagerly. "I go to a private school right now. All girls. I hate it." She makes a face. "I definitely want to go to college. Not an all-girls college either though that's what my parents want." She rolls her eyes. This girl is freaking adorable. "I'd like to go somewhere on the east coast I think."

"Why the east coast?" I've never been to the east coast. I've never even been out of California.

"Well, I was born and grew up in the south—Texas—and we moved to Los Angeles when I was eleven. I figure I've never lived on the east coast so why not? I'm looking for something different. A change." Her gaze meets mine, full of expectation. For what, I'm not sure. "I'm looking for an adventure."

My entire body goes still. I almost feel like she's aiming that statement directly at me. "Bored doing the same old thing?"

"Uh huh." She nods, her gaze dropping for the briefest second to my lips. I wonder what she's thinking.

I wonder if we're thinking the same thing.

"You're being pretty adventurous tonight," I say as I lean across the table a little bit, toward her. I'm tempted to touch her hand again but I restrain myself. I don't want to push too hard or be too forward. This girl is nothing like Krista. I could reach over and grab Krista's boob and she wouldn't even flinch.

Hell, she'd probably encourage me.

"Don't you think your parents are looking for you?" I ask.

Reverie waves a hand as if dismissing my words. "They're too busy celebrating my mom's birthday to worry about me. They think I'm pouting up in my room remember?"

"Are you sure they won't check on you?" You'd think they would keep her under lock and key. I know she's been pretty sheltered.

"My bedroom door is locked." She shrugs and I study her bared shoulders. The delicate gold necklace she's wearing with the smooth round locket that rests against her chest. What's in that locket? A photo of an old boyfriend? I hope to hell not. "Trust me. They won't come and check on me. Mom's probably glad I'm not there to ruin anything."

Those words are said so bitterly I almost want to question her further but I don't. Let that be her business. "Are you saying you snuck out on purpose? Like hopped out a window or something?" I'm impressed if that's true. And surprised.

A tiny smile teases the corners of her lips. "Kind of."

"How?" She might be a good girl but it seems Reverie has a rebellious streak.

That smile grows. "I have my ways."

So she's not going to tell me and play the mystery card instead.

And just like that, I want her even more.

Chapter
TEN

Dear Diary,

(July 3rd, 11:49 p.m.) I can't even begin to describe what happened tonight. What started out as completely awful turned into one of the most incredible nights of my life. It's Mom's birthday and of course, she'd been on a rampage all day. Demanding everyone treat her like a queen (like she doesn't get enough of that treatment already) and that it was her SPECIAL DAY. She started screaming at Dad for not paying enough attention to her (which is true—he never pays attention to her anymore, not really).

Evan flat out left. Just flipped her off and walked out of the house, which of course, left her fuming. Me too. I was so jealous. I wanted to be my big brother at that very moment. Bold and defiant and doing whatever I wanted. That's how it's always been. Evan gets away with everything and I get away with nothing.

Right before her party, I came down the stairs and she glared at me. Started yelling when she saw what I was wearing. It's no big deal. I've seen plenty of girls wear practically nothing compared to my dress. She didn't like that it was strapless. I might've been pushing my limits but the dress covered me pretty well. Not a hint of cleavage and my legs were covered almost to my knees. I thought I looked nice.

I don't think Mom liked seeing me look cute. I'm not saying I think I'm beautiful or whatever, but Daddy said when he saw me that I looked pretty and that made her mad. She wanted all eyes on her.

Not me.

She called me a whore and that made me start to cry. She said only whores wore red. Daddy shushed her, grabbed her arms and asked her how much did she have to drink before he turned to glare at me, the message in his eyes all too clear.

I was nothing but trouble. He wanted me gone.

So I left. Locked myself out of my room, hid the little key on top of the door frame and left the house through the back door where no one noticed me. All they cared about was her stupid party anyway so what does it matter, where Rev is?

I ran toward the woods. I always went to the woods by the house when I was upset. I cried there a lot. I would read there sometimes too. It smelled good, all the pine trees and fresh air, the salty scent of the ocean lingering. Always lingering.

There's a clearing in the middle of the pines with an old fallen tree I like to sit on and cry like a stupid baby. But it was fine if no one caught me, you know? I could ball my eyes out and no one was the wiser except the birds and the bugs and maybe a stray squirrel or deer.

But he followed me. I don't know why. I didn't notice him, as unbelievable as that sounds. He breathes and I usually sit up and take notice. Not this time though. He followed me down the path, through the trees and found me at the clearing.

Nicholas Fairfield.

I was so angry at Mom and what she said to me. How she treated me. I was sort of hysterical when Nick found me and I told him to go away. Can you imagine? Why would I tell him to go away? I flipped out in front of him. Just completely lost it and tried to take off my dress (!!!) because I hated it. I wanted to get myself something beautiful and Evan helped me and all it did was cause problems. So I tried to take it off like a crazy person. I'm pretty sure I flashed my underwear at him.

So embarrassing. I've never lost it like that in front of anyone, especially a boy.

He calmed me down though. Invited me to leave with him so I did. He took me to the Snack Shack down by the ocean and bought me a burger and fries. It smelled so good that I ate practically all of it because Mom never allows me to eat food like that.

It was delicious. Being with Nick, talking to him, all of it was delicious. Wonderful. He smiled at me. Touched my hand with his. His hand is big and kind of rough and his fingers are so long. A shiver moves through me every time he touches me.

Every time.

His mom died a few months ago. Isn't that sad? I almost wanted to cry. He's so young and strong. I'd fall apart if something like that happened to me. I even think he lives alone. He's already graduated from high school and he works. He's like a seventeen-year-old kid living an adult life.

I can't even begin to imagine.

Spending those few hours with him, staring at him from across a picnic table, wishing I could touch his face, his hair, his lips (he has the most beautiful mouth I've ever, ever seen), I knew right then I wanted him to be mine. That sounds greedy and foolish but it's true. I want a boyfriend, but not just any boy.

It's always been this unattainable goal. This ethereal, dreamy kind of yearning for a boyfriend with no real substance behind it. Watching romantic movies I'd think, I want that. Sneak reading all those books on my Kindle, I'd sigh at the happy ending and think I want THAT.

I think I know who could give me that. I look at him and my entire body tingles. He smiles at me and my heart feels like it's tripping over itself. He touches me and the strangest sensations flood my lower body.

Nick. I wonder if he likes me? He acts like he does.

But I don't know. I'm not good at this sort of thing. I have zero experience with boys, especially extremely good looking ones like Nick.

He drove me back home and dropped me off sort of close to the house, which I thought was risky but he insisted. Wanted to make sure I got into the house safe, he said. It was so sweet, I couldn't protest. So I didn't.

For whatever dumb reason I was hoping he'd kiss me goodnight but he didn't. Of course, he didn't. Silly of me to believe he would because we don't know each other that well but a girl can hope. I've never been kissed. Ever. I feel so stupid and inexperienced but I have a feeling Nick wouldn't make me feel dumb. He would probably touch my face and give me a soft, sweet kiss. One that would make my heart skip about a thousand beats and my skin feel like it caught fire.

I need to spend more time with him. I need to not be shy and talk to him. Figure out a way to get him to like me as much as I like him.

I hope I can.

Chapter
ELEVEN

Fireworks: an exciting or spectacular exhibition
The Fourth of July

I'M setting off explosives and I have no idea what the hell I'm doing.

Michael's doing most of the launching of the bottle rockets and all that other shit and he's having so much fun I'm starting to wonder if he's a secret pyromaniac. He hoots and hollers like some sort of good ol' boy, a beer clutched in his hand as he stares up at the sky. Heather is nearby, clutching a beer as well though she's barely eighteen and she's wobbling on her feet, looking a little sloppy. I wonder how many she's had.

Hell I wonder how many Michael has had. The moment we made our escape from the house, we cracked open a couple from his secret stash. He's been pounding them, especially because Heather showed up and that made him nervous.

The grins Michael shoots her way every freaking five seconds tells me he is desperate to get into her panties.

I feel his pain though it's not Heather I want.

My problem? I can't stop thinking about Reverie. I couldn't sleep last night. Krista was waiting on my doorstep when I got home, wearing an American flag bikini that just about showed all her goods. Tiny triangles strained across her tits and I knew if she turned around her ass would be hanging out.

Didn't matter though. I was still on a high from my stolen time with Reverie. I had zero interest in Krista. The more time I spend with Reverie, the more everyone else starts to fade. Looking at Krista, all I feel is shame. Shame for using her. Shame for how she puts herself on such blatant display to try and entice me. It used to work.

Not anymore.

Krista flattened herself against my door when I said I wasn't interested, her hand covering the door handle, which only pissed me off. She then whisked off her bikini top, her tits on display for anyone to see if they happened to pass by and I shoved her away, making her yell and curse at me like some sort of hardened biker.

Considering her dad is a former motorcycle gang member, this shouldn't come as a surprise.

No way could I even touch Krista after spending a few hours with Reverie alone. Just…No. Way. So I locked myself in my apartment, stripped off all my clothes and jacked off to thoughts of Reverie. Flashing me one of those shy smiles. Touching me. Kissing me. I can't imagine her being so obvious and crass like Krista but I could imagine her being sweet and trembling in my arms. Telling me to go slow and make her feel good and I'd promise I would. I'd do my damnedest to help her forget everything but just the two of us.

Yeah. I'm a total goner over a girl who took off with me because I'm her one rebellious moment. Do I really want to be that to Reverie? A meaningless act of defiance against her parents? Because I know that's all I am. That's all I can be.

"Fucking Fairfield, what is your problem?" Michael yells, knocking me from my thoughts. "You afraid of getting burned?"

I turn to glare at him and gave him the finger. I know he's referring to the fireworks but his statement could be taken in so many ways. "Light another bottle rocket, asshole."

Michael laughs and does exactly that, making Heather squeal and jump, clapping her hands like some sort of Independence Day cheerleader.

We're on the opposite side of the Hale property, lighting the fireworks for the guests that still remain at Hale House, and there are a ton of them. The party started at straight up noon and hasn't lessened. In fact, I think it's gotten busier, if that's possible. There are so many people spilling out of that house, onto the back patio, near the pool, all over the freaking place, I've never seen such a huge party.

I've been hanging on the peripheral all day. I started out directing cars into the drive and making sure they parked right without blocking each other in. Then I made an ice run to the local grocery store. Twice. Restocked the soda buckets. Brought in the empty platters and bowls from the buffet tables.

I didn't hang out much close to the house, which was probably best. I caught glimpses of her. Reverie. Smiling and laughing with a group of kids her age, which only filled me with irrational jealousy. She wore some sort of cover-up that covered her too much and I know her suit is black. Thicker straps than I'm used to seeing but considering I'm used to Krista's hooker bikinis made of thread, that's no surprise.

If I saw Reverie splashing around in the pool in a swimsuit I'd probably make an ass of myself by staring too long. So I avoided the pool as much as I could.

Best I stay away.

After a hard day in the hot sun, dealing with painfully perfect people having a good time while I slaved to take care of all their needs, I was ready to let off some steam. By making fun of Michael and setting off fireworks. Though I've pretty much left that responsibility to him since he's enjoying it so much.

"They're all oohing and aahing over there," Heather says, pointing toward Hale House. "I can hear them."

I could too, faintly. "Why aren't you over there?" I ask, swiping the beer out of her hand and taking a huge swig.

She glares with those intensely dark eyes of hers, mutters *asshole* under her breath when I finish it off. She really is pretty and she seems at ease in any situation. I can see why Michael's hot for her. "Valerie—Mrs. Hale finally said I could go. I was so scared she might change her mind, I practically ran out of the house."

"She have you running all day or what?" The woman has a reputation. We all gripe about it. She makes up work just to watch us bust our asses to ensure she's happy, I swear.

"You wouldn't believe the stuff I had to do. Including sober her up." Heather rolls her eyes when she notices my shocked expression. "She's a total drinker, you know."

"Really?" I frown, turning my attention to Heather more fully. Michael doesn't need my help lighting fireworks. He's doing a mighty fine job of it on his own so I'm going to dig for information. "Like…has a problem with drinking-type drinker?"

Heather nods slowly. "She got into a huge fight with her daughter last night right before her birthday party started. I saw it all happen and it was ugly." She mock shudders.

Now I'm really interested in what she's saying. "What about?" I keep my voice casual. I already knew what it was about, at least according to Reverie. But maybe it involved something more.

"She'd been drinking all day." Heather lowers her voice, like we're surrounded by a ton of people and she doesn't want them to hear. Considering we're only hanging out with Michael and his stash of fireworks, she doesn't have to worry about that. "And she was mad at everyone. Just on a total rampage, calling Rev a whore, accusing Reverend Hale of cheating on her." Heather's eyes went wide, as if she couldn't believe she just said that. "God, you really have to make sure you never say anything about this to anyone. I'd lose my job in a heartbeat."

"I swear." I cross my heart with my index finger. Cheating? That was a pretty damn harsh accusation. "This doesn't go beyond me and you." If I was sitting down, I'd be hanging by the very edge of my seat, waiting to hear what Heather has to say next.

"What doesn't go on beyond you two?"

Everything inside of me goes still at the sound of that voice. That very sweet, very female and very familiar voice. The look on Heather's face says it all. Holy shit and every other cuss word I can think of.

We almost got caught spilling some very private information.

Slowly I turn to find Reverie standing in front of me. Looking fucking hot as sin in a white tank top that makes her tits look huge and faded denim shorts that I wish were way shorter.

But I'll take what I can get.

"Reverie." I smile at her dopily, feeling a little buzzed and not just because she's in my presence though that's definitely a major influence. I chugged that beer Heather had only just cracked open plus the first one Michael handed me. And I haven't eaten anything in hours. I'm a total fucking lightweight at the moment and it doesn't help that the girl of my jack-off dreams is staring at me like I'm her favorite ice cream and she wants to lick me up.

My entire body tightens and I breathe deep.

Jesus. I need to be careful with where my thoughts go.

"Nicholas," she returns, flashing me an equally dopey smile.

This gives me hope, as much as I tell myself to knock that shit off.

"What are you doing here?" I ask, glancing around to make sure she didn't bring anyone else with her. Like her rude as hell brother and all of his rude as hell friends.

I don't like those punks. The majority of them are older than me and I see the judgment in their eyes when they look at me. They think they're so much better than me. Jerks. The only difference between me and those assholes is that they have money and I don't.

"Um, I live here?" She glances around before her gaze lands on Heather. "Hi."

Heather steps up to stand beside me and I'm instantly afraid we're giving off the wrong vibe. "Hey, Rev. You wandered off from the party? Get a little lost?"

"Heather," I warn, shocked she would talk to her boss's daughter in such a snide tone. I don't even know Heather but no way am I going to let her speak to Reverie like she's some dumb little girl.

"I was looking for Nicholas." She hesitates, her smile falling from her face as she sinks her perfect white teeth into her perfect lower lip. "But maybe you're busy?"

Michael chooses that moment to light off the biggest bottle rocket he had in his collection, along with a bunch of little ones, all at once. Not quite sure how he did that but he yells out an enthusiastic *fuck yeah* as they all shoot into the sky, exploding with bursts of color that casts Reverie's face in a rainbow of red, white and blue.

Fuck yeah is right. Just looking at her hurts. What if I actually got a chance to get my hands on her? I might not be able to stand it.

"I'm not busy," I say as I take a step toward her. Heather follows me and I shoot her a look that says what the hell?

Because really. What the hell?

"Rev!" Michael jogs over and stops in our circle of three, making it four, which fills me with relief. Heather's being totally weird and I don't like it. She came here for Michael but she's following after me like she wants to be with me or something. Is she trying to make Michael jealous? Or maybe even Reverie? That makes no damn sense. "Whatcha doing? Come to watch the master at work?"

61

"You know it." Reverie shoves him on the shoulder, all easy flirtatious girl, not resembling the timid, crying girl I'd rescued not twenty-four hours ago.

"Everyone like the show? That was the grand finale, if you were paying any attention." Michael puffs up his chest, as if he's looking to make a career out of lighting fireworks. Reverie giggles and Heather sends her a deathly stare before moving away from me and going to Michael's side, curling her arm around his and looking nice and cozy.

"You did an awesome job," Heather murmurs to Michael, her face so close to his I swear her lips are brushing against his cheek as she speaks.

Michael looks stunned and thrilled. He's been after Heather since the moment she started working for the Hales and she constantly plays hard to get. I have no idea what she's doing tonight but it's weird. Like she's jealous of Reverie or something.

"I'll uh, let you guys get back to whatever you were doing. I just wanted to say hi." She offers a tremulous smile, once again the unsure girl of last night. My chest aches. I hate how uncomfortable she seems. "I should head back to the house before they send out the search and rescue." Reverie starts walking backward, offering us a little wave. "See ya."

"Bye," Heather calls, all sugary sweet as Reverie turns on her heel and practically starts running away from us.

"Reverie, wait," I say, shooting Heather a dirty look over my shoulder before I take off after Reverie.

Second time in twenty four hours that I'm literally chasing this girl. She's fast I'll give her that but I catch up with her quick.

"Reverie." I grab hold of her arm and turn her around so she's facing me. She looks upset, her eyes narrowed into slits as she yanks out of my hold and crosses her arms in front of her chest. The move only makes her boobs look bigger and my gaze drops. Lingers.

Wishes.

"What do you want Nick?" She sounds irritated. Sweet but irritated.

I jerk my gaze back up to hers. "Why did you leave just now?"

"I didn't want to disturb you." She practically spits the last two words out.

"What are you talking about?" I think I know exactly what she's talking about.

"Are you with Heather?"

"What? No way." I shake my head, shocked she would come out and ask me point blank. "Michael's hot for her, not me."

Her expression softens though she still sounds skeptical. "Well, she seemed *very* interested in you."

"It was nothing, I swear. We were talking while Michael was lighting the fireworks. He let me set a few off but after a while, he wanted to take over completely. So I let him." I shrug. "He was just showing off for Heather. Trying to impress her."

"She acted like she was trying to impress *you.*" She sounds jealous. And sick ass that I am, I like it.

"Not even," I scoff because yeah. I doubt she's interested in me. Maybe she was trying to rile Michael up?

Heather had acted pretty weird when Reverie appeared. But she's a girl. They always act weird. And I rarely understand them and their motives. Look at Krista. Though really she's a terrible example because that girl is flat out crazy.

"Are you sure? Gosh, I feel stupid for asking. And insecure. You must think I'm overreacting, which I probably am." Reverie's voice softens even more until she's practically whispering. "I just…after last night…I don't know." She shakes her head. "I thought…"

"You thought what?" I encourage when she stops talking. I'm dying to know what she was going to say.

"I thought you…" She presses her lips together and shakes her head again. Closes her eyes for the briefest moment before she pops them open. She's struggling with something and I wish I knew what. "Never mind."

I step close. Closer. And she doesn't back up. I'm invading her space, I can smell her, feel the heat radiate off her body and mine reacts. My skin tightens and I break out in a sweat. I take her hand and entwine my fingers with hers, notice that they're trembling. She doesn't pull away, doesn't even seem to be breathing and I realize I'm holding my breath too.

Letting out a ragged exhale, I wonder what the hell is happening between us. The air is charged, heavy with unspoken declarations. I shouldn't push her. She's innocent. Sweet and virginal and sheltered. But I want to know what she's thinking, what she's feeling. I can only hope it's about me. "Say it," I murmur, needing to hear her confession.

It won't mean anything though, what she's going to say. It can't. Not really. We're the last two people who should be interested in each other.

"I like you. And I thought you liked me." The words come out in a rush and she closes her eyes again, her expression pained. "Stupid right?"

My heart speeds up as relief floods me. She likes me. "Not stupid," I murmur, dipping my head, my lips so close to hers that I…

Go for it.

And I kiss her.

It's light. A kiss but not a kiss at all because I barely feel her lips. But I know from that one singular moment when my lips touched hers that they are soft. And warm.

And perfect.

A shaky breath escapes her, I feel it waft across my face and her eyes crack open when I withdraw from her. She's staring at me with a horrified expression. Looking scared out of her ever-loving mind. Not the look I want a girl to wear after I kiss her for the first time.

She touches her mouth with her free hand, her fingers shaking when they brush against her lips. Without a word she releases her grip on my hand, turns around.

And runs.

Chapter
TWELVE

Dear Diary,

(July 4th, 11:32 p.m.) I did the dumbest thing ever. EVER. I got jealous when I saw Nick standing there talking to Mom's assistant. That girl doesn't like me. Heather. The minute she saw me approach, she got all friendly like with Nick. Then Michael.

And I got jealous. Not over Michael but over Nick.

He belongs to me.

I was mad. Feeling dumb. Feeling like a little girl who doesn't know how to keep a guy's interest, which is sort of true. I wanted to leave so I did but Nick chased after me.

Again.

I let him catch me. I let him talk to me, take my hand and connect us. He...

Oh my God, I can barely type this. When I look back at this diary years from now I know I'm going to want to slap myself for what I did but here it goes:

deep breath

He kissed me. My first kiss. Ever in my life from the one boy

I wanted it to be from. It was nothing and everything all at once. A mere touch of his lips upon mine. They were firm and soft. How can lips be firm AND soft? His are. I told him that I liked him (ack). That I thought he liked me (I still can't believe I said that) and then he kissed me.

How I wish I could relive that moment and do things differently. I should've touched him. His face. His hair. I should've grabbed hold of his shirt and pulled him to me but I'm not brave enough. What if I did something wrong? What if that kiss had somehow been an...accident?

I want to roll my eyes at myself. How can a kiss be an accident? I'm looking for any excuse to tell myself I'm not worthy. I might've proved myself unworthy because of what I did next though.

I ran away. Like a complete idiot I RAN. AWAY. How can I ever face him again? Will he even want to look at me again? I don't know. Did I blow it? Does he hate me? Is he over this before it ever really begins?

I hope not. I hope I didn't ruin my chance though it feels like I did. He didn't chase after me again. Didn't call my name. He just let me go and maybe that's a sign that he's not really interested after all.

That hurts.

You know what I like though? I like how he always calls me Reverie. Not Rev. Everyone calls me Rev, even my family.

Not Nick. He calls me Reverie. And I love it.

I want to be his Reverie. All his.

Chapter
THIRTEEN

Guilt: a feeling of remorse for some offense, crime, or wrong
July 5th, early morning

I DREAMED. Of brimstone and hellfire. Of Reverend Hale standing behind a pulpit, pounding his fist so hard the wood shook and I was afraid it would splinter into tiny pieces with the force of his blows.

He was yelling at me. Screaming at me. His face red, his voice booming as he threatened me for touching his daughter. He grew and I shrunk. Until it felt like he was ten feet tall and I was about five years old.

You're vagrant filthy scum! Keep your disgusting hands off my daughter!

Those words—or a variation of them—were slung at me again and again. Until I was nodding in agreement, until I promised him I wouldn't touch her. I wouldn't so much as look at her.

I wake up drenched in sweat, my heart racing, my phone lit up as a text message comes in. It's two in the damn morning. Who the hell would text me?

Grabbing my phone, I check it.

Krista. Of course.

Get your fine ass over her and lick my snatch. I miss your tongue.

I grimace. Gross. She really thinks that's going to work on me? She must be drunk. I don't even bother replying. Within sixty seconds she's texting me again.

Nick!!!! I need you!!!

Groaning, I flop back down on the bed, staring up at the ceiling. I'm straddling two worlds. The one here, in my shitty little apartment with a master bedroom that is still filled with all of Mom's stuff and dealing with my sex-crazed ex-girlfriend, and there, at Hale House, where I pretend to be an upstanding citizen, do my job and secretly lust after a freaking reverend's daughter.

Straddling two lines while I lie directly in the middle, bad on one side and bad on the other. I don't know which side is worse. They're both equally crap.

My phone dings again and I give it a quick glance.

I nEeD yOuR bIg DiCk NiCk NoW!

Christ. How long did it take her drunk ass to type that nonsense?

Stop texting me, I reply quickly, my fingers flying as if I can hardly stand to text her, which is sort of true. Just reading what she wrote makes me feel…dirty. Stupid considering I'm just as low as Krista. I probably whispered similar words in her ear when we first got together. The both of us were young, experimenting, getting down and dirty, believing that's what sex is all about.

Not that there's anything wrong with getting down and dirty but damn. We were kids. And she was whoring herself out to every guy available when I thought she was my girlfriend. She even fucked my best friend.

And then my best friend fucked me over.

I don't want to stop texting you. I want you. Why can't I have you?

Because I don't want you.

I know how to suck your dick real good. Don't deny it.

Maybe I don't want my dick sucked by you.

Why? You got somebody else?

Maybe I do.

I wish I did.

No one knows you like I do. NO ONE.

She's not too far off the mark. And that's what scares me the most.

What if Krista's right? What if no one else knows me like her? What if she's the only one in this world who truly understands me?

A scary thought.

Krista's words feel menacing. Like a threat. I don't like it.

Leave me alone, I type just before I drop the damn phone by my side. Screw this. I don't need to have a text battle with Krista tonight. With my luck she'd show up on my doorstep and kick the door in. She'd probably do it naked too, she's that crazy.

Not what I need.

I think of what I really need. What I want. Who I want.

Reverie.

I still can't believe I kissed her. It wasn't much of a kiss. More like an accidental brush of lips though it was no accident. She'd looked so upset and I wanted to reassure her. A totally impulsive move.

And then she bailed on me. Didn't say a word, she just ran.

Weird. Her leaving made me feel guilty. Like I shouldn't have touched her at all. She came out there to see me. I know she did. But she didn't like how Heather talked to her, followed me. This entire night went down in flames and there's no one to blame for it but me.

You'll miss me you fucking douche. And when you come back begging for a taste of my body and I tell you no? You'll cry like the big baby you really are. FUCK YOU ASSHOLE.

Great. Krista's pissed at me. Maybe she'll stop harassing me once and for all.

A guy can wish.

Chapter
FOURTEEN

Frustrated: disappointed, dissatisfied
July 8th

I'VE worked my ass off the last four days straight with no time off. I get two days off starting tomorrow and I'm freaking exhausted. Every night since the Fourth, I get home late, scarf down whatever fast food I picked up on the drive home and then collapse into bed. Sleep like the dead until I have to wake up and start all over again.

On a few of those nights though, I dreamed. Of Reverie. Of taking that little kiss between us further. Of touching her, slipping my fingers into her hair to see if it's as soft as it looks. Pulling her closer until her sweet curves mold to my body and she wraps her arms around my neck, moaning against my lips as I take the kiss deeper…

Yeah. Dreams. Definitely not my reality.

Last night Michael came over with a twelve pack of beer and we polished it off quick. Too quick. I'm not usually a big drinker. Alcohol causes nothing but trouble. Considering that Reverie's been ignoring me since the Fourth of July, I've been frustrated.

So I drowned my sorrows in beer.

Unfortunately, Michael met Krista. She can't stay away, even though she's still pissed at me. Within five minutes of us arriving she was knocking on the door, as if she could scent new meat. The dirty looks she shot me when I opened the door didn't stop her from pushing her way inside like she owned the place, her eyes alighting on Michael as if she just discovered a pot of gold at the end of some sparkly rainbow.

She flirted with me, she flirted with Michael and then after about ten minutes of that bullshit, I grabbed her arm and escorted her pretty little ass right on out of there. Krista whined and complained, Michael even shooting me a look that said *let her stay* but I ignored him. Ignored her too as I shoved her right on out of the apartment and slammed the door behind her.

"She's trouble," I told him when he expressed interest. "Trust me. You don't want to get tangled up in that mess."

He left it alone and so did I. We drank. And drank. Michael moaned and groaned over Heather and I let him. She'd been all into him after the fireworks show. They'd made out in his truck and she'd even given him a hand job. The dude had been ecstatic, talking about her nonstop the day after she jerked him. How this was going to be the best summer ever because for once, he nabbed a girl early in the season.

His words, not mine.

Two days off and she shows up yesterday acting like he didn't exist. Heather had barely looked at him, let alone spoken to him. I felt his pain, not that I'd told him. No way I could let him know how far gone I was over Reverie. How I barely kissed her and she ran like I shoved my hand in her panties.

We were good and drunk within an hour. I refused to let Michael drive home so he crashed out on my couch. We woke up hungover and grumpy as shit. I drove to work wincing against the sun, pissed that I lost my sunglasses somewhere at the Hales yesterday. And later that afternoon, when I realized it was my turn to clean out the horse stables, my grumpy mood went straight to quietly furious. Downright fucking hostile.

Yeah. This week went from full of potential to absolute bullshit, just like that.

Glancing around the stables, I let forth a growl, pissed that I gotta clean this mess. I whipped off my shirt just before I walked inside since I knew it was gonna be hotter than balls in here. I rest my hands on my hips, surveying the area, making mental notes of what I need to take care of.

Mostly all of it since there's chaos everywhere. Guests had come for the holiday and their kids loved to ride the horses every day. Lucky me.

I'm shoveling horse shit within minutes, sweat dripping down my face and chest, the air so close and sticky I feel like I can hardly breathe. The old khaki shorts I pulled on this morning because everything else I own is in the laundry basket are slipping low on my hips. I forgot to put on my belt before I left for work and with one wrong move the shorts could fall to my feet in an instant. I'm constantly hitching them up which is driving me crazy.

This entire day is driving me crazy. I just want it to be over and done with.

After I finish cleaning out the manure, I replenish the hay and refill all the water buckets. I shuck my work gloves and even groom the damn horses, not that I mind that job. I like brushing their coats and murmuring soothing words to them in the hopes that I'll gain their trust. It soothes me too and considering how riled up I'd been when I first got there, I'd needed to relax as much as they did.

I even brought them carrots to chew on, trying to get on their good side because a couple of them are old and cranky. It works. Soon they're all snorting and neighing at me, demanding my attention, and when one in particular leans over to snatch the carrot right out of my fingers that was not meant for him, I start laughing.

It feels good to laugh. I've been tense for days. Frustrated. Hungover. Riled up.

"He's always been greedy."

I jump about a mile at the sound of Reverie's lilting voice and turn to find her standing directly in front of me, wearing…God. She tries to kill me every single day with her wardrobe I swear. A sky blue T-shirt that stretches across her chest, the fabric so thin I can see the lace trim of her bra. Denim shorts again, these a little shorter and revealing her long, tanned legs, her feet encased in dark brown cowboy boots.

She doesn't even try to be sexy. She's more on the modest side but every time I see her, she gets to me. Makes my entire body go on high alert. Just having her close sends a crackling energy between us, one I can't control no matter what I do. It's just…there. Like we have no choice but to either ignore it or deal with it.

I prefer dealing with it though I know I should ignore it. I get the sense Reverie would rather deal with it too.

"You like sneaking up on me don't you?" I ask when I finally find my tongue.

She slowly shakes her head, a little smile curling her dark pink lips. Damn, just seeing that smile sends a surge of want through me. The urge to grab her and give her a real kiss threatens to take over me. "I was coming out here to do exactly what you're doing."

"Clean the stables?"

Her smile grows. "Groom the horses."

"Ah." Heaven forbid Princess Reverie gets her hands dirty. That was kind of a crappy thought but there it is. She *is* a princess. And I'm the lowly grunt who works for her daddy the king. "Well, I beat you to it."

"Yeah, you did. Looks like they like you too."

More than you like me, I want to say to her but don't. Instead I don't answer her at all and start putting everything away instead. The brush I used, the broom and the shovel and the buckets and all the miscellaneous cleaning supplies. I keep myself busy, not wanting to look at her, talk to her, get distracted by her. Don't want to get my hopes up either because that's the biggest waste of my time ever. I'm done chasing after Reverie.

Maybe Krista's right after all. Maybe no one else really does get me but her. Maybe Krista's all I deserve.

"Are you mad at me?" Reverie asks after almost five minutes of stone cold silence on my end.

I pause and hitch up my damn shorts again, noticing how her gaze drops to my hips then jerks back up to my face. I refuse to read anything into that. She's not checking out my underwear or my naked chest or any of that. More like she's scandalized that I'm wearing hardly any clothes. I'm probably freaking her out completely. "Why would I be mad at you?" My voice comes out colder than I mean it to and I clear my throat, feeling like a jerk.

She clasps her hands together in front of her and sways to and fro like a little girl caught doing something bad and trying to sweet talk her way out of it. "I ran away from you the other night."

My heart leaps to my throat. Well, look at her just coming right out with it. I'm shocked. "Yeah, you did." I decide to be just as straightforward as she is. "I get why though."

She blinks. "You do?"

"Sure." I shrug but don't say anything else. What could I say? Sorry for pushing myself on you and giving you a two second kiss? That just sounds…ridiculous.

Reverie starts walking toward me, making me nervous. This girl gets too close to me and I don't know what I might do. "I don't know why I did it," she blurts, then presses her lips together.

"Did what?" I frown and back away a step, wishing I had a towel or something to wipe away the sweat on my forehead. I must smell ripe. And I'm all dirty and shirtless and if anyone walked in on us right now, my job would be toast.

"Why I ran away." Another step toward me, close enough that I can smell her now. Sweet and innocent and so damn seductive I wish I could bury my nose in her hair or her neck and discover exactly where that delicious smell is coming from. "It was dumb."

"Dumb?" I'm not quite sure what we're talking about. I've lost track. Just having her come closer and closer is sending me into the land of stupid. Zapping brain cells left and right with her pretty looks and determined glare.

"I shouldn't have run from you," she admits softly as she bends her head, her hair falling forward to conceal her. Like she doesn't want to face me.

"Hey, if I did something I shouldn't have done, I get it," I say, trying to play this off. "Because that kiss…it wasn't a big deal you know? It lasted what? Two seconds?"

Reverie lifts her head, her eyes clashing with mine. "No big deal?"

I shrug, nervousness filling me, making my stomach cramp. She looks mad again. "It was just a little kiss," I offer weakly.

"Just a little kiss." She makes a face. "Why'd you do it then?"

"Why did I kiss you?"

"Yes, why?" She points a finger at me. "And don't you dare say it's because you felt sorry for me. That would be the absolute worst thing ever for you to say."

"That wasn't the reason," I say, my voice low. One of the horses gently neighs as if encouraging me to go on. "That wasn't the reason at all."

"Then why?"

I rest my hand on my hips, hating that we're having this serious conversation in the middle of the stables, me wearing hardly anything and stinking to high heaven and her perfectly dressed, perfectly beautiful, just flat out…perfect. "You said you thought I liked you."

Her cheeks color the faintest pink and she nods. Doesn't say a word.

"You also said that you liked me," I add.

Now her cheeks blaze red. She nibbles her lower lip but still doesn't say anything.

"And you seemed sort of worked up over it." When she parts her lips to surely offer a protest I cut her off. "So I wanted to show you that I…felt the same way."

She clamps her lips shut. Then parts them again, her tongue darting out for a quick lick.

She is straight up killing me and doesn't have a clue.

"You feel the same way?" Her voice is the barest of whispers. "I-I don't believe you."

"Hey, you're the one who ran," I point out. "Not me."

We don't speak for what feels like an eternity but really is only two minutes tops. I hear the horses rustling around in their stalls, the buzz of an airplane flying overhead. A soft little sigh escapes Reverie and she tucks her hair behind her ear, running her fingers through the rest of it so it flips out behind her shoulder.

I catalog every little thing about her. The tiny gold hoop in her ear, the thin gold chain bracelet around her right wrist and the ring on her middle finger. It's a simple gold band with a single pearl in the center and tiny diamond chips flanking either side.

This girl likes jewelry. Gold jewelry. Her clothing isn't fussy. No crazy patterns or frills or lace beyond what I spy on her bra. She reeks of money and class, of a girl who could have everything she could ever want. While I'm a guy who struggles for every little thing, who can never, ever have what he wants.

And right now, what I want is…

Her.

"You're staring," she whispers, startling me.

I smile sheepishly. "Busted."

"Did you know that was my first?"

"Your first what?" I'm frowning again. Damn this girl is making my head spin, how she keeps changing the conversation.

"My um, first…" Her voice trails off and I watch her struggle. "My first kiss. From a boy."

I'm shocked. Then again, I'm not. From what I can figure, she's lived a sheltered, protected life. She hasn't done much. Lived much. She's terribly shy but so achingly beautiful it hurts for me to watch her too long.

And I'm the one responsible for her first kiss. A really crappy kiss too.

"Really?"

She nods but doesn't answer.

"Huh," I finally mutter because I don't know how else to respond.

"You think I'm lame," she says flatly.

"No." I shake my head. "Not at all." That is the last thing I think of when it comes to Reverie.

"Pitiful then." She throws her hands up in the air and whirls on her heel to start walking away from me. "Pitiful Reverie Hale, never been kissed, never gone on a date, never done anything but live vicariously through books and movies like some sort of big loser."

Speaking of big losers, I'm losing my chance with her here. Despite my earlier promise to myself, I'm chasing Reverie one more time, grabbing her by the crook of her elbow so I can spin her around to face me again. "You're not a loser," I tell her.

She blinks up at me. "I'm not?"

"No. I'm the loser." I jerk my thumb at my chest. "I'm the one who gave you a crappy first kiss."

"It wasn't crappy," she murmurs.

Well, what else does she have to compare it to? "I can do a lot better than that." I sound way more confident than I feel but come on.

I can absolutely do a lot better than that two second kiss.

"Oh really?"

"Yeah. Definitely." I'm crazy. Flat out losing my mind if I think I'm really going to get this girl to kiss me again. She should shove me as hard as she can and run. Or I should walk. This isn't right, playing around with her. She's a girl who deserves someone better than me. Some respectable kid her father approves of.

Not me.

"Okay then." She pauses and my gaze meets hers. Watch as her gaze drops to my mouth and lingers there.

"Okay what?" My blood heats at the way she's looking at me, and my hands itch to grab her. Pull her to me and show her exactly what kind of kiss I can really give her.

"Prove it."

Chapter
FIFTEEN

Daring: adventurous courage; boldness
July 8th

*P*ROVE *it.*

She's practically daring me and I'm not one to back down from a dare. Provoking me while I'm all sweaty and dirty, still feeling a little irritable, the girl is flat out playing with fire.

And I think she likes it.

"Come here," I tell her, my voice deceptively soft while inside, I feel anything but soft.

Reverie takes those last remaining steps toward me and I grab her hand, pulling her to me. She gasps when I maneuver her into the position I want her in. Her back is flat against the wall and I'm standing in front of her. We're a short distance from the horses and they're watching us, a built in audience for Reverie's new first kiss.

"Wh-what are you doing?" she asks shakily.

"I'm going to give you a redo on that first kiss," I say as I brace my hands on the wall on either side of her head, caging her in. She inhales sharply and some of my bravado crumbles at that telltale sound. "I'm probably all sweaty," I mutter, immediately wishing I never said that.

"I-I don't mind," she admits quietly.

Okay. This girl is just…fuck. What is she doing to me? "I should put my shirt on." I don't even remember where it is. Inside? Outside? I honestly don't know.

"Don't." She shakes her head, then tentatively reaches out to settle her hand on my shoulder. Her touch is electric, her nails grazing my skin and making me shiver. "You're hot."

Hell yeah, and so is she but I think she's meaning literally. "Keep that up and I'm going to get hotter."

"Oh." A shuddery breath escapes her and my gaze drops to her chest, watching as her tits rise and fall with her quickened breathing. Slowly I let my eyes wander up. Along her shoulders, her throat, her chin, my gaze settling heavily on her mouth for a beat too long before I finally look into her eyes. I tuck one stray strand of blond hair behind her ear, let my finger trace the tempting curve. She closes her eyes, lush lips parting in anticipation and my blood heats just looking at her.

I want it. Want her bad. But I'm going to draw this out for as long as I can.

"You smell good too," I whisper, pressing my nose against her hair. It's silky soft, the feel of it on my skin ratcheting my need for her another million notches. "Sweet." I inhale deeply. "Like candy."

Her eyes remain closed as she smiles. She turns her head toward mine, her nose nuzzling my cheek and I don't know how much longer I can hold out. "Are you teasing me, Nicholas?"

"I'm trying to make this good, Reverie." My voice is hoarse. I sound like I can barely hold it together, which is pretty damn close to the truth.

"It's already good," she confesses so softly I almost don't hear her. "So, *so* good."

Our cheeks are pressed together and I move away from her slightly, repositioning myself so our mouths are more aligned. Warning bells are going off in my head, clanging loudly till they're all I can hear. Telling me I shouldn't do this. Shouldn't play with her. Shouldn't even look at her, let alone touch her. She deserves so much more than this.

So much more than me.

I push the warnings out of my head, determined to do something for me for once. I've done everything for everyone else for so damn long. I took the fall along with David all because of his lies. I took care of Mom because she was dying. What about me? What about what I want?

It's my turn to take. And to give, all at once, with Reverie.

Touching her cheek, I drift my fingers across her satiny soft skin. She opens her eyes, her gaze meeting mine and I swear she's holding her breath.

"Close your eyes," I tell her and she does so without hesitation, licking her lips once more. I study her for a long, quiet moment, taking in every tiny little detail. Her smooth skin, her rounded cheeks, her thick, dark lashes. They flutter, as if it's taking everything within her to keep her eyes shut and a surge of unfamiliar emotion floods through me, making me feel wobbly.

"Nick," she whispers, and that needy, pleading little sound pushes me over the edge.

I lean in and settle my mouth on hers. One kiss. Two. Soft. Gentle. I kiss her bottom lip, her top lip, one corner of her mouth, then the other. I drag my lips up her chin, teasing her, kissing her again, drinking from her perfectly sweet, perfectly lush lips. She remains completely still, her hand still braced on my shoulder, my hand still cupping the side of her face. I tilt her head back the slightest bit so I can rain kisses on her chin, her jaw, her throat.

A shuddery breath escapes her as her hand curls into my skin, clutching me almost desperately. I step closer to her, our feet tangling together, my chest brushing against hers as I slip my hand behind her neck. Lifting my head, I look at her, the riot of pink color in her cheeks, her lips damp from mine, her eyes still tightly closed.

"How was that?" I ask, my voice low, my thoughts chaotic. That was nothing. A minor kiss in the scope of things.

So why do I feel all twisted up in knots? Like the most momentous thing of my life just happened, all within about ninety seconds' time? It was just a kiss.

Yet it was more than that. Way more.

She slowly opens her eyes, her expression dazed as she blinks up at me. "That was…"

"Okay?" I smile, trying to keep it light so I don't expose how much that just…what? Moved me? I kept it slow on purpose so I wouldn't freak her out and instead I feel completely pushed off my axis. What the hell would've happened if I'd slipped my tongue into her mouth, let my hands wander, let myself get out of control…?

I wouldn't be able to stop, that's what. Not with Reverie. I want her too damn much.

"It was good." She nods once and I cock an eyebrow at her, earning a tiny smile from her in return. "It was perfect," she adds.

"Perfect? So I set myself up to fail next time?" I slide my fingers into her hair, savoring the silky softness.

"I-I don't know." She closes her eyes again and thunks her head against the wall behind her. "I'm so not good at this."

"You're perfect at it," I whisper against her lips before I kiss her again. I can't resist. Our mouths linger and I angle my head, tempted to deepen the kiss. I shouldn't. I just told myself I shouldn't but…

Yeah. I rarely follow the rules, even my own. And that's what usually gets me in trouble.

Carefully, I dart my tongue out and lick her top lip. Once. A quick little swipe to test her and she whimpers, slips her arm around my neck and draws me even closer to her.

Looks like she just passed my test with flying colors. And that means I need to break this off quick.

Pulling away from her, I smooth her hair away from her forehead, stroke my index finger along her hairline. She blows out a harsh breath from between pursed lips, her eyes still closed as if she's afraid to open them. I take a step away from her, then another, creating some much needed distance between us.

"Nick." She swallows hard and opens her eyes. "Would you…"

"Hey douchebag, you in there? Better not be jacking the horses you fucking pervert!"

Christ. It's Michael. Accusing me of jerking off horses in front of Reverie, no doubt. Way to make an impression.

I spring into action, moving away from Reverie with lightning speed. "Go over to the horses," I whisper-hiss at her, not bothering to slow down as I head toward the giant industrial sink in the far corner of the room. I crank on the water at full blast at the exact moment Michael strides into the stables, whistling some popular rap shit song that he was playing at full blast earlier this morning.

My back is to Reverie as I wash my hands, wash away the scent of her from my skin. My lips still fucking tingle from kissing her and my mind is officially blown. I've never reacted that way toward a kiss before.

Ever.

"Whoa. Rev. What are you doing in here?" Michael asks as he skids to a stop.

"I came down to feed the horses," she says, sounding a little breathless. And a lot guilty.

I glance over my shoulder to see her patting the old palomino aptly named Trigger. She has a couple of sugar cubes in the palm of her hand and I wonder where she found them. Maybe she'd brought them in her pocket?

"And you found loser in here all alone shoveling shit?" Michael laughs, jerking his thumb toward me. He finds his greatest joy in not having to clean out the stables. It's the worst job on the property. Definitely my least favorite.

Though if it helps bring me closer to Reverie, then maybe I won't protest after all.

"Hope he's been treating you all right," Michael continues as he ambles toward me, his gaze still stuck on Reverie.

"He hasn't even really said a word to me beyond hi," she replies, sniffing a little as she turns toward the horse and whispers something to him, holding her palm out flat with the sugar cubes presented as a treat. The horse gobbles them up, his giant teeth making her giggle as they scrape across her hand. The sound of her laughter dances across my nerve endings, making me long to go to her and I glance in her direction to find her studying me with the same yearning I'm feeling in her eyes.

Michael would have to be a blind man not to notice what's happening here between us.

"Well, aren't you a rude bastard?" Michael nudges my shoulder and I jerk my gaze away from Reverie, sending him a deathly glare in answer before I return my attention to the sink. I shut off the water with a fierce jerk and then tear off a couple of paper towels without a word, dry my hands and start to head out.

"See ya, Reverie," I say with a curt nod as I stride out of the stables, Michael chasing after me.

"Bye Nicholas." Her soft voice makes my heart clench. She sounds sad and damn it, I don't want to make her sad. I just kissed her for God's sake. I wanted to keep on kissing her too.

Not good.

Eyeing my shirt hanging on the railing in front of the stables, I snag it and slip it on, wrinkling my nose when I smell it. I need a shower fucking stat. What I really need is to dunk my head in a cold bucket of water and purge all thoughts of Reverie from my head.

"What's your prob bro?" Michael asks.

"Nothing," I mutter as I start toward the house. I figure if I keep moving I won't give Michael enough time to ask me questions I don't want to answer. "It's got to be past quittin' time, right? I'm beyond ready to clock out."

"Yeah, me too. I was just coming to tell you that and help you out if you needed it so we could get out of here." Michael pauses. "Looks like you found plenty of help already though."

I stop and whirl on him. "What the hell are you talking about?" The deadly edge to my voice takes me back to when I was in jail. Constantly having to defend myself. I'd been on high watch every single day I spent in that hellhole. Funny how easy it is for me to go right back into that mode. No matter how much I don't want it to be, it's still in me, buried deep. An experience I can never escape.

"You and Rev alone in the stables? She sounded all breathless and weird dude. I know the horses don't get her going that good." Michael rocks back on his heels. "Don't tell me you're fucking around with Hale's daughter."

"I'm not fucking around with Hale's daughter," I toss out as I start walking once more, slowing my pace so I don't seem so angry. I don't want Michael to suspect shit. He's my friend, I trust him with some stuff but not everything.

And right now, Reverie is my secret. Just like I'm hers.

"If you were, you'd tell me right? So I could keep lookout for you? Her parents would kill you if they found out you were making moves on her. She's innocent man. I know that girl's never been on a date. And I can sure as shit guarantee she's never been kissed, let alone any other stuff," Michael says as he falls into step beside me. "Daddy Hale keeps her under lock and key. I hear that ring she wears is some sort of purity promise she made to him. They had a ceremony and everything."

I stumble over nothing at Michael's words and save myself from falling on my ass, hoping like hell he didn't notice. Whatever he's saying sounds like a big load of crap. "Are you for real?"

"As real as anything. Haven't you heard of those purity ceremonies girls participate in? They've been around for a while and they were getting all sorts of media attention there for about five minutes before some other new fad started," Michael explains. "I know Reverie participated in one. That's where the pearl ring comes from."

Purity ceremonies. I've never heard of such a thing. Granted I hang out with girls like Krista who gave up their virginity when they were too young but hell, so did I. We were kids fucking around. We didn't know what we were doing. It sucks. I sometimes regret using Krista like I have. But then I remember how she uses me too and then I don't feel so bad.

That's what the two of us are. Users. No wonder we should stick together. No one else would probably really want us anyway.

"How do you know she's vowed chastity or whatever to her daddy?" I ask with an eye roll added in for good measure. I hope he believes I'm blowing this entire thing off. Can't have him know how curious I really am. "This all sounds like a total crock."

"I know it's freaking true because they held a celebration dinner here last summer." Michael kicks at a rock and sends it flying. "Weird right? They invited a few close friends and some other girl who also made the same vow to her father. They were one big happy family of virgins swearing their virtue to their daddies."

Hell. Here I went kissing a girl in the stables—fucking shirtless—and she's made a vow of purity to her father to remain a virgin until... what? She marries? Or is she stuck with her dad as a virgin forever?

Okay that last thought is just flat out creepy.

"So I'm warning you. There's nothing there when it comes to Reverie. Nothing. Even if she flirts with you, you don't stand a chance," Michael says. "She's a good girl. She does what her parents say. She has an entire congregation on national television watching her every move."

"She's hardly on the show anymore," I say in annoyance, my thoughts in turmoil. I can hardly comprehend what Michael just told me. It's all so damn weird.

"That you even know this proves to me you already know too much." He points his finger at me. "Leave her alone, Fairfield. Find some other chick to sniff after. Some girl who'll give it up to you easily and doesn't have all that baggage. Rev's sweet and she's a freaking hottie, but she won't put out. And even if she did—which she so won't—you will never come first. Her family does. And after her family comes God. She's the real deal man."

His words linger in my head long after we say goodbye and leave

Hale House in separate cars. They haunt me for my next two days off. After I fight off Krista multiple times when she tries to freakin' accost me. When I find myself in my room, in my bed late at night staring at the ceiling, thinking of Reverie. Remembering how soft her lips were, how she whispered my name, her hand on my skin, fingers curled around the back of my neck. Her tongue…

Jesus. Her tongue.

I need to stay away from her. What I want, I'm not going to get. I should tell Krista to come over and take out all of my sexual frustration on her. She'd be a more than willing participant.

Instead it's just me and my hand, with thoughts of Reverie floating through my mind. These two days off give me much needed distance.

And almost make me want her that much more.

In other words, I'm completely screwed.

Chapter
SIXTEEN

Dear Diary,

    (July 8th, 7:45 p.m.) He kissed me.

    Again.

    I can hardly find the words to describe how wonderful it was. How incredibly romantic and sweet and sexy…

    His lips are so soft. The way he touched me, the things he said, the hitch in his breath right before our lips touched, his fingers in my hair. Tangling, tugging a little bit. As if he somehow wanted to pull me close. Closer. Like he couldn't get enough of me.

    I felt the same way.

    I'm changed. Completely changed. I thought my crush on him was overwhelming and all I did was watch him. Yearn for him. Wish he would really look at me, talk to me, get to know me.

    But now, it's all different. Now I know what it's like to be held in his strong arms, to feel his mouth on mine, his taste…

    No one ever told me it could be like this. Of course, none of my friends have boyfriends, just innocent crushes. I felt the same way about Nick. That's all it was. A silly crush, a slight obsession, I've done this countless times. Lots of hopes and wishes and dreams wasted on pretty boys who never noticed me. Who never noticed any of us because first, we go to an all-girls' school and they didn't even know us. And second, I'm part of a...bookish crowd.

Wow. Just looking at what I wrote I feel like an old lady. 'Bookish crowd.'

Fine. Some might call us nerds. We call ourselves highly educated and properly informed. Old lady words.

Well, my tiny circle of friends would die if they saw Nick and knew that I kissed him. DIE. I want to die right now just thinking about him. His smile. His eyes. His body (OMG his body). His hair...

It was a mess earlier. Overgrown and curling at the back of his neck, sun-kissed from all the time he spends working outside. It's like it doesn't know whether to be straight or curly so it sort of goes everywhere. I love it. I wish I'd touched it. Just gripped his head and plunged my fingers into his hair, holding him close as he kissed me again and again.

I'm getting ahead of myself. Michael almost caught us out in the stables, and Nick moved away from me so fast it was almost impressive. I could hardly stand, my knees were shaking so bad and everything inside of me quaked and burned. I watched him walk out of the stables barely looking at me, Michael following after him and the second they were gone I fell to the ground like I was boneless. A crumpled heap on the floor and my skin buzzing as if I'd been electrocuted. I couldn't stop touching my lips.

I felt like I'd died and gone to heaven. All because of a kiss. A touch.

All because of Nicholas Fairfield.

If I play my cards right, I'll have a boyfriend for the summer. A real, bona fide boyfriend. Someone to create memories with, to do things with.

Someone to fall in love with.

That's what I want more than anything. I want to experience... everything. I want to do it all with Nick. I want him to be mine.

All mine.

Chapter
SEVENTEEN

Dear Diary,

(July 10th, 9:17 p.m.) It's been two days since I last saw Nick and I feel like I'm slowly, quietly freaking out, especially because I have no one to talk to about this. At first I worried. What happened to him? Where did he go? Is he okay? Did I somehow drive him away?

That was the one thing that scared me most of all.

When I was finally brave enough to ask Heather if she'd seen Nick lately, she gave me a dirty look and said it was his day off in a really snotty tone. I was relieved to know why he was gone, but then again I got mad.

Why didn't he try and reach out to me? It's so stupid that I don't have my cell phone. I got it taken away from me at the very beginning of summer because my grades weren't up to Mom's standards. I had all B's. Pretty decent, right? But no, not good enough for Mommy Dearest. She took my iPhone away from me and I've been without it for weeks. I miss my phone. If I had it, I could give him my number and Nick could text me any time. I could make plans to sneak out and meet him somewhere. Maybe out in the woods where he first found me? Maybe he could take me to the beach, to the Snack Shack again.

But that would mean I'd probably need a new swimsuit because the one I own is so boring. One piece and black and just blah. I hate it. I look terrible in it. Not that I'm confident enough to wear a two piece in front of him. At least, I don't think I am…

As usual, I'm getting ahead of myself. It's a bad habit of mine, I swear.

So that's how I spent most of yesterday, pining away for Nick. Evan invited me to the movies with a group of his friends but I declined. I wondered if Mom put him up to asking me.

Then Mom slipped into my room and had a long talk with me and I knew she put Evan up to asking me to go with him because come on. I'm the biggest pain in his butt ever—that's what he always tells me at least. But anyway, Mom told me that I'm closing myself off from others and not wanting to spend time with kids my age. She said I needed to spend more time out of the house, not moping over missing my friends from school and constantly reading.

If she only knew what I was reading…she'd probably flip out. Romances with descriptive sex scenes that set my imagination wild, especially after that kiss with Nick…

Then Mom hit me with how I shouldn't inquire about the hired help. I got so mad. Heather ratted me out. I couldn't believe it. When Mom asked why I wanted to know where Nick was, I made up some dumb excuse. Told her I lost my necklace and I knew he was around that night so I wanted to ask him if he'd seen it. A total lie but I didn't know what else to say.

Well, it was the absolute wrong thing to say. Mom got all crazy thinking he might've stolen it. I had to reassure her again and again there was no way that could be possible and I even went over to my jewelry box and dug out the so-called missing necklace. Let it dangle from my fingers and acted like I was brainless. Oopsie, here it is after all!

That calmed her down some. She seemed so rattled and then she took a couple of deep breaths, smiled at me and she was back to her old self. Like she flipped a switch between her moods. I've seen her do this before but it usually took longer…

Monica Murphy

Then she gave me another speech on how I have to be careful around some of the people Daddy hired this summer. Some of them are...unsavory, including Nick. What did she mean by that? I want to ask him but how? He's so sweet to me. I'm not scared of him. He's one of the few people I spend time with and actually feel comfortable around. Mom made him sound like some sort of criminal but I find that hard to believe.

And really, what can I say to him? Hey Nick, my mom said you're 'unsavory' – ha ha, funny word right? Well, anyway, I'd like to know. Ever been to jail? Are you a criminal?

That wouldn't go over very well.

I have to be careful around Heather though. I can't tell her anything, but you know what? I think I'm going to have a little chat with her. Tell her I'll let Mom know she's getting a little too close to Michael during work hours. I caught them hanging all over each other on the backside of the stables the day before Nick kissed me in there. Mom would flip if she knew that.

I'm also going to ask for my phone back. It's almost my birthday. A sort of early birthday present then? I don't even want any presents. Just my phone. I need to find a way to communicate with Nick so no one else will know.

The more I think about it, the angrier I get. I'm going to be seventeen and I never get to do anything. All I want is my phone. Oh, and a secret little summer romance with Nick.. Lots of girls my age do way worse.

But my parents don't let me do anything.

I have one more year of high school and then I'm gone. I can't live under their rules anymore. Mom and Daddy are too strict. I love them. They mean everything to me, even when Mom treats me so terribly and Daddy ignores me because he'd rather take care of his 'followers' than his family. But I'm almost an adult. I need to experience my own life, do what I want, not what my parents expect of me.

Being away from Nick, even for two days, makes me worry. What if he's changed his mind? What if he doesn't care about me any more? The kiss could've been just that....a kiss and nothing else. A way for him to experiment and see if he was interested in me or not. So what if he's not? What if he hates me? What if he thinks I'm a terrible kisser, that I have bad breath, that I'm some weird

89

little obsessive girl who has zero experience when he's looking for
a girl with lots of experience? Someone sexy and confident.

    That is so not me.

    I wish it were though. I wish I were sexy and confident. Just
for Nick though.

    Just for Nick.

Chapter
EIGHTEEN

Longing: strong and persistent desire or craving
July 10th

I DID nothing on my two days off but think of Reverie.

Oh, I did other stuff. Mindless, sometimes stupid stuff. I washed my truck. Got drunk Saturday night with Michael when he came over with a bottle of tequila and margarita mix plus a blender. Who travels around with a blender?

Michael, that's who.

The massive hangover from all the tequila just about did me in come Sunday morning. I felt like absolute shit when I first woke up, my head pounding, my mouth as dry as cotton balls and my stomach protesting every time I even thought about food.

So I was lazy and watched TV all day. Even found Reverend Hale on his Sunday televangelist show, punching his fist in the air after every word he said, like some sort of weird, gotta-drive-my-point-home punctuation. He was talking about the youth of today. How they don't listen. How they think they know everything and refuse to respect their elders. How they don't follow the gospel of our lord Jesus Christ and think they're invincible.

I wonder who he's referring to. The episode is a repeat, they take the summer off, but something must've set him off for that sermon. I can't help but wonder if it was his son. Evan. That guy is constantly doing whatever the hell he wants and doesn't give a damn what his parents think. And no way can he be talking about Reverie. She's the perfect girl. I think she's scared to death to disappoint them.

Her spending even a minute of time with me would surely disappoint them. That's why we have to keep what we're doing secret. I don't even know what exactly I'm doing. I should've never kissed her in the stables. I still feel like a jerk for just leaving her there, never saying anything to her again.

She probably hates me. She should.

Late in the afternoon there's a knock on my door and I automatically think it's Krista. No one else comes over unannounced. Michael always calls or texts me first and I don't really have any other friends, not anymore. Krista needs the element of surprise on her side because she knows I'm avoiding her as much as possible.

So when I decide fuck it and throw open the door fully expecting to find a half naked Krista waiting for me, imagine my surprise when I see David standing in front of me.

David. My former best friend, he was like a brother to me. The guy I would do anything for. The kid who lied and said I was with him that one night when we supposedly beat a man to death after going on a drunken binge. The one whose lies sunk me, sent me to jail, cost my mom money she didn't have and nearly ruined my life.

Yeah. That David.

I don't say a word, start to shut the door on him but he throws his hand out, blocking me. Fucker was always stronger than me too. Broader, bulkier, though I got him beat in height. Didn't help me in situations like this though.

"Move," I practically growl, not letting my eyes meet his because damn it, I don't even want to look at this asshole.

"We need to talk," David says, his palm flat against my front door, his body leaning slightly forward. He's putting all his weight into holding that door open and I'm putting all of my weight into trying to close the damn thing.

And I'm freaking losing which frustrates me even more.

"I have nothing to say to you," I say through gritted teeth.

"Well, I have plenty to say to you. Stop being such a stubborn ass and let me in so I can tell you," David says.

Curiosity washes over me and I wish I could quell it. But…I can't. I want to hear what he has to say. I need to hear an apology, a reason why, something so I can start to understand why he did what he did. If I can ever understand what he did. I don't know if that's possible.

Giving in, I move away from the door and David practically falls inside, stumbling forward before he catches himself and stands up straight. I slam the door behind him, hoping like hell Krista doesn't know he's here. She'd run right over if she found out.

Something I absolutely do not want to deal with right now.

"You've got ten minutes," I say as I turn to face him, my arms crossed in front of my chest. I'm trying my best to look tough while facing my former best friend for the first time in years, wearing a battered old T-shirt and equally battered shorts, both having seen better days.

"Ten minutes?" David thrusts a hand through his black hair, sending it straight into chaos. An old tell that lets me know he's nervous.

Oddly reassuring since I am too.

"And the clock is ticking," I say with a nod.

"Fine." He blows out a harsh breath before he starts talking in earnest. "I'm really sorry. I heard about your mom and how you uh, lost her." He pauses, sounding a little choked up. "She meant a lot to me and it about broke my heart to hear she was sick."

I swallow hard, past the swell of emotion threatening me. "How'd you find out?"

"My dad." David shakes his head and collapses in the chair closest to him. Mom's old chair. How fitting. "I cried when he told me."

"Are your tears supposed to make me feel better? Give me some sort of peace since I lost her?" I feel like a jerk for saying it but come on. "At least I was able to be with her during her last few months." *No thanks to your lies putting me in jail in the first place.*

"Yeah, thank God for that." David clears his throat. "Listen, I'm sorry for everything else too. For lying. For…getting you arrested. For ruining your life and mine too."

Great. Now he's the martyr. I want to punch him in the nuts for saying this crap. "When did you get out?"

"Two days ago." He studies me, all solemn sincerity. "I fucked up. I don't know why I did it."

Anger rises within me, making my skin hot and my blood boil. He thinks he can come see me and not give me a real reason as to why he did what he did? "So that's all you've got?" I yell, making him wince. I feel like I'm going to explode. "You fucked up? You don't know why you did it?"

He shrugs, his expression uneasy. "They pressured me."

"Who? The cops?"

"Well, yeah. I told those detectives who questioned me we were out drinking that night in the park. Not too far from where that guy got beat up. You remember how it was, when the police talked to you? They questioned me for hours. They wouldn't let up, asking me the same thing over and over again. Telling me we were the ones who did it. That they *knew* we did it. I was so tired, freaking delirious really, and I finally said yes, we did do it, just to make them stop." He pauses and I notice there are unshed tears shining in his eyes. I've known this kid since we were six. I don't think I've seen him cry in ten years. But those tears are not gonna move me now. Besides he's giving me details I already know. "I'm sorry bro."

"Don't call me bro." I tip my head back and stare at the ceiling, the water stains there, the wisps of long abandoned spider webs. The detectives questioned me relentlessly too. Doesn't mean I gave in to their harassment and said that we did it. We didn't. No matter what they said to me, I wasn't going to cave. Why would I? We were innocent. "I didn't do that to you. They questioned me just as long as they talked to you. I stood by the truth."

"Maybe you were the stronger one then. I was young. Stupid."

"We're the same age, asshole." I study him, really look at him. He appears way older. And tired. So freaking tired. Do I look that tired and old? Hell, we're not even eighteen yet. David looks like he's lived a thousand lives already. "How did you get out anyway?"

"They tried to make other charges stick, about my making false statements to law enforcement when they're the ones who filled my head with lies. Dad threatened to sue them all, which sprung them into action. When they realized they had nothing to hold me there, especially once they let you go, they dropped all charges and released me," David explains.

He's lucky he has his parents to stand by him. I don't have anyone. "Is that all you've got to say then?"

David stares at me, his jaw hanging open like he's trying to catch flies. I don't know what he expected. A sappy reunion? My instant forgiveness? He wronged me like no one ever had or probably ever will. He said I helped him kill someone. "I guess so," he mumbles. "I thought..."

"You thought what? That I'd welcome you back into my life with open arms? That we'd resume our friendship just like it was before you started spewing lies and accusing me of fucking murder?" The rage that consumes me is near overwhelming. I'm shaking, I'm so angry. "You were wrong."

"I guess so," David says quietly as he gets up. "I'm sorry, Nick."

"Fuck you," I practically spit out. "Your ten minutes are up."

Without another word David leaves my apartment, closing the door behind him, the sharp click echoing in the otherwise quiet room.

I stand in the center of the living room, my breathing ragged, like I just ran twenty miles. My lungs burn, my eyes sting and my heart... it fucking hurts.

Never could I admit this out loud, especially to David's face, but I miss my best friend. I wish I could accept him back into my life with open arms. I wish we could pick up where we left off. There's so much I could tell him, so much I'm sure he could tell me.

But I can't. He screwed me over and I don't mean that lightly. The guy—my so called best friend—told the damn cops that he and I got drunk. That we went out looking for trouble and found it with some chubby middle-aged guy getting off work after pulling a late shift. That we took a tire iron to the dude and beat the shit out of him until he collapsed and...died by the side of his car. In the middle of an otherwise empty parking lot.

I remember seeing it on the news. I remember thinking how close we were to that parking lot the night before. We had gone out drinking at the city park not far from that dead guy's work. David had brought a twelve pack of beer, one he'd stolen from his dad. We drank it fast and were buzzing pretty hard. We were trying to bond after our fight about Krista.

My best friend and my girl, fucking. I'd been pissed. Not hurt so much by Krista's betrayal, but from David's.

Then he went and betrayed me even further.

I collapse on the couch and sling my arm over my eyes. My chest aches. Everything hurts and it's not a physical pain. More like a throbbing deep in my bones, buried in my heart.

Scarred all over my soul.

I need out of this place. It's no good here. I stay in this apartment, in this town, hanging out with the same people, I'm just spinning my wheels. Going nowhere.

Hale House is my one glimmer of hope. Gaining some work experience there could help get me out. If I'm careful, I could even save enough money to take a couple of classes at the community college this upcoming fall, if I can still somehow enroll. Probably can't do it till next spring though, which is probably better. That way I can have even more money saved. I need an education. I need an advantage to get me out of here for good.

Before I'm forever stuck.

Chapter
NINETEEN

Conflicted: contradictory, a struggle
July 11th

I ARRIVE at Hale House early so I wait in my car the last fifteen minutes before I'm scheduled to clock in, slugging back some cheap-ass coffee I bought at the gas station and listening to the radio. I slept like hell last night after my conversation with David and I'm desperate for a distraction. And at the moment, the distraction I'm most looking forward to is seeing Reverie.

Despite telling myself I don't deserve her, despite replaying my conversation with Michael over and over again in my head, I still want to see her. Just…breathe her in. See that shy smile. Let myself get lost in her presence for a little bit. She takes all the ugly in my life and makes it beautiful, at least for a few stolen minutes.

I can look right? Just for a little bit?

What's so stupid is I'm nervous just to freaking look at her. What we shared in the stables feels like it happened months ago. Or maybe that it didn't happen at all. Like it was some sort of awesome dream I conjured up.

But it wasn't a dream. I kissed Reverie. She kissed me back. If I'm an idiot, I'll try and kiss her again even though I shouldn't.

Yeah. I shouldn't.

So here I sit, too amped up and anxious to actually see her because I have no idea how she's going to react when she finally lays eyes on me. Is she pissed at how I just left her in the stables? I had no choice but girls are weird. As in, I never know how they're going to react. They can get upset over the smallest things. And maybe that wasn't so small. I was kissing her. She seemed to be really getting into it too.

I know I was.

Memories come at me, one after another and I lean back in my seat and revel in them. Her soft lips. Her wet tongue. The taste of her, sweet and addictive, hooking me instantly. How she felt in my arms, how I wanted to come out of my skin when she touched me...

I hear Reverie before I see her, her voice knocking me from my thoughts. I slouch low in my seat, not wanting her to see me sitting here staring at her like some sort of stalker.

That doesn't stop me from wanting to get a look at her though. Just...soak her up a little bit before I have to go to work. She's in the front yard standing next to her mother, talking animatedly. Her hair is down and a little wild looking this morning. She's got on a sunny yellow dress and with her golden skin and blonde hair she's like a flash of intense hot summer in the otherwise cool Monday morning.

Reverie throws her arms up in the air, her long blonde hair flying out behind her. Her mom says something in response and Reverie rests her hands on her hips, tapping her sandaled foot on the grass impatiently. I can feel the tension in her from all the way over here. Whatever she's talking about, it's got her riled up. I don't think she's angry but she's certainly...passionate. She's always pretty meek and quiet, especially around her mom so I gotta admit...

I like seeing this.

They're standing among the various rose bushes that Valerie Hale tends to. And they aren't looking in my direction either so I lean forward, wrapping my arms around the steering wheel as I rest against it. Reverie seems to calm down and she reaches up, running her fingers through her hair again and again, as if she's combing it.

My fingers twitch. I remember how soft her hair is. I'm dying to touch those silky strands again...

I punch the steering wheel and mutter a curse under my breath. I'm an idiot. I'm driving myself insane by watching her. Longing for her. It's fucking stupid.

I'm fucking stupid.

By the time I'm climbing out of my car to head toward the house, Michael shows up, parking next to me and hopping out of his tiny car full of boundless energy as usual.

"What are you doing? Spying on the Hale ladies?" Michael asks as he approaches. He flicks his head in their direction and I look to see that they're heading toward the back of the house, their backs to us as they walk side by side.

Thank Christ. I have no desire to explain myself to Michael. He'll just twist it around to make me sound like some sort of pervert anyway.

"I was waiting for your late ass," I drawl, playing it off, praying Reverie won't turn around and see me. Or worse, what if she said something to me? Not likely that would happen since she's with her mom but still. I'm paranoid.

"Gimme a break. I got here right on time," Michael says as we walk toward the house. "Your days off were good?"

"Yeah." I don't give him any more details because while for the most part my two days off were fine, yesterday's visit with David still leaves a sour taste in my mouth.

"I saw Heather." Michael drops this tidbit like it's nothing. No big deal. But I know it's a huge deal because I've seen him chase after her like crazy while she continues to ignore him.

"No shit?"

"Yeah. I practically attacked her in the back seat of my car Saturday night," he says with a shrug, that cocky smile on his face telling me he's pretty pleased with himself.

"She live with her parents too?" Michael comes home every summer to work, though he lives on his own during the school year, when he's away for college. He's told me more than once he's sick and tired of being under his parents' roof, always having them tell him what to do.

I say nothing. I'd look like a total wimp if I confessed I wished I still lived with Mom. Yeah, I lost her only a few months ago but still. I need to man up. I can handle this on my own.

"Yep. She's going away to school in the fall, just like I am," Michael says, our feet crunching on the graveled driveway. "This is definitely going to be a summer romance, nothing more."

"And you're okay with that?" I ask, shoving my hands in the pockets of my shorts.

"Do I have a choice? Besides, it's not such a bad thing, walking into a relationship knowing it won't last beyond a few months. So yeah, I'm good with it," Michael says with a shrug. "Really it's perfect. No strings attached. We walk away from each other at the end of the summer and no one's feelings are hurt."

Not a bad idea, approaching the relationship knowing it's going to end for good in a limited amount of time. Something I could consider with Reverie though I wonder how she would feel about it. She's not someone to trifle with. She deserves more than a summer fling with a loser like me.

Not that I can do something like this with her anyway. I'm supposed to be giving up on that angle and I need to remember it.

"Plus, working with her, we can sneak off during breaks and get some personal time in if you know what I mean." Michael waggles his eyebrows at me like he's some sort of cartoon character, making me laugh. I'd been in such a bad mood since yesterday it felt good.

I shove him away from me. "I better not walk into the storage barn or whatever and find you half naked with Heather, tumbling around in the hay."

"Like I found you with Rev in the stables?" More waggling of the brows on Michael's end. "Besides, hay's too damn scratchy."

My lungs freeze, making it hard to breathe. "What the hell are you talking about?" I wave my hand, trying to blow off his statement but it feels forced. Phony.

"I'm not blind, dude. She may have been clear across the room from you but something was going down between you and Rev in the stables." I can feel Michael's eyes on me, steady and pointed.

I stop walking and so does Michael. "It was nothing," I lie.

"Bullshit," Michael says cheerfully. "Deny it all you want. I saw the way you chased after her on the Fourth. And I freaking felt the tension between you two in the stables. You're still pursuing that even after everything I told you? Are you crazy?"

No way can I answer him. Instead I start walking fast, headed toward the shed near the patio where the Hales keep all their lawn equipment. Michael chases after me like the persistent dog he is, chattering the entire way.

"Listen, if you're gonna go all balls to the wall and go for it anyway, I'm not going to stop you. Who am I to get in the way of true love? But I need to warn you dude. This isn't going to be easy."

"I have no idea what you're talking about," I say between clenched teeth, glancing around to make sure no one else is listening. Michael's volume is always high. The guy doesn't know how to be quiet. The last thing I need is someone else hearing him give me permission to go for Reverie.

"It's all good if you do like her, dude. I won't tell a soul. Not even Heather."

I turn on him, thrust my finger in his face. "Especially not Heather," I practically growl.

Michael's smile fades as he throws up his arms in surrender. "Don't worry. I won't blow your cover."

Irritated with my reaction, I drop my hand and turn away from Michael. "It's nothing between Reverie and me. Nothing."

"You're the only one who calls her that you know," Michael says.

I turn to look at him again. "What?"

"Reverie. No one else calls her that. She's just Rev." The smile is back, not as shit-eating as usual though. More like he can see right through me and is realizing that I really do like her.

Which just leaves me feeling weak and vulnerable. And I hate that.

"Rev. It doesn't fit her," I mutter, headed toward the shed once more.

"Whatever dude," Michael calls after me but I ignore him this time. We don't need to get caught by Valerie Hale talking. She'd love nothing more than to give us twice the work to finish in half the time.

I start my daily washing of the patio, a mindless chore I like to do first thing in the morning, when I'm not one hundred percent awake. Though at the moment I'm hopped up on that extra large cup of coffee I had and I feel all jittery. Or that could just be nerves. I still have no idea how she'll react the first time she sees me after we kissed. Will she act casual, like it was no big deal? Ignore me completely? Yeah, that would probably be for the best. It sucks though.

Maybe I should go seek her out and get this over with. Be the one to approach her, tell her it was all a mistake and hope like hell she understands. This was all just a fluke. It had to be. Kissing the reverend's daughter is the stupidest thing I could've done since getting out of jail with all charges dropped. I'm supposed to be on the straight and narrow, not playing with danger.

"Nick."

I about jump out of my skin at the sound of Valerie Hale's voice and glance over my shoulder to find her watching me with an expectant look on her face. What is up with these Hales always sneaking up on me and surprising me?

I'm both relieved and disappointed to find that she's alone. Reverie is nowhere to be found.

"Morning, Mrs. Hale." I turn to face her, making sure the hose isn't aimed in her direction. I don't think she'd like it if I accidentally splashed her expensive leather sandals.

"Turn that off." She waves a hand at the hose, her gesture impatient. She seems irritated. I can't help but wonder if it has to do with that conversation she just had with Reverie.

Without a word I go and turn off the faucet, then start hurriedly rolling up the hose. "You wanted to talk to me about something?"

"I do." She approaches me, her steps evenly measured, her back ramrod straight. Her dark blond hair is pulled into a low ponytail and she's wearing a sleeveless white shirt and matching skirt. She looks extremely put together, not a wrinkle in sight, not a hair out of place.

She's intimidating as hell. I usually deal with her when Michael's around. Rarely do we talk alone. I prefer it that way. Why, I'm not sure.

Maybe because every time I look at her, a steady stream of guilt pours over me, making me feel like crap.

Hey Mrs. Hale, what's up? Oh, you found out I kissed your virgin daughter in the stables? Yeah, no problem. Hope you don't mind. I just couldn't resist her. You have to admit she's pretty damn cute.

Yeah. That wouldn't go over well.

"Did you steal my daughter's necklace?" she asks, her voice laced with just enough venom to make me feel like she's merely scratching my neck with the tip of the knife, not full on thrusting it into my flesh.

I'm so shocked by her question I gape at her like an idiot for a second, unable to form words. "W-what are you talking about?"

"On Saturday, Rev wanted to speak with you. Something about a missing necklace. Do you know anything about a missing necklace?" She raises her eyebrows, waiting for a logical answer from me.

But I don't have one. "I have no idea what you're talking about, Mrs. Hale," I say, slowly shaking my head. What the hell? Was Reverie going around accusing me of stealing her necklace? This is the last sort of trouble I need. Is this some sort of revenge plot on Reverie's part? Because this sort of accusation could royally screw me over.

As in, cost me my job.

"You didn't *steal* her necklace did you?"

"I would never put my job at risk like that, Mrs. Hale. I swear to you. This job is everything to me. I need it. I would never steal from any of you," I vow, hoping like hell she believes me.

She studies me, her gaze razor sharp, almost as sharp as her words. Crossing her arms in front of her chest, she purses her lips and I notice the faint lines around them, the bright red of her lipstick. I can see where Reverie got her looks. I remember what Michael said. How she grabbed him last summer and hit on him. I wonder if he was exaggerating.

I hope like hell she never tries to pull something like that on me.

"Glad to hear this," she finally says. "I'll be frank. I don't like that my daughter is asking about you."

I swallow hard and say nothing.

"I want you to stay away from her," she continues as she takes a step toward me. Then another. "I don't know exactly what she's doing, inquiring about you. Making up stories about missing necklaces and then miraculously finding them. She's young and curious and naïve. Someone like you could easily take advantage of her."

Anger flares inside of me at her words. Someone like me? What is she accusing me of? She's making me sound like some sort of creeper rapist.

"So I suggest you stay away from my daughter." Mrs. Hale taps me on the chest with one red lacquered red fingernail. Her finger presses into me, lifts away and then does it again. Like she's testing me out or something.

Weird.

"I have no plans of going after your daughter," I tell her firmly because damn it, it's the truth. I don't need the trouble. I don't need some crazy girl going after me, accusing me of things I didn't do, getting me in trouble with her parents, my employers.

"Good." Mrs. Hale tilts her head back, her gaze meeting mine. She smiles and presses her entire hand against my chest, her fingers curling ever so slightly into the fabric of my shirt. "Because I will *ruin* you if you so much as lay a finger on her."

With those final words, she shoves at my chest and then turns, walking away without a backward glance. I watch her slip back inside the house through the French door and take a deep breath the moment she disappears from view.

A mixture of frustration and anger swirls within me and I breathe deep, wishing I could punch something. What the hell was that all about? Stolen necklaces? Veiled threats? The woman sounded like she wanted to chop my balls off and then turn around and play with them. And that is scary as shit.

I'm starting to think spending even a minute with Reverie Hale isn't worth the risk.

Chapter
TWENTY

Dear Diary,

(July 11th, 7:52 p.m.) I don't know what I did wrong. Nick ignored me all day. Any time I tried to get his attention, he looked away from me. Not that I saw him much. Mom kept him and Michael busy and then she forced me to go with her while she ran a bunch of errands, which really turned into us going out to lunch and going shopping. An early birthday present, she told me.

For once in my life, I wasn't in the mood for shopping. All I wanted was to see Nick. Talk to Nick. Find out what happened, see how he's feeling after we kissed. Because I was alternating between feeling great about it and then worried. Now though. Now I'm just...

Confused.

I'm also tired. I don't have anything to say. Nothing good happened today. My expectations were so high that I think I'm crashing. In fact, I know I'm crashing. If I keep writing about how disappointing this day was, I think I might start crying.

I'd like to avoid that so I think I'm going to lie in bed and read. I'd rather lose myself in a book than worry if Nick hates me or not.

For so long I wanted a boyfriend. I wanted to know what it would be like, to kiss a guy, talk with him, flirt with him, touch him. Hold hands, go out on a date, talk about meaningful things, make each other laugh. I wanted all of that. I thought for a quick minute I would get that with Nick.

I wanted too much too soon I guess. Or maybe I put all my focus on liking him and not realizing he wasn't feeling the same way. Whatever. I must say this though.

I didn't realize liking a boy, kissing a boy only to have that boy ignore me would hurt so much. Because it hurts.

A lot.

Chapter
TWENTY-ONE

Dear Diary,

(July 17th, 8:05 a.m.) I am now seventeen. I don't feel different but I never do. When you're little you think birthdays are magical moments. Perfect days where nothing can ever go wrong. And even if it does, cake and ice cream and prettily wrapped presents can solve all your problems.

It's not true. Don't get me wrong. I still love cake and ice cream. Presents too. Mama and Daddy have already been so generous. She took me shopping and bought me so much stuff. Pretty things. I didn't get the, 'Don't be vain,' or 'Remember to pick something modest,' lectures either.

It was nice.

But I still don't have what I want most. He's still ignoring me. I think I know why too and it must have something to do with Mama. I think she talked to him. Told him to stay away from me. He steers clear of me completely. Won't even look at me. It's so weird.

I miss him.

This morning though, I woke up feeling hopeful. Feeling

strong. *Before I even got out of bed I made a wish. Closed my eyes tight and squeezed my hands together, almost in prayer.*

I wished for one more chance with Nick.

Tonight is my birthday party. I'm going to wear my new dress and put on the makeup Mama allowed me to buy. I'm going to put my hair up and try my best to walk in those new heels. Most everyone coming to the party are friends of Daddy's but that's okay. At least the Williamsons are coming. Glenn Williamson has always had a crush on me. I used to have a tiny crush on him too.

Not anymore. This may sound mean but I'm going to use that crush to my advantage. Maybe my flirting with Glenn will make Nick sit up and pay attention. I feel like a mean girl for using Glenn but he won't mind. He's too sweet to mind.

Here's to new adventures. To capturing my dreams. To becoming a woman.

Here's to turning seventeen.

Chapter
TWENTY-TWO

Jealousy: resentment against a rival
July 17th

"You look ready to tear his arms off and make him eat them for dinner," Michael mutters.

I jerk my head toward him, glowering at my friend. "What are you talking about?" I clench my hands into fists, barely able to keep my focus on him when all I can hear is Reverie's happy shouts as she splashes around in the pool.

With a guy.

"Douchebag in the pool with Rev." Michael waves his hand toward them. Reverie's laughter rings out, light and sweet and it's killing me that I'm not the one making her laugh like that. I've blown my chance thanks to her witch of a mom. "Though I'm pretty sure he's harmless. You could take him on."

"I don't want to take him on," I lie between clenched teeth, feeling like an idiot for even acting this way. Thinking this way. I have no business feeling so possessive. She's not mine. She never was mine. I talked to her a few times. Kissed her a couple of times. So why do I feel so strongly for her? The pull I have toward her is undeniable.

And frustrating as hell.

I've done so good. All week I've ignored Reverie. I refused to look at her, talk to her, even think of her and focused solely on my job. The job I can't risk losing for showing any interest in my boss's daughter. Ever since my enlightening talk with Valerie Hale a few days ago, I've avoided Reverie. We haven't talked. She won't approach me and I sure as hell won't approach her.

It's all working out perfectly. Just like Mrs. Hale wanted. So why the hell am I so miserable?

Because you still want her, jackass.

And now there's some guy here, some dude who's her age and more her speed. An old family friend who came to visit with the rest of his clan, Glenn Williamson and his parents arrived yesterday, just in time for Reverie's birthday.

She's splashing around in the pool with him right now, playing some sort of game that looks like grab ass to me. She's laughing and yelling at him every time he splashes her, which only makes him do it more. When he's not splashing her, he's trying his best to grab hold of her. Constantly. Puts his hands all over her.

She must've gotten a new swimsuit for her birthday because there isn't a thick black strap in sight. All I see is skin. Her shoulders, her chest, her stomach and those sexy long legs, all on display since she's wearing a colorful bikini that manages to cover all the important parts up pretty well but still fuels my imagination.

"You're a fucking liar, bro. That guy is all over your woman." Michael pauses, scrutinizing me a little too closely. "Or are you two on the outs already?"

I shrug and look away, my gaze snagging on Reverie yet again. After going days without looking at her at all, now she's all I can see. All I can hear. She's treading water in the deep end, her hair slicked back from her face, water droplets still clinging to her cheeks. Glenn's running around the pool like he's ten and ready to do a cannonball right in front of her, which is probably what he's planning to do.

Her gaze meets mine and she flashes me a little smile. A smile that says, *look but don't touch.* Diamond studs sparkle in her ears and I wonder where the hell she got those.

Probably Daddy's the one who got his precious baby girl earrings that could pay my rent for at least two years, maybe more.

How nice.

Her smile falters a little bit but she doesn't look away and I can't either. We stare at each other, even though Michael's still talking to me and the obnoxious Glenn is yelling her name. She mouths 'hi' at me and gives me a little wave.

I look away from her and focus on Michael. "I decided you were right," I say, interrupting him.

Michael's eyebrows went up. "Yeah? That's a first. No one ever thinks I'm right."

I chuckle. Even when I'm thoroughly pissed off, this guy can still make me laugh. "Yeah well, in this situation you definitely are. She's nothing but a goody goody virgin. I gave up on her." The words leave a sour taste lingering in my mouth the moment I say them. Because I don't mean it. I only gave up because I had to. And yeah, she might be a virgin, but I have a feeling it would've been real easy for me to show Reverie a thing or two. She would've been a more than willing participant. She melted every single time I got her in my arms…

But I'll never know what could've happened because that is over and done with.

"You sure about that? You look kinda wound up. Not that I can blame you since Rev looks pretty damn hot in that bikini. Who knew she was hiding such a bangin' body?"

Just like that, I go from appreciating Michael's sense of humor to wanting to bash his face in. This isn't good. I'm not the jealous type. I need to get my shit under control.

"I'm sure," I say, my lips barely moving. Breathing deep, I tell myself to get a grip. Wanting what I can't have is getting me nowhere. "Besides, look at her. She has a new guy to play with."

"Please. Glenn Williamson has been coming here every summer with his parents since I've worked here. He chases after her for a few days, she tolerates him, they have fun but it's nothing serious. That guy is a complete loser." Michael makes a dismissive noise but it doesn't ease the jealousy tearing up my insides.

I need to face facts. I'm not over Reverie. I still want her. Bad. So bad, I feel ready to beat some innocent dude's face in just so I can prove a point. He needs to keep his hands off her.

"Come on, the party is gonna start in a little over an hour and they want us to finish arranging everything over at the tent," Michael reminds me.

I follow him away toward the rose garden, keeping my gaze straight ahead versus looking at the pool one last time. But I can feel her eyes on me, watching as I leave. I wonder if she's flirting with that guy on purpose. Does she want to drive me crazy or is she innocent in all of this? I'm not sure.

She's unpredictable. That's half the reason I'm attracted to her.

A tent for the small dinner party they're having in celebration of Reverie's birthday has been set up in the garden. A long table awaits inside, lavishly set with a deep pink tablecloth and a scattering of lit votive candles. A local florist brought in colorful arrangements that run down the entire center of the table. There's even a freakin' chandelier hanging from the highest point of the tent, casting a rich golden glow that makes the entire setting look like something out of a fairytale.

I bet Reverie is going to love it. She seems like the type of girl who still believes in the fairytale.

Michael and I need to do a few little things to prep for the dinner, including set up the torches around the tent and light them, then wheel over the portable bar, which is a heavy son of a bitch. Once we're done with that, we can head back to the pool to clean up and then we can make our escape.

Thank God. I'm ready to get the hell out of here. I can only handle so much torture before I'm pushed beyond my limits. And I'm pretty sure I already hit that mark a couple of hours ago.

We work silently, Michael and I. Even the people from the kitchen are quiet as they finish setting the table with the fancy china and making sure everything's ready. All I can do is think about the birthday girl. I don't know if I could stand watching Reverie at her special dinner. She'll probably wear something amazing and look gorgeous. Her parents will shower her with more gifts. Stupid Glenn Williamson will give her something too. Something expensive and out of my reach and she'll give him a big hug for it. Maybe even a thank you kiss.

My blood boils just thinking about it.

"Uh oh," Michael utters under his breath.

"You two!" I hear hands clap twice, a sure sign that Valerie Hale has blessed us with her presence. "Hurry up! I don't want you around when Reverie arrives."

"We're almost done," Michael tells her as I shoot her a quick look. I don't dare stare at her too long for fear she says something to me. Like, *you're fired.*

Yeah. I know she's not happy with me. Feeling's mutual. I did what she asked me to do and I stayed away from her daughter. What more could she want?

"You. You're done," Valerie says as she stops directly in front of me. I'm lighting one of the last torches, holding the lighter to the thick wick before it finally catches. "You can go."

"Are you dismissing me?" Ah hell, I didn't mean to talk back but I'm holding on by a thread here. My temper is this close to exploding and I'm not one to explode.

She crosses her arms in front of her chest, plumping up her boobs. I figure she's doing it on purpose but I refuse to ogle her. I don't know what's up with this woman but I don't like it. "I am," she says coldly. "Now go. Before our guests see you."

I feel like a lowly hideous servant she wants to hide. My hand curls tight around the lighter and I feel like I could bust the plastic into a million little pieces with my fist. Instead I turn and leave, muttering a low 'see ya' at Michael as I stalk away toward the house.

"You need us to still clean up the pool?" I hear Michael ask her.

"Just you. Let him go. You don't need him." The contempt in her voice when she says *him* is more than obvious. "You can handle everything on your own, right Michael?"

What a bitch. She dismisses me and unloads an unfair amount of work on Michael. God, I hate her. Maybe I should quit. It's probably what Valerie Hale wants. She treats me like shit in the hopes she can get rid of me and normally, that would make me want to stay even more.

I'm not sure if it's worth the trouble though. I'd rather give her the satisfaction and get away from her smug ass than have to deal with her every day.

That would also mean I won't see Reverie anymore, but maybe that's okay. It's better for me actually. A couple of days ago I viewed this job as my saving grace. Now quitting Hale House is the perfect excuse for me to get away from Reverie once and for all.

No matter how much I need this job and how much I would miss Reverie I know it's what's best. I gotta look out for myself. No one else gives a crap about me. I have no one.

No one at all.

I'm planning my giving notice call to Reverend Hale when I run into her. Reverie. Just plow straight into her slender body so hard I almost knock her on her ass. Her startled gasp reverberates through me and I reach out to grab her upper arms. My fingers tingle as I hold her steady and she finds her footing. "God, I'm sorry. Are you okay? Did I hurt you?"

She lifts her head, her gaze meeting mine and I'm stunned silent by her beauty. Fucking corny as hell but it's the truth. She must be wearing makeup because I've never seen her eyes look that intense before and her lips are this glossy, tempting pink. Her hair is slicked back into a tight bun that sits practically on top of her head and she's wearing a dress that is almost…indescribable.

Short. Strapless. Gold and lace and a black ribbon wrapped around her waist as a belt. Slender arms on display, long legs on display, she's the hottest thing I've ever seen. A sexy fairy princess who's come to me in my dreams, only this is my fucking reality.

I let my gaze linger as I drink her in. Slowly I ease my grip on her arms but I don't release her. It's like I can't. "I'm fine," she finally answers. "Are you all right?"

That she cares about my wellbeing says a lot. I've treated her like shit all week and she still asks. When she should kick me in the shins with those sexy shoes she's wearing and tell me to go to hell.

"I'm fine," I say as I realize I'm slowly stroking her upper arms with my thumbs. I immediately release her, glancing around to make sure that her mom is nowhere in sight.

"Are you leaving?" She sounds disappointed.

"Yep. Work day's over." I offer her a grim smile as I step away from her, creating some much needed distance between us. Of course, all this does is allow me to see her even better and man, is she a sight to see. It's like a transformation happened in the last few days. She went from sweet, innocent Reverie to sexy, all grown up Reverie.

I don't know which version I like better.

"I haven't seen you much this week," she says, getting straight to the point, as is her typical style.

"Been busy." I shrug.

"More like been avoiding me."

I don't say anything because she's right.

"Did I do something to make you mad? It's like we haven't even talked since…the stable." She looks worried. I did that to her and it makes me feel like shit. "I was afraid that maybe what happened… wasn't good. For you. Or whatever." She waves a hand, her cheeks coloring a pretty shade of pink that reminds me of a summer sunset. "I'm being stupid. Just ignore me. Have a good night, Nick." She starts to walk away.

"Wait a minute." I grab hold of her arm again to keep her from escaping and turn her to face me. "I'm not mad at you."

"You seem mad."

"Other shi—stuff is making me mad. It's not you. I'm sorry that I ignored you." *What are you doing, asshole?* "And just to let you know, it has nothing to do with what happened in the stables."

"Um, okay," she whispers, nodding. Looking like she wants to believe me but she's not quite sure if she can.

"And you're never being stupid. *I'm* the stupid one," I reassure her because damn it, it's true. What I'm doing right now is so stupid, so risky. Her mom sees us and I'm done.

Fired. Gone. Out of her life.

Reverie smiles a little at that. "No you're not."

"Yeah, trust me I am. Just…don't ask me to explain what happened. It's all me. My own issues. You're perfect. I hope you realize that. " I return her smile, just basking in her presence. If that's all I can get then I'm going to enjoy every minute of it. "Happy Birthday, Reverie."

"Thank you," she says, her voice so soft I almost don't hear her. "I wish you could go to the dinner with me."

My entire body tenses. She's offering me something I can never have. What sucks worse is I want it. So bad, I'm tempted to say screw it and accompany her to that dinner. Wouldn't her mom just shit if I pulled out a chair and sat right next to Reverie? If she put her hand on my arm and told her parents, "He's my guest and he's staying."

It would never happen. But a man can dream.

"I don't belong at that table," I finally say, facing my truth. I'm not worthy. Of her, of her family, of any of them. We live on opposite sides of the world and the divide between us is so wide I don't know why I'm even attempting this.

"Yes, you do. You're my friend. I want you there."

"Just your friend?" I ask, pissed at myself for even saying it.

Walk away, walk away, walk away.

I don't move. My entire body is frozen as I wait for her answer.

"I…" She smiles prettily and lowers her lashes, like she can't look straight at me when speaks. "I'd like us to be something more. I made a birthday wish this morning but I don't know how you feel."

I want more but I can't tell her that. Can I? "A birthday wish?"

"It's dumb. Completely immature." She huffs out a sigh and glances over her shoulder. "I should probably go. My mom will come looking for me."

"Tell me your birthday wish." I should let it go but I can't. I want to know what she wished for.

I want to know if it has to do with me.

"Really?" She flashes me a tremulous smile and I feel it to the very depth of my soul. Her uneasiness. Her fear that I'll laugh or worse, reject her.

"Tell me." I grab her hand and entwine our fingers, pressing my palm flat to hers. "And make it fast before your mom shows up and ruins everything."

She giggles. "I wished for another chance with you," she whispers, her eyes wide and full of fear. "I've missed you."

I can't do this. I shouldn't do this. I don't measure up. But I can't hurt her. I don't want to. I love how direct she is. She's a total contradiction. Shy and direct. Sweet and sexy. "I've missed you too," I admit, wishing I hadn't the second the words fall from my lips.

Too late.

"I'd rather be with you tonight than that stupid dinner my mom planned," she confesses.

My heart starts racing triple time. No way can she mean that. "I've seen what she planned for you. Trust me, you don't want to miss it."

"Meet me later then." She squeezes my hand, her slender fingers strong. I can literally see her gain more strength with every word we exchange. I'm giving her hope and that is the last thing I should be doing. "In the woods by my house. In the clearing where you found me last time."

A matching hope lights within me and I tell it to get lost. "Reverie... no way. It'll be too late and you can't sneak out like that. Not on your birthday."

"Why not? I've snuck out before remember? They won't know. I'll give them an excuse and bail early. Tell them I'm not feeling very well." She smiles and the sight of it strikes at my dumb with lust heart. "Please Nick? Do this for me? For my birthday?"

"I didn't buy you a birthday present." And I feel like a real ass for it too.

"Don't you get it? *You're* my birthday present." Her smile grows.

"Come on, you have to say yes. You're what I want for my birthday. Nothing else."

Damn. When she puts it like that…

"Won't it be too dark to walk the trails?" I sound like an overly concerned grandma with all my protests but shit. It's to protect her. I don't want her to get hurt.

"It's a full moon. You haven't noticed how bright it is?" She steps closer to me, the scent of her enveloping me in a heady rush. With the heels on, she's much taller. It would take nothing for me to lean down and kiss her. "I can find my way and so can you. Meet me at ten?"

"Uh…" My brain is scrambling for an excuse to give her. Anything. But I've got nothing but a yes waiting to spring from my lips.

She stands on tiptoe before I can get another word out and brushes her mouth against mine, leaving a smudge of lipgloss on my lips. It smells like watermelon. "Don't say no," she whispers. "Please?"

How can I say no to her? It's humanly impossible. "Are you sure?"

Reverie nods and kisses me again, a gentle press of her mouth against mine that makes my head spin. "I'm sure. See you in a couple of hours?"

I lick my lips and taste watermelon. "All right. But Reverie?"

"Yes?" She releases my hand and steps away from me.

"Don't wear those heels when you walk in the woods," I tell her.

"You don't like them?" She kicks out one foot, swaying it this way and that. I'm practically drooling as I stare at her leg, imagining exactly what I could be doing with those legs later tonight.

"Oh I freaking love them. I just don't want you to break your ankle later." I pause. "But don't change. I like the dress. And the hair." Hair up means I have better access to her neck, which I'm dying to kiss.

She laughs and shakes her head. "So I'll see you later? Promise?"

"I promise."

Chapter
TWENTY-THREE

Anticipation: expectation or hope
July 17th, later that night

I'M nervous. Pacing around the clearing, waiting for Reverie to show up. I went straight home after talking to her, my head spinning over what happened the entire drive to my apartment complex. I took a shower, gathered up a couple of thick blankets and pillows, found an unopened bottle of wine in the cabinet that must've been Mom's. I put it on ice in a small ice chest, threw in a couple of plastic glasses and stashed it all in the trunk of my car.

I shaved, wore my best jeans and a button up shirt. I tried to tame my hair but it was no use. Only a haircut would save that mess. So I combed it as best I could. I'm trying to look my best for her because she's so damn pretty and I'm just...

Me.

It's past ten and she's not here but I'm not surprised. I figured she might be late. She's trying to escape her birthday party. They're all going to want to keep her there. Feed her cake. Give her presents. Hell,

Glenn Williamson is probably trying to cop a feel at this very moment and that thought alone makes me want to sock him in the nose so hard I can feel the bones crunch beneath my knuckles and see the blood spurt from his nostrils.

I'm not a violent guy despite what I've been accused of. I got into a couple of fights at school when I was in junior high but they were minor. Nothing serious. I'm not one to get majorly pissed off, it's just not part of my personality.

But I will defend what's mine. And right now, I'm feeling so proprietary over Reverie Hale it's almost scary.

Shoving my hands in the front pockets of my jeans, I stare up at the sky. Reverie definitely hadn't lied about the full moon. It's so bright outside I can see almost everything. It cooled down nicely too and there's a breeze coming off the ocean, bringing with it the salty scent of the sea.

I'm anxious. I need to keep myself busy so I rearrange the pillows, straighten out the blankets and check the ice chest. I'm close to breaking out the bottle of wine and drinking it but I don't want to get ahead of myself. Will she even want to drink any? Am I being too presumptuous in bringing alcohol? I was just looking for a way to celebrate. I brought something else for her too. A little present for her birthday. It's nothing major and the best I could come up with in such a short amount of time so I hope she likes it.

My phone beeps in my pocket and I pull it out to find a text from Krista. Fucking great.

I miss you.

Yeah. I don't miss her at all. I don't reply and turn off the volume, shoving the phone back into my pocket. Krista is the last person I want to think about right now. Tonight is all about Reverie. I still can't believe we're actually doing this. That I'm actually going to see her. Touch her. Spend time with her. Alone.

I hear her before I see her, walking along the trail, her feet snapping a branch much like I did the first time I found her here.

And then she appears, still wearing that gorgeous as hell dress, her hair still up and flat sandals on her feet, just like I requested. The moment she spots me a giant smile spreads across her face and she increases her pace, practically running toward me. I meet her halfway, grabbing hold of her so I can pull her into my arms.

"You came," she breathes against my chest as she wraps her arms around me, her breath warm even through the fabric of my shirt.

"I said I would." I press my lips against her forehead and close my eyes, savoring the feel of her. I touch her shoulder, drift my fingers across her skin and she shivers. "You got away okay? No one's suspicious?"

"They think I have a headache. Chocolate does that to me sometimes." She pulls away slightly to smile up at me.

"Chocolate?" I frown.

She laughs. "My cake was made out of all this rich, decadent chocolate. I couldn't even finish my piece and it was tiny. I started complaining that my head hurt and my mom said I should go lie down. So I ran up to my room, changed my shoes and here I am."

"I'm glad," I murmur, staring deep into her eyes. My luck has changed for the better. I'm embracing this. Embracing what I share with Reverie. "You look so pretty tonight."

"Thank you." We study each other for a long, tension filled minute. I'm about to kiss her but then she steps out of my hold and turns away from me to look at the blankets I spread out. "You've been busy."

"Yeah. I have." I'm suddenly feeling self-conscious. I want to impress this girl. It matters to me, what she thinks. "You like it?"

"I love it." She flashes a smile at me from over her shoulder. "Looks cozy."

"Come on." I take her hand and we sit on the layers of blankets, me closer to the ice chest. I pop open the lid and pull out the bottle of wine. "You want some?"

"Um, sure. Did you bring a corkscrew? Glasses? Or are we going to have to break the glass over a rock and sip out of the bottle?"

Shaking my head, I chuckle. "Don't worry, I brought it all. I'm classier than you think."

She laughs in return but says nothing. I wonder if she realizes how true my statement is. I don't want to seem like some sort of dumbass loser in her eyes. I want to impress her. To be someone. Someone important.

I get to work on opening the bottle of wine, having a hell of a time with the corkscrew at first but I finally figure it out, yanking the cork out of the bottle with a loud pop. I grab one of the glasses and fill it, then hand it to Reverie before I fill one for myself. I watch as she takes a sip, grimaces a little then takes another one.

"You like it?" I ask.

"I'm not much of a drinker," she admits as she takes another sip. "I had a glass of champagne at a wedding once."

Ah jeez. I'm not a big drinker either but I've been doing it more lately with Michael. Not wine though. Mostly beer. "If you don't want to drink it…" I start but she shakes her head, cutting me off.

"I do. I love that you brought this for me. Thank you." She takes another swallow, a bigger one this time and I take a swig as well, hoping the alcohol will calm my nerves.

Ridiculous but I'm nervous around Reverie. I want this next hour, couple of hours, whatever, to be perfect. This might be my only chance with her so I'm going to make it as good as I can get.

"I have something else for you," I tell her, watching her closely as she keeps drinking her wine. The surprise that flashes in her eyes makes me smile.

"You do? I thought you said you didn't get me a present."

"Well, I did." Reaching into the ice chest, I pull out the wrapped package that I kept safe in a plastic shopping bag. I hand it to her, pleased at the eager way she plucks it from my fingers and holds it in front of her, smoothing her thumb over the already wrinkled wrapping paper.

"What is it?" she asks.

"Open it and find out."

Slowly, she tears the paper away, revealing the dark pink decorative bottle that I found on Mom's dresser. I think it held lotion in it at one point because when I unscrewed the top, I could still smell it. Faint and floral and reminding me so much of Mom, nostalgia hit me strong, right in my chest, directly at my heart.

The color of the bottle reminded me of Reverie. I stopped by the local Walmart and bought a jar of iridescent glitter. The girl at the checkout counter helped me create a label out of a plain white sticker she had and let me use her pink glitter pen. I've known her since we were in Kindergarten and she's one of the few people from my past I've bumped into since I was released from jail who treated me like normal.

"Dreams," Reverie says as she reads the label on the bottle. She lifts her head, her gaze meeting mine. "You made this?"

I nod, suddenly embarrassed. It's a cheesy gift, clearly made by someone who's broke. "The bottle was my mom's."

"Oh." She studies it again, smoothing her fingers over the bottle, the label. She's cradling it like it's the most precious thing she's ever held when really it's just an old empty bottle of cheap lotion now filled with messy glitter. "I…I love it."

"Really? I just…" I let out a ragged breath, trying to find the right words. "I didn't know what else to get you and I don't have a lot of money but I wanted it to be something meaningful. I know it's not much—"

"Stop." She rests her fingers over my lips, silencing me. Since when did she get so close? And how does she smell even better than usual? I breathe in her scent, my head starting to spin and it's not from the glass of wine I just sucked down. "I love it. You made this for me. I almost don't feel right in taking it since it's something that once belonged to your mom."

"It's not much," I start but she presses her fingers firmly against my mouth, silencing me again.

"It's everything," she whispers. "You made it. For me. No one ever makes me anything. They buy me stuff. But that's not the same. This is…this gift came from the heart."

My damn heart starts to beat so hard I feel like it's going to pound out of my chest. "The color of the bottle reminded me of you," I admit. "And every time I hear the word dream, I think of you."

"It's beautiful." Her hand drops from my mouth as she studies the bottle once again. "I'll use it to capture all of my new dreams."

"New dreams?"

She lifts her head, those luminous blue eyes meeting mine. A cool breeze washes over us, sending a stray strand of her hair across her face and I reach out, tuck it behind her ear. "I have new dreams," she whispers. "They involve me and you."

Ah hell. How do I respond to that? *Don't waste your time, we probably won't last long anyway?*

Yeah. That sucks. I can't say that to her.

"And one of them is coming true tonight. Right now." She leans in closer to me and rests her head on my shoulder. "This is the best birthday present I've ever received."

I make a noise, dismissing her remark. "Give me a break."

She lifts her head to glare at me. "I'm serious, Nicholas Fairfield. You created this romantic setting tonight just for me. No one's ever done anything like this for me before. Ever."

I dip my head and kiss her before I ruin the moment and say something stupid. Cupping her face, I run my thumb along the smooth curve of her cheek and drink from her lips, tasting the wine there, and the underlying sweetness that's Reverie. She opens easily for me and I slide my tongue inside, circling it around hers. She scoots closer, her hand going to the back of my head, fingers plunging in my hair as she holds me to her and we kiss like that for long, tongue-filled minutes.

Until I finally break away from her first, pressing my forehead against hers. "Want more wine?" I ask, needing the break from her addicting lips.

She laughs, the soft huff of her breath brushing against my chin. "Okay."

I reluctantly pull away from her and top off her glass, then fill mine. I sneak glances at her as she drinks, the way she's curled up on the blanket, her legs tucked under her, her knees peeking out from beneath the hem of her skirt. Her bare shoulders gleam under the moonlight, making me want to lean in and kiss her there but I restrain myself.

For now.

"Look at the stars," she says, her voice soft, her head tilted back.

I glance up at the sky. "All I can see is the moon."

"And a few stars, right?" She leans into me again, rubbing her cheek against my shoulder. "Let's lay down on the blanket and check them out."

I grab the pillows and arrange them so we can get more comfortable. We stretch out next to each other and I grab her hand, intertwining our fingers. Her shoulder brushes against mine as we both lay there quietly, staring up at the sky. The moon is bright, casting its silvery glow over everything, including the pine trees that surround us. The night is so silent, I can almost hear the ocean in the far distance.

"This is the best night ever," she says on a sigh, her fingers curling tight around mine.

"Come here," I tell her, releasing my hold on her hand and lifting my arm. She scoots even closer to me, laying her head on my shoulder and using me as her pillow as I slip my arm around her shoulders. She feels good nestled up close and I stroke her shoulder and arm with my fingertips, making her shiver.

"Keep doing that," she whispers, turning her face into the crook of my neck. Her lips move against my skin and I close my eyes, savoring the sensation. "You smell good. Fresh and clean."

"Irish Spring working its magic," I joke and she laughs, the sound and movement tickling, making me squirm.

She hums against my neck then kisses me there. One little peck after another, until I'm pulling her closer with a growl and slipping my fingers under her chin to lift her mouth to mine. She tilts her head back, her lips part for me and I dart my tongue out, teasing as I lick at her, then suck her lower lip between mine.

I could do this all night. Stare at her pretty face. Touch her. Hold her close. Kiss her until our lips are raw. I pull away from her a little bit so I can study her. The delicate arch of her brows. The kissable tip of her nose. Her swollen lips, her slightly pointed chin…

Slowly her eyes open to find me staring at her. Her brows wrinkle. "What?"

"You're beautiful," I whisper as I carefully roll her onto her back so I'm hovering above her. "I feel like it's my birthday too and you're my present."

A smile spreads across her face and her eyes go soft and hazy. "Kiss me, Nicholas," she murmurs.

So I do.

Chapter
TWENTY-FOUR

Dear Diary,

(July 18th, 1:12 a.m.) This was the best birthday of my life. I'm in love. Totally and completely in love with Nicholas Fairfield. I know it must be love because no one makes me feel like he does. He looks at me and my stomach flutters. He touches me and my skin burns. And when he kisses me...

I want to melt.

I think all the splashing around with Glenn in the pool earlier this afternoon upset Nick because I caught him staring at me and he looked so angry. But not at me. More like at Glenn. I know he hated how Glenn tossed me around, his hands all over me. Nick's glare and hard jaw said it all.

And I liked it. I know it's wrong of me to admit and I'll probably need to say extra prayers asking for forgiveness before I fall asleep tonight but if it worked and got Nick's attention, did I really do something wrong?

Probably. But I don't regret it.

I lucked out and ran into Nick as I was going to the rose

garden where Mama and Daddy were holding my birthday dinner. He looked at me, in my new dress with the makeup on and my hair up, like he wanted to eat me up, and that made me feel strong. I'd been so bold with him. I even kissed him and asked him to meet me in the woods. When he promised he would, I felt triumphant but also scared. What if he didn't show? I would be devastated.

The entire dinner, all I could think about was him. I was so distracted, everyone noticed though no one really said anything to me but Daddy. I reassured him I was fine, just tired and I had a minor headache from the too-chocolatey birthday cake and he seemed to accept that answer.

The minute I could make my escape though, I did. Oh, and it was worth escaping for. It was worth the risk of getting caught too. When I showed up at the clearing, Nick was there, looking so unbelievably handsome he made my breath catch. He wore a blue and white plaid shirt and dark jeans, his usually out of control hair somewhat tamed. He was nervous, I could tell from the way he was pacing back and forth and I thought that was so cute.

He brought wine and set up a spot with blankets and pillows. He gave me a present, a pretty little bottle filled with glitter that he labeled dreams.

So incredibly sweet, I almost wanted to cry when he told me the bottle belonged to his mom.

We drank some wine and kissed. I felt very grown up, even though I didn't like the wine very much. I had a whole cup though and I could feel the alcohol buzzing through my veins. That was kind of weird but it also felt good. The wine helped me relax.

Then we were lying on the blankets and staring at the stars for all of a minute before he started to kiss me. Well, maybe I was the one who kissed him first. His neck...he smelled so delicious and I couldn't resist.

I think we kissed for at least an hour. Maybe more. I don't know. I lost count of time. All I know is there is nowhere else I'd rather be than in his arms. He felt so good. So solid and warm. At one point I pushed him onto his back and spent about fifteen minutes just kissing his face. His eyebrows, his nose, his cheeks, his chin, his amazingly perfect lips...

At the end of the night I asked him what this meant. What I meant to him. He cupped my face with his big hands and stared *into my eyes. He said he wanted no one else. He just wanted to be with me. I thought my heart would soar right out of my chest, hearing him say that. I told him I felt the same way. It's not like he officially declared, 'You're my girlfriend' but what else could that mean?*

We're together, Nick and I. I know Mama and Daddy won't approve so it'll still have to be a secret. But I'm going to work up the nerve to tell them. I have to.

After all, I'm in love with him.

Chapter
TWENTY-FIVE

Confession: acknowledgement, admission
July 27th

"**W**HERE are you taking me?" Reverie turns her head in my direction, the wind blowing her hair everywhere. We have the windows down, trying out the new truck I just bought yesterday.

I smile at her. "It's a surprise."

She settles back in her seat, her hands clutched together and resting in her lap. Looking sexy as hell in a thin pale green sundress that tempts me to slip my fingers beneath the hem and stroke her thigh.

But I keep both hands firmly planted on the steering wheel, staring straight ahead at the road. I've spent the last ten days with Reverie, sneaking time with her wherever and whenever I can. Now that she's so firmly in my life, Reverie has become an even bigger distraction.

One I'm welcoming rather than running away from.

"I love your new truck," she says again, for about the twentieth time. She's running her fingers along the inside of the passenger door and I wish those fingers were doing the same thing to me. "I especially like the color."

My truck is silver. And old. Well, it was made this century, but just barely—I bought a 2000 Chevy S-10 with over 150,000 miles on it. No air conditioning and it has a stick shift but that's okay. I got it for twenty two hundred dollars so I'm not complaining. The truck is exactly what I was looking for. Now I've got Mom's car up for sale on Craigslist and I've already had a lot of calls on it. I'll get rid of it soon and put more money in my pocket. Money I need because this summer is just flying by and next thing I know, I'll need to find a new job.

Not looking forward to looking for a new one. Not looking forward to missing Reverie after she's gone either. My heart pangs just thinking about it.

"Thanks, but you don't have to pretend you like it." I give in to my urges and squeeze her knee, caressing her lightly just with the tips of my fingers. Goosebumps follow in their wake, I can feel them. "I know you're used to your fancy, expensive cars."

"Oh please." She settles her hand over mine. "I don't care what kind of car I'm in as long as I'm with you."

She says things like that and I never want her to leave my side again. "You tell me that now but some pretty rich boy will come along in his tricked out Mercedes and you'll leave me in a heartbeat."

"Do you really think I'm that shallow?" She sounds sad as she starts to pull her hand away. I turn my hand up, grasping her fingers tight so she can't escape.

"Not at all. You know this. I'm sorry. I'm just being an ass," I say, feeling like shit. My insecurities come into play every time I'm with Reverie. She wants to be with me and I don't quite understand why. I'm just a guy. And she's this beautiful, perfect girl…

She brings our linked hands to her mouth and gently kisses my knuckles. "You don't have to worry about me leaving you for someone else. I'm not like your ex-girlfriend, you know."

Yeah, I know. And thank Christ for that. I told her about Krista. Well, not everything. I didn't tell Reverie I had sex with her not even a month ago. I didn't tell her Krista lives in the same complex as me. I also didn't tell her that my best friend double-crossed me and I ended up in jail because of his lies.

One step at a time.

"You are the farthest thing from her." I disentangle my hand from hers and settle it on her leg once more, this time directly on her thigh, my fingers flirting with the hem of her dress. "I'm going to make you dinner tonight."

"Wait, what? Where?" She sounds excited. Almost as excited as I feel.

Tonight is special. Her parents went out of town for a meeting in regards to their evil empire, AKA The Flock of the Lambs corp. They'll be gone for three days and two nights and left Evan in charge.

This means Evan bailed the moment their parents' car pulled out of the driveway. He'd told Reverie straight up, "I don't care what you do, just don't get beat up, raped or kidnapped." Then he left.

He's just about the worst brother ever, I swear.

So Reverie is all mine. There are no prying eyes around the house. Most of the staff was given the same time off that the Hales are gone. Including me. Including Michael and Heather. Reverie invited me to stay with her at the house for the evening but I'd rather she see where I live.

It's not much but I know she won't judge. She's not like that. She's pure and accepting and she likes everything that's a part of me. If I lived in a broken down shack near the ocean, she would've smiled and told me she liked it. And she would've meant it too.

"I'm taking you to my apartment." Taking a chance too, because if Krista catches wind of this, she will have no problem coming over and putting on a big show for Reverie's benefit. Or she'd turn into a jealous wench and attack Reverie. Spill all of our dirty little secrets, making everything we've done sound sordid and cheap and totally wrong.

Which it was. I feel bad for what I did with Krista, to Krista. She's an unhappy, unstable person and I knew this. But I continued to fuck around with her anyway.

Not cool. I gotta make it better between us but how? I have no clue. And right now is not the time to figure that out.

"I can't wait to see your place," Reverie says, her sweet voice interrupting my thoughts. "Are we almost there?"

We've been driving for almost twenty minutes but traffic is shitty and I live clear across town. Not on the good side, close to the spread out neighborhood the Hales' summer home is at.

No, my little apartment is located on the more gritty side of town. Where drug deals go down in parking lots in the middle of the day and cars are stolen in the dark of night.

"It's nothing much," I say with a shrug. "But it's home. My mom tried her best to make it nice. She worked hard."

"She sounds like she was a really great mom."

"My mom was the best," I say firmly.

"I think that's so sweet." Reverie leans over and plants a kiss right on my cheek, her sticky with gloss lips lingering and making me smile. "You're sweet," she whispers in my ear before she moves away from me.

She's got it all wrong. She's the sweet one. The one who fills me with light that chases out the darkness. The one who listens to me, who talks to me, who holds my hand and offers comfort when no one else has done that for me in so long.

Reverie has become my everything. And that's both scary and wonderful, all at the same time.

"And I'm sure I'll love your place," she continues as she settles back in her seat. "Especially because you're making me dinner. What's on the menu anyway?"

"My specialty of course," I say, being purposely vague.

"That's no answer." She shoves at my shoulder and I laugh.

"You'll find out." It's nothing major. I'm no cook but I learned how to fend for myself from a young age, when Mom had to work late hours. I've really had to kick that skill into gear since I lost her, though most of the time I pick up fast food on the way home from work.

She'd hated that. Even Reverie gives me grief about it. Says I need to eat healthier.

"So mysterious." Her flirtatious tone makes my smile grow. "You're a man of many talents aren't you?"

Ha, if she'd let me show her all my many talents, I'm sure I could blow her mind. Not that I want to push. We're taking it slow, though she's so responsive it's difficult for me to remember that. The minute she gets in my arms we're kissing. Her hands everywhere, mine everywhere…

Yeah. I've become reacquainted with my hand and solo performances in the shower again. The girl gives me a serious case of blue balls.

I know though, that she'll be worth the wait.

"I'm impressed." I watch Reverie rinse the last of the dishes and stack the plate in the dishwasher before she shuts it.

She turns off the faucet and then dries her hands with a paper towel before she tosses it in the trash. "With what?"

"With you. And that you actually know how to wash a dish." She sticks her tongue out at me, making me laugh. She hassled me for knowing my way around a kitchen. How could I tell her that most of what I learned I picked up when I was in jail? "Seriously. I didn't think you knew much about manual labor. But you know your way around a dishwasher."

"You keep giving me a hard time." She approaches me, her steps light since she's barefoot. I glance down, studying her pale pink painted toes, let my gaze wander up her ankles, her calves, her knees. I really love her legs. Every chance I get I'm touching them. The temptation to get my hands beneath the dress and caress her bare skin is near overwhelming. "Do you really think I'm that spoiled?"

My laughter dies when I see how serious she is, her earnest expression. "Yeah, I guess I do," I say.

She goes completely still, her expression frozen. "Um, wow. Are you serious?"

"Hey. It is what it is right? You can't help the way you were raised." I'm trying to blow this off. I didn't mean to offend her. I don't want to ruin this night. It's important to me. Pretty sure it's important to her too.

If all goes as planned, she's staying the night with me. All night long with Reverie in my arms, in my bed. I won't push for anything more than she's willing to give. I've been patient with her because I know she's worth it. She means something to me and I thought I meant something to her too.

Fighting with her is the last thing I need.

"Right. So you'd think you wouldn't hold that against me. I can't help who my parents are. Just like you can't help how you've been raised either," she says pointedly. "I don't judge you, Nick. I'd really appreciate it if you didn't judge me."

"I'm not judging you," I start but she shakes her head, cutting me off.

"You totally are. And I don't get it. I thought you knew that I accepted you. I'm putting everything at risk to be with you, Nick. Everything. Are you sure this is what you want? Because if my mom or dad caught me with you..." Her voice drifts off and she shrugs.

"You're the one who treats me like I'm your dirty little secret," I point out, grimacing the moment the words leave my lips. I shouldn't have said that.

Too late.

"You do the same thing! Oh my gosh, I'm leaving." She starts toward me, keeping a wide berth as she walks past me so I can't even reach out and grab her.

"Where are you going?" I ask, my gaze tracking her as she makes her way toward the front door. Panic races through me and I can't believe how fast this escalated.

"I'm leaving," she tosses over her shoulder. She plucks her tiny purse from the back of the couch where she left it and goes to throws open the door.

"How are you getting home?" I jog toward her, grabbing the door before she can slam it in my face. "Reverie, come on."

"I'll find a ride. I…I'll call my brother." She steps outside and turns to face me, her arms wrapped around her waist, looking a little lost. "He'll come and get me. I know it."

She looks uncomfortable. This is definitely not her kind of neighborhood. It's dark, especially since most of the lights that are scattered throughout the complex are either out or busted. There's a couple of shady looking dudes bent over the front of an old car parked across the lot with the hood up as I assume they're trying to figure out what's wrong with it. I hear a baby crying in the distance. A door slams and I swear I recognize Krista's voice, yelling at someone, probably her newest victim or maybe her dad. I can only hope she's given up on me.

"He won't come rescue you." I reach out and take her hand, forcing her to face me. "I'm sorry. I didn't mean to hurt your feelings," I tell her bent head, stroking the inside of her wrist with my thumb.

"Well, you did." She shrugs, tries to jerk her arm out of my grip but I won't let her. "You were honest. You think I'm a spoiled brat. I can't change how you feel."

"Reverie." I tug her hand and she steps toward me, her head still bent. "There's nothing wrong with you. I like you just as you are."

She lifts her head, her eyes wide and full of hurt. I feel her pain like a kick in the gut, especially because I'm the one who caused it. "You do?"

Her insecurities slay me every time. "Come on, get inside." I pull her into the apartment and shut and lock the door before I press her against it. She gasps, her purse hitting the floor with a thud. I wrap my arms around her waist and hold her, reaching to tug on the ends of her hair so she tilts her head up, our gazes meeting. "You know I like you," I say, keeping my voice low. "I like you for who you are. I'm not trying to change you."

"I-I like you too." She touches my cheek, drifts her fingers along the line of my jaw. "I don't want to change you either. I think you're... perfect."

I am so far from perfect it's not even funny. But if this girl thinks so I'm not complaining. "You're the perfect one."

"I'm a mess," she says without hesitation.

"A perfect mess." I smile, my fingers still tangled in her hair. "My perfect mess."

"I don't know if I should take that as a compliment or not," she says warily, though I can tell by the way her eyes are sparkling that she's teasing.

"It's definitely a compliment." I study her, overwhelmed with the fact that Reverie wants to be with me. That she thinks I'm perfect. How did I luck out so good? What did I do to deserve her? "I'm sorry for hurting your feelings."

She presses her lips together, her gaze unwavering for a long, almost tense moment before she finally speaks. "You're forgiven." She breathes deep, her chest expanding with the motion. "Was that our first fight?"

"I think it was." I lean into her and press my lips to her forehead, letting them linger. "You forgive me?"

"Of course. There's really nothing to forgive." She pulls away, a tiny smile curling her lips. "Maybe we should kiss and make up though? For like...hours?"

I touch her hair, smoothing it back from her cheeks, letting the silky strands sift through my fingers. We've already spent the last few days kissing for hours. It's our favorite pastime. "Is that what you want?"

An eager nod is her answer, making me chuckle. "You aren't tired of kissing me yet?" I ask.

Her eyes widen. "Are you tired of kissing me?"

Pushing her more firmly against the door, I release my hold on her and put my hands on either side of her head, caging her in. "I don't think I could ever get tired of kissing you," I murmur against her lips before I do just that. Long, wet kisses with plenty of tongue and those little soft whimpers she makes that drive me wild. Until the both of us are panting and I need distance yet again before I lose all control and tear off her clothes.

I've dreamed of it endlessly. A naked Reverie beneath me. She's all I want. I'm consumed with the idea of making her mine. I should win a medal for how patient I've been. Everything in my life has always moved fast. Incredibly fast. I hardly had a chance to be a kid, what with how I had to grow up since I spent so much time on my own while Mom worked. I had to take responsibility. And funny thing was, I wanted it all to happen fast.

Now I'm forced to take things slow and though it's driving me straight out of my mind most nights, I'm also enjoying it. Savoring my time with Reverie because I know it's not going to last.

It can't. And I think she knows it too.

"Do you want me to take you home?" I ask when I can finally find words. My heart is racing, it's like I can feel my blood pumping in my veins and my entire body feels like it's a live wire, buzzing and electric. All from a few heady kisses.

I'm trying to do the right thing here but it can be so damn hard sometimes.

She shakes her head, her slender hands coming up to cup my cheeks. "I want you to show me your room."

"What about this?" I grasp hold of her hand and hold it up between us, flashing the ring she's wearing at her.

Her eyes widen in shock and she drops her other hand from my cheek. "What about it?"

"Your father gave it to you right?" I keep my gaze level on her, watching as conflicting emotions wash across her face.

"How did you know?" She sounds surprised. Good. The girl always keeps me on my toes and uses it unknowingly to her advantage.

"Michael told me."

A soft sigh escapes her and she gently tugs her hand from mine, staring down at the pretty ring on her finger. "My father made me promise myself to him," she admits quietly. "More like he made me promise that I would save myself for marriage and pledge myself to him and God until then."

Right. So her being here makes absolutely no sense. "What are we doing, Reverie? Why are you here? With me?" I need an answer. What's happening between us feels like more than a few stolen kisses here and there. I like this girl. A lot.

Too much probably.

"It was easy to make that promise. Back when I was fifteen and never really talked to a boy. I knew nothing about the opposite sex. About sex in general. My dad wanted to use me as an example to the rest of his congregation. He worried that girls were falling prey to using their bodies to get what they wanted and I agreed." She rests her hand on my chest, stroking absently, and my eyes want to cross at how good her touch feels.

"I don't want to make you do anything you don't want to," I say. It pains me to say it, but I don't force girls to be with me. Mom taught me to respect women no matter what and I sure as hell respected her. I respect Reverie too. She stands by her beliefs and she's not ashamed to admit them to me. She knows what she wants.

But the way she's looking at me right now, I'm thinking that what she wants is me.

"You're not forcing me to do anything, Nicholas." She smiles as she slips her hand beneath my shirt and touches my stomach, her fingers lightly tickling. "Show me your room."

Anticipation curls through me, and that electric feeling intensifies. I know she's trying to change the subject. She doesn't want to talk about the promise she made to her father. Neither do I. "You sure?"

"Yes." She kisses me, her lips soft and damp and I immediately want more. More kisses, more touches, more Reverie. "Please?"

We're quiet. My brain is going a hundred miles a minute and I can only imagine what she's thinking. "I won't force you to do anything that you're not comfortable with," I say, wanting to reassure her. "You understand that, right? You can say no. I won't be angry."

"I know. But I...I *want* to do things. With you. Only you." She slings her arms around my neck and clings to me. "I want you to teach me."

Damn, this girl... "Teach you what?" I ask hoarsely.

"Everything. I want to know everything. About intimacy and love and...sex." She stumbles over the last word, which I think is kind of cute. And I swear there's a faint pink flush in her cheeks. She's blushing. Even after everything we've shared. And everything we're about to share.

"We'll take it slow," I tell her. "And I'll make it good for you, whatever happens. I promise."

"You already do that," she says, her smile shy, yet her voice sultry. I don't know how she does that, the innocent plus sexy thing she has going on, but I love it.

Probably a little too much.

"Come on." I withdraw from her, not letting go of her hand. I want to keep us connected. This moment we're about to create feels…larger than life. Like we're about to turn another corner in our relationship. "Let's lock up and get ready for bed."

"Bed?" She flashes me that same shy smile, though it's a little bigger this time. "That sounds so…"

"Scandalous? Wicked?" I waggle my brows at her, trying to lighten the moment.

She bursts out laughing. "I was going to say normal." Her laughter dies as she stares at me. "You make me feel so normal. There's always a label on me. Reverend Hale's daughter. The little girl who used to sing hymns on TV. The religious girl at school other girls are afraid to talk to for fear I'm some preaching freak who wants to talk about God all the time." Her voice drifts off, the sad expression on her face tearing me up inside. I hate it when she's sad.

"Do people really think that?" I ask.

"Oh yeah." She nods. "But you never have. You didn't even know who I was." And she sounds downright thrilled by it too.

"I knew you were the prettiest thing I'd ever seen," I admit softly, making her smile.

She pulls me to her and kisses me right on the jaw. "Come on," she whispers. "Let's go to bed."

We walk through the small apartment shutting off lamps and hitting light switches. She grabs her purse and brings it with her as we go to my bedroom, smiling shyly at me as I open the door. I'd left the bedside lamp on last time I went in there and now it casts a gentle glow throughout the room, which is small but somewhat decent thanks to some massive cleanup I've been performing the last few days when I could find the time.

"It's nice," she says as she steps inside, looking everywhere. At the walls, at my tiny desk, at the bookshelf Mom and I put together when I was in the eighth grade. "It's so small."

"My mom's stuff is still in the master," I say. "I just…don't have the heart to change it. Not yet."

"Oh." She turns to face me, pity and sadness etched all over her delicate features. "I'm so sorry. I'm sure you're not ready to move everything out yet."

"No, I'm not." She gets it and I love that about her. I don't think anyone has ever understood me like Reverie does. "It's still too soon. It's not even been six months."

"That is way too soon. You can clean it out when you're ready. Don't worry what anyone else thinks," she reassures me, her gaze dropping to the bed. She chews on her lower lip nervously. "Your bed looks... comfortable."

A simple navy blue comforter covers it. I've had the bed since I was twelve. It's seen better days and it's a double so it's not very big but Reverie and I will fit. We'll just have to lie real close together.

Such a hardship.

"It's all right," I say. "You want to test it out?" Her jaw drops and I chuckle. "What? Isn't that why you're here? To test out my bed?"

"I'm here because I want to spend time with you." She reaches out and pulls at the bottom of my T-shirt, her hand sneaking underneath it, fingers tickling my stomach and making the muscles flinch. She flashes a knowing glance and just like that I'm hard. "And because I want to spend the night in your bed."

"I knew it. You're just using me for my bed." I grab her by the waist, shocking her when I take her down with me so we're both falling onto the mattress in a tangled heap. She's struggling to get out of my hold, hitting my chest, laughing as I tickle her ribs. I coast my hands up, up further until they're just below her breasts, and I'm smoothing my thumbs along the bottom of her bra.

She stills, her breath hitching in her throat and I stare at her, waiting for some sign of approval. Not even a minute in and I might've already pushed her too far. I start to withdraw when she subtly arches her back, filling my hands with her breasts.

There's my answer.

Relief flooding me, I crash my lips onto hers, the touch of her tongue against mine sends a shockwave pulsating through my body. Her arms come up to weave around my neck, her fingers tunneling in my hair and holding me to her. Like I'm going to escape or something and she needs to grip me tight.

As if she has to worry about that. Wrapped around her on my bed is the only place I want to be.

I'm hungry. Fucking starved for more of her. I deepen the kiss, rolling her over so she's on her back and I'm above her. All I can hear is our accelerated breaths, the creak of the mattress beneath us as we shift and move, the gasp that escapes her when I break away from her intoxicating lips to run my tongue along the length of her neck. Fuck, she tastes amazing.

"Oh," she chokes out, sounding as overwhelmed as I feel.

The thin straps of her sundress are barriers I can definitely conquer. I ease one off her shoulder, along with the thin, lacy strap of her bra, my mouth blazing a path across her skin. She shivers, her hands falling to my shoulders and squeezing. Clinging to me.

I'm moving too fast. I can sense it. I need to slow down but I can't seem to control myself. She's not stopping me either. The sounds she makes, the way she moves against me is nothing but pure encouragement and I grab hold of the hem of her skirt, lifting it. Slow and easy, until it's bunched around her waist and I see nothing but legs.

And thin, lacy little pale pink panties.

Closing my eyes briefly, I shake my head and lift away so I'm on my haunches in front of her. She lays there, unmoving, her eyes wide and luminous as she watches me. She props herself up on her elbows, her long hair swaying as she tilts her head to the side. "Everything okay?" she asks shakily.

"I should be the one asking you that." I press my lips together, my gaze falling to her panties. My blood runs hot and straight between my legs and a pained sound escapes me. She is pure temptation. I want to slip my fingers beneath the lace. Touch her and find out just how hot and wet she is. Drive her wild until she's writhing and gasping out my name.

"I don't want to stop." She shifts up and pulls her sundress over her head, throwing it onto the floor. The bra matches the panties. Seeing her like this, the reverend's sexy daughter half naked and ready to give her body to me, I feel like I'm going to die. "Take off your shirt?" Her voice goes shy and soft and without hesitation I do as she requests, tugging my shirt off, relieved that the cooler air soothes my heated skin.

I'm on fire for her. Absolutely on fucking fire. The front of my jeans strain and I'm scared to strip off any more clothing for fear I'll freak her out and send her running.

"You have the most beautiful body I've ever seen," she whispers as she scoots closer and rests her hands on my chest. Her gentle touch makes me flinch and she jerks away but I shake my head.

"Don't stop," I murmur, almost repeating what she said a minute ago.

Smiling up at me, she comes even closer, her hands on my chest, pushing me gently so I fall back onto the bed. She follows after me, her mouth at the spot where my neck meets my shoulder and I sink my hands into her hair, holding her close. Her bare, soft skin on mine is like nothing I've ever felt before. Sparks ignite where her mouth presses and I close my eyes, reveling in the sensation of her silky hair dragging across my chest as she moves over me. We shouldn't be doing this. But I'm sure as hell not going to stop.

I don't know if I can ever stop.

Chapter
TWENTY-SIX

(July 28th, 4:23 a.m.) I'm writing this in the notes section of my phone because I want to remember this moment forever. The moment where I fell into Nicholas Fairfield's arms. In his bed. Where I let him take off my clothes and I took off his and we did things. Incredible things that made my body feel like it broke into a million tiny little pieces and he's the only one who can put me back together again.

I'm forever changed by this experience, and I don't regret doing it. I know I made a promise to my father and to God that I would remain pure but it's so difficult. Nicholas Fairfield is pure temptation to me. Delicious, perfect, wonderful, sexy temptation.

Now I understand why people do what they do for love and sex. I finally get it.

We didn't go all the way because I wasn't ready and Nick respected that. But we did just about everything else. The way he touches me...with his hands. His mouth. OMG his mouth. I've never experienced anything that felt so deliciously good. And the way he looked at me when he pulled off my dress and saw my bra and matching undies. I've never had someone look at me like that. Ever.

I'm in love. Definitely in love with Nick. I can't deny it. He's the perfect one for me. The only one for me.

I can only hope I'm the perfect one for him.

Chapter
TWENTY-SEVEN

Sin: a deliberate violation of a religious or moral principle
July 28th

I WAKE up to sunlight blasting through my cracked open blinds. I throw an arm up, warding off the bright light and I sink my head back onto my pillow, tugging a sleeping Reverie closer. She's wearing one of my T-shirts and her back is to my front, her butt nuzzled right up against me and damn, minus the semi-open blinds, this is the best possible way to wake up in like, forever.

A knock sounds on the door, startling me and I wonder if that's what woke me in the first place.

"Who is that?" Reverie asks, her voice sleepy and so damn sexy.

"Don't know and don't care." I bend down and press a lingering kiss to her bare shoulder. She has the smoothest, most fragrant skin in the whole entire world. I could spend hours kissing her everywhere.

I did just that last night and long into the early morning too. Just remembering the sounds she made, the way she looked when I made her come for the first time...

Another knock sounds on my door, this one longer and harder.

"Sounds like they certainly care," Reverie says, pointing out the obvious. "Maybe it's important? Someone you know?"

I hope to hell it's not someone I know. There are only a handful of people who'd be knocking on my door and I don't want to see any of them. "They can come back later. Or call me. The people who matter in my life have my number." The moment I say it I realize there's really no one in my life who matters. The only person who really does is lying with me in my arms. I've become wholly dependent on Reverie.

Fucking scary.

We're quiet for a moment. I almost feel like I'm holding my breath, waiting for the knocking to start up again. But it doesn't. Whoever was at my door must've left.

"I don't have your number," she finally says, her voice almost as soft as her fingertips on my skin. She's tracing circles on my chest and it's driving me crazy. "You've never given it to me."

Surprise fills me. "I didn't know you had a cell. We've never talk about it." Kinda weird. She's a girl. I thought they all lived on their phones.

"That's because my parents took mine away. I begged my mom to give it back for my birthday but she didn't. Until a few days ago. She called it a late present." She's silent for a moment and then she continues hesitantly. "She said I-I finally earned their trust back."

She sniffs and dread fills me. I slip my finger under her chin and tip her face up. Her eyes are luminous and her lower lip trembles. "What's wrong?"

"I feel guilty." She shakes her head, a tear falling from the corner of her eye and sliding down her cheek. I stop it with my thumb. "I earned back their trust when really I'm being s-so b-bad. I've committed a sin, Nick. My parents would be so disappointed in me if they ever found out."

Guilt fills me too. We've been almost borderline obsessive with each other these past few weeks. Sneaking glimpses of each other where we can. Kissing behind the stables, behind the house, in the woods, in my truck, on the beach…

And now she's spent the night at my place. We've gone farther than we ever have before. Our fooling around is putting her relationship with her parents at risk. Putting her relationship with God and herself at risk too. Making her question her morals…

I didn't have a religious upbringing. I know about right and wrong but I never had the fear of God put in me. I have no idea what that's like, to have such strong beliefs.

"I should take you home," I say firmly, moving away from her so I can sit up.

"Okay." She scoots back until she's leaning against the wall, freaking adorable wearing my T-shirt, her face bare of makeup, her hair a disheveled mess around her head. "I-I'm sorry, Nick."

"For what?" Shit. Is she sorry we got involved? Sorry that she spent the night? Sorry that she's going to have to break it off? My mind is awhirl with possibilities, all of them terrible.

"I don't know. For being such a good girl? I can't even rebel properly I swear." She climbs out of bed and starts pacing. Her legs look amazing and I wonder exactly what she has on beneath my T-shirt. "You must think I'm completely ridiculous."

I run a hand through my hair, then scratch my chest. "I think you're completely normal. I'm not surprised you feel guilty. You never rebel. You're always the good girl." Until she met me. And that means I'm no good for her.

"Good girls are boring." She throws her hands up in the air, which makes the T-shirt rise. Her back is to me and I catch a glimpse of her ass cheeks and my body instantly reacts.

Well. That confirms she's wearing nothing under the shirt.

"You are definitely not boring," I tell her, my voice low, my thoughts dirty.

Reverie whirls around, her hair flying out behind her as she faces me. "Do you like me, Nick?"

Her abrupt question surprises me, knocking aside my dirty thoughts. "Well, yeah…I like you, Reverie."

"How much do you like me? I know you said before you don't want to see anyone else but…what are we doing exactly?"

"I don't know," I admit quietly. "I like you. I love spending time with you. We've had a lot of fun together. But you're going back to L.A. at the end of the summer. Going back to school. And I'll be here. I don't know what's going to happen."

"So what you're saying is this is temporary." She crosses her arms in front of her, the T-shirt riding up and my gaze drops.

"How can it be anything else?" I ask, my eyes locked on her upper thighs.

She emits an irritated noise and dips down, plucking her dress off the floor before she storms out of my bedroom and into the tiny bathroom down the hall, slamming the door behind her. I flop back on the bed and stare at the ceiling, blowing out a harsh breath.

I was honest with her. What's wrong with that? This is for the best, I tell myself. I care for her. What we've shared these past few weeks has been...mind blowing in the best way possible.

But it's not meant to last. It can't. No matter how much I don't want that to be true.

I crawl out of bed and shuffle through the apartment, the sound of running water coming from the bathroom telling me that Reverie is taking a shower. I go to the front door and open it, surprised to see a taped folded note fluttering in the breeze.

Tearing it off the door, I open the piece of paper and read it.

You wouldn't answer your door. I'm guessing you were too busy with the pretty blonde who stayed the night? Who's the lucky girl? Maybe all three of us could have a little fun sometime...
  xoxo
  Krista

I crumple the note in my hand as I slam the door, fury racing through me. Fucking Krista. When did she see us? Is she spying on me? What the hell is wrong with her?

My phone rings from where I left it on the kitchen counter the night before and I jog over to answer it, grimacing when I see who the caller is.

"What do you want?" I answer, my voice low.

"Ah, there you are. I'm guessing you slept in with your little love bug?" Krista's voice is extra sweet, edged with obvious sarcasm and a hint of anger.

"Fuck off."

She laughs. "I love it when you talk dirty."

"I'm serious, Krista. Stay out of my business. We're not together. We haven't been together for a long time."

"Do you think you can just use me whenever you want, then toss me aside when you find someone prettier and sweeter? Because she looks terribly sweet, Nicky. So sweet she gave me a toothache when I first saw her. Does she know about your past? About your time in jail? I mean, we know you weren't guilty of any crime, but spending that much time locked up with criminals has to affect a person and not in a positive way. I bet she'd be shocked to hear that story." Krista continues laughing and I grit my teeth, wishing I could reach through the phone and strangle her.

"Leave her alone. Stay away from us." I hang up before she can get another word in. I toss the phone on the counter like it burned me, biting out a curse before I turn to see Reverie standing in the hallway, her damp hair pulled into a ponytail, wearing yesterday's sundress, clutching her hands in front of her.

Shit. How much did she hear? Hopefully none of it.

"Hey," I say softly, starting to approach her. "You ready to go?"

"Who were you talking to?" She shifts from one foot to the other, nibbling on her lower lip.

"No one," I say dismissively.

"You sounded pretty angry for it to be no one." I stop right before her and she tilts her head back, her gaze meeting mine. "Who was it Nick?"

"I told you. No one important," I insist, nerves eating at my gut. She must've heard plenty. I don't want to tell her the truth. She might freak out.

"It was Krista," she says quietly, her expression emotionless. "I heard you say her name."

Dread sweeps over me. "Why did you ask when you knew all along?" I thrust both hands in my hair and hold the back of my head in frustration. I'm pissed. Frustrated. Not at Reverie but at myself. And Krista. Everything's coming to a head and there's nothing I can do to stop it.

She flinches. "You don't have to yell at me."

"I'm not—" I drop my hands and blow out a harsh breath. I can't deny I'm yelling because I totally am. "Look, I need to get you home. Are you ready?"

"Why did you tell her to stay away from us? Is she threatening you? Threatening me? I'm not scared of her and you shouldn't be either." She reaches out and grabs hold of my hand in both of hers. "Is there something you're not telling me? Be honest with me, Nick. That's all I want. All I ask for. Please."

I stare at her, my stomach churning. I can't tell her the truth. Not like this. She'll hate me. Or worse, be disgusted by me. Disappointed. "There's nothing to tell," I lie.

She's eerily quiet as she studies me. "Why did you tell her to leave us alone then?"

"Because she's a jealous bitch who's mad that I found someone else," I practically spit out.

"Why is she jealous? I thought you two broke up a while ago."

I blow out an exasperated breath. I can't keep hiding this from her. She'll keep badgering until I give her something. "Fine, you wanna know my little secret? I hooked up with Krista over a month ago. It was nothing. It meant nothing. But I guess she thought it meant we were together again. I don't know."

Reverie's eyes widen and she drops my hand, taking a step back. "You had—you had sex with her a month ago?" Her voice is small, her eyes wide.

I feel mean. Backed into a corner and I don't like it. I don't want to hurt Reverie's feelings but she's giving me no choice. "Yeah. I made a mistake. I do that sometimes you know." More like a lot of the time. As in right now. "Sorry to shatter any illusions you might've had about me but guess what? I'm *not* perfect." I'm reminded of our conversation last night, all the perfect talk and what she said. Just a big sham if you ask me. None of us are perfect, least of all me.

She flinches again, the hurt expression on her face unmistakable. "You don't have to be so mean about it," she murmurs.

I can't win for trying, I swear to God. I immediately feel like shit. "Are you ready to go or what?"

"Let me grab my purse." She lifts her chin, looking both defiant and sad. I ache to draw her in my arms and tell her I'm sorry. Bury my face in her hair and breathe deep her sweet unique scent. Let it wash over me and ease my anger over Krista.

And how scared I am to tell Reverie the truth.

But I don't. Instead I go to my room, throw on some clothes, slip on shoes and grab my keys.

Chapter
TWENTY-EIGHT

Dear Diary,

(July 28th, 3 p.m.) I don't know what to say. What started out as an amazing night turned into the worst morning ever. I thought what Nick and I shared last night meant something to him. I know it meant something to me. We practically had sex. I've seen him naked. He's seen me naked. We did things to each other that I've never, ever done to anyone else. It was the most amazing experience of my life. I had zero regrets. None. I know what we did was a sin but when you love someone so much, it can't be wrong.

Or so I told myself.

Daylight makes everything different. You can lose yourself in the darkness. It's so easy. Forget all your troubles and become someone else. Darkness and secrets go hand in hand. When the darkness fades and the secret comes to light, there's no turning back.

So in the morning I actually faced what I'd done and had some...regret? No, that's not the right word. I had an attack of guilt. My parents finally trust me again and look at what I'm doing?

Sneaking around with a boy they probably wouldn't approve of at face value, though if they just got to know him they'd see how truly wonderful he is...

I want to trust Nick but he acted so weird. And then when I heard him on the phone yelling at that stupid tramp Krista...I didn't know what to think. Is he still seeing her? Why does he feel so connected to her? I don't understand the link that they share.

I'm so confused. Love shouldn't be like this right? It's supposed to be pure and beautiful and all encompassing. Not ugly and hurtful. I feel like Nick is still keeping secrets from me but I don't know what they are. Something more than his having sex with Krista a month ago. I'm sure of it.

Even writing those words hurts my heart so bad. I hate that he's had sex with other girls. I hate that this Krista girl is still in his life. I want her gone. I wish she didn't even exist. Our lives would be so much easier without her around.

The entire drive back to my place Nick was quiet. So was I. He dropped me off and didn't give me a kiss. Didn't want to make plans for later. Nothing. I entered my number in his cell phone when we first got into his truck but other than that, nothing really happened.

Let's see if Nick texts or calls me. I can't call him so I'm completely dependent on him making the next move. I don't like that.

At all.

When I walked into the house, Evan was sitting at the kitchen counter, the look of amusement on his face hard to miss. He asked in that dry, sarcastic tone of his that I sometimes hate if I was playing around with the help.

I sent him a dirty look but didn't answer. Just went up to my room and closed the door. Then I had a good, long cry in the shower.

Mama and Daddy will be home tomorrow. I wonder if Evan will tell on me. I wonder if my guilt will become too overwhelming and I'll end up telling on myself. I don't know. I'm so conflicted.

Maybe I need to pray. Maybe I need to talk to Evan, though he'll probably just laugh at me and give me bad advice. Our relationship hasn't been very strong lately and I'm scared to tell

him what I did.
I don't know what to do.
I guess I have to wait and see what happens.

Chapter
TWENTY-NINE

Evil: morally wrong or bad
July 30th

SHE's late. I'm pacing back and forth in my living room, waiting for her to arrive, getting madder as every minute passes by. I don't want to do this. I'd rather pretend it never happened but I can't ignore it.

If I want to get back in Reverie's good graces, I need to face my troubles head on. This is the first step.

When the knock finally sounds on my door, I rush to answer it, throwing open the door so quick, Krista's hand is still raised, her hand in a fist.

"Wow. That was fast." She smirks. "Are you that happy to see me?"

I roll my eyes, not in the mood for her games and sexual innuendos. "Come in," I say gruffly, opening the door wider.

She strides inside, her hips swishing, the denim mini skirt she's wearing hanging so low I swear it's gonna fall off. The bracelets stacked on her left wrist jangle loudly in the otherwise quiet of my apartment and she turns to face me as I shut the door, the smile on her face huge.

I know she thinks she's won. She probably believes I'm her prize and she's come to claim it. I don't want to be mean and I don't want to hurt her feelings but I can't let this go on any longer. She can't be my friend, my hookup on the side, my ex-girlfriend, none of it. I need her out of my life before she ruins it completely. What's scary is she has that power and I think she knows it.

"Looking good as usual Nicky." She snaps her gum. "I like what you've done with your hair. The messy look works for you."

I don't bother saying anything, not even a thank you, which is what she wants. "We need to talk."

Her smile fades and she slowly shakes her head, the oversized double hoop earrings she's wearing clanking. "Talking's overrated. Let's get naked."

Jesus, she's persistent. "That's never going to happen."

"It's happened before." She rushes me, her hands going to my hips, fingers hooking into the belt loops of my jeans. "And it can definitely happen again. You know you miss me. After seeing that little virgin you had over, I'm not surprised you were bored. Or is she here and you called me over to play? You know I'm game for anything, Nicky. *Anything.*"

I'm disgusted. What happened to this girl I've known since we were little kids? She's become this predatory creature who uses sex to get whatever she wants. She's nothing like the Krista I remember from fifth grade, who was sweet and fun and always up for a little trouble.

Nothing.

Her fingers brush against the skin of my stomach and I shove her away from me hard, disgusted by her touch. She takes a staggering step backward, her expression full of shock. "Asshole! What the hell are you doing?" she screams.

"Don't insult her," I mutter. "You know nothing about her."

"I know enough to figure out exactly who she is." The triumphant smirk is back. "Reverie Hale. The Reverend Hale's daughter, who just so happens to be your boss." She slowly shakes her head, making a tsking noise. "You're one crazy motherfucker, you know that? Screwing around with a girl who's practically a saint? What happened last night when you felt her up? Did her angel wings pop out of her back when you took her shirt off?"

Shit, shit, shit. This changes everything. I don't know what to say. I don't know what to freaking do. "How..." My voice trails off and I clamp my lips shut, afraid I might say too much and Krista will use it against me.

"Google is my best friend, though I had my suspicions when I saw her. I knew I recognized her from something, I just couldn't place it at first." Her smile returns and she clasps her hands in front of her in mock delight. "Did you know that when I was little, my mom watched Reverend Hale's show all the time? I was fascinated with the daughter. I thought she was so pretty, with her perfect little dresses and her long blond hair. She wore a different dress and matching ribbons in her hair every Sunday. I was so jealous."

Just my fucking luck. What are the odds that Krista's mom was a Hale disciple? "You recognized her."

"I sure did! Unbelievable right?" She exhales a dreamy little sigh. "I used to think her big brother was hot. Is he still hot?"

I make a face. "I don't know. I don't check out dudes."

"Right. Of course you don't." She waves a hand. "Well, whatever. Evander Hale will just have to remain my not-so-secret dream boyfriend. And Reverie Hale—such a stupid name by the way—is your real life girlfriend. How exciting is that? What do her parents think of you? Are they happy their little girl found true love?"

I say nothing. Krista already knows the answers anyway.

"Wait a minute, are you telling me they don't know you two are involved? Ooh, that changes everything. The daughter messing around with one of the summer employees—a guy originally implicated in a murder case—well, they'd probably flip the fuck out, right? That's some major scandal right there, yo."

"Krista," I warn but she's on a roll. She completely ignores my protest.

"So you have a secret. One you need kept." Her eyes go round and so does her mouth. She reminds me of an owl. "Actually you have a couple of secrets don't you Nicky? You'd think Google was her best friend like it's mine. She could enter your name and bam, find out everything in a matter of seconds. It's a wondrous thing, that Google. Though she doesn't need Google at all if she has me calling her and telling her everything. Or maybe I could tell the Hales how you two are together…so many possibilities!"

Reverie didn't have her phone until a few days ago. I've never seen her with a laptop, at a computer, nothing. What if she does Google me?

I'm fucked, that's what.

"I've filled your head with so much information, I'm sure you have a lot to think about tonight." She approaches me, patting me on the chest before she curls her fingers, her nails digging into my skin. I jump back from her with a curse and she smiles benignly. "I suggest you sleep on it and approach me with a solution tomorrow. What do you think? We meet same time, same place?"

What am I going to do? How can I fix this?

You can tell Reverie the truth.

Hell. No. Not yet. I'm not ready. She's mad at me. I let her know I've been in jail and she'll really hate me. I can't risk it.

"Fine." I blow out a frustrated breath. "We'll meet tomorrow."

"Perfect," she practically purrs. She takes a step toward me, grips my shirt in her fist and pulls, planting a quick kiss on my lips. "See you tomorrow."

She practically runs out, slamming the door behind her. I can still hear the jangle of her jewelry, her overpowering scent lingering in the living room. I wipe the back of my hand across my mouth, like I can rid the evidence of her kiss.

I can't erase it though. Can't erase what she said to me either. It's like her words are on repeat in my head, reminding me how much of a mess I'm in. How hard it's going to be to climb out of it.

When I was released from jail, I felt like a man reborn. I was given a second chance and I planned on doing things right. No more mistakes. No more making stupid choices. I made that promise to myself.

Here I am a few months later and I'm no better than I was before I was arrested and falsely accused of a crime I didn't commit. I think I'm actually in worst shape, minus my time in jail, which was the most fucked up period of my life.

I'll never learn. Krista was right. I can't escape where I came from. I can't escape her. I need to remember where I belong. Here. In this stupid apartment, in this stupid town, with that stupid girl who'll do whatever it takes to sink her claws in me and never let me go.

I need to remember this.

No matter how badly I want to forget.

Chapter
THIRTY

Dear Diary,

(July 31st, 6:58 p.m.) Mama and Daddy came home and I was so glad to see them. I always feel anxious when they go out of town because it doesn't happen very often. I'm not used to it. The sense of relief I feel when I hear their voices as they walk through the door is overpowering every single time.

I thought I would feel differently this time around, with the guilt hanging over me after what I've done with Nicholas, but I didn't. I ran toward Daddy when I first saw him, wrapping him in such a huge, clinging hug he laughed with surprise and held me tight. Then murmured close to my ear how much he loved me and missed my smile.

It felt good. Reassuring. I've said a lot of prayers since what happened with Nick. Had a lot of conversations with God, searching for answers but not really finding any besides my ever present guilt. I love Nick. That I don't doubt for a minute. What happened between us felt good and right and so wonderful, I never wanted it to stop.

But in the eyes of the Lord, what we did was wrong. It was a sin. I made a promise and I broke it. I was no longer pure. I fell asleep crying, my heart aching with confusion and remorse. I hated feeling so conflicted.

This morning though, I woke up feeling cleansed. Ready to face anything and everything. I steeled myself, waiting for the blow. For the confrontation. For the big speech they would give me, how they would ground me, take away my phone forever and hold me prisoner in my room for the rest of the summer.

None of that happened. Mama ignored me and Daddy seemed distracted. He locked himself up in his study the moment he came home. Mama poured herself a giant glass of wine and sat out on the patio alone, clutching her cell phone tight as she talked intently for well over an hour to someone. I don't know who.

She didn't even say hello.

Evan took off the moment he realized they weren't paying him any attention. I'm in my room by the open window, staring at the night sky, wishing I was anywhere else.

Wishing I was with Nick.

I might've entered my number in his phone but I didn't get his. What a mistake. Now I can't get a hold of him. I have to wait for him to reach out to me. But he was so mad when he dropped me off, I don't know if that's ever going to happen.

So I wait. My night with Nick still vivid in my mind, my body tired, my spirit defeated.

Was he just using me? Maybe I was a novelty for him to toy with. The famous reverend's daughter who'd never been kissed. Never had a boyfriend. The poor, naïve girl he could easily trick into his bed.

I don't want think that's the case but I don't know.

And the unknown is the worst.

Chapter
THIRTY-ONE

Realize: to grasp or understand clearly
July 31st

I'm lying in bed, wallowing in my own misery like a sullen idiot. I miss her. I hate that she's not with me. Reverie. I can worry about Krista and what she's going to do to us to ruin everything I want, but it doesn't stop me from missing my girl.

And she's mine. I can't deny it. I was such a shit, the way I dropped her off at her house without saying a word. Like she didn't matter to me. I'm a complete liar. She matters to me more than I ever want to admit, even to myself. She's everything to me.

As I spend too much time alone with my thoughts, I'm realizing denying my feelings for Reverie is pointless. When I take a cold hard look at my life, I know I have nothing. No hope, no purpose, only darkness and despair and a life ahead of me filled with constant disappointments. All sorts of strikes are against me and I don't even bother trying to conquer them. I'm just rolling with it because this is all I expect. All I think I could want.

Meeting Reverie, seeing her smile, hearing her say my name, tasting the sweetness of her lips…she gives me purpose. She makes me want to change and become better. To actually do something with my life and rise above it all, you know?

More than anything else, she gives me hope.

I grab my phone off the rickety old bedside table that belonged to Mom when she was little and I search through my contacts, looking for Reverie's number. I can't find it though. Panic strikes as I scroll through the relatively small list again but it's not under R and I know she entered it. I watched her do it.

But then as I go back yet again and search, I find something that makes me smile. She didn't enter it under her real name. She put it under D.

For Daydream.

My girl is tricky. And I love it.

I hit send text as my option and stare at the blinking cursor, wondering how the hell I should approach her. I'm taking the coward's way out already by sending her a goddamn text but like a baby, I'm afraid to call her. What if she doesn't answer? She doesn't even know my number and there's no way I'll leave her a voicemail. Her parents could monitor that crap and we'd be caught.

Fuck it. I type a quick message and hit send.

Not even ten seconds later and I get a reply.

Nicholas? Is this you?

Yeah it's me. Are you okay?

I chew on my lower lip as I wait for her answer.

Not really.

Those two words make my heart crack open. I wish I was with her. I wish I had her by my side and my arm around her shoulders, holding her tight. I wish I could take away all her pain and make it go away. Until all she can focus on is me and her and the two of us together.

But I can't. All I can do is send her a text message.

Tell me what's wrong?

Anxiety races through me. I want to fix whatever's bothering her but I don't know how. I'm not even sure if she'll let me.

Something's wrong with my parents. They seem upset but I'm pretty sure it's not at me. I can't figure it out.

I'm relieved it has nothing to do with me, which is sort of shitty but I can't help it.

Well that's a good thing right?

I guess.

Are you mad at me?

No. Just a little sad over how we parted.

I smile despite her words. My girl is such a romantic and I'm afraid I ruined all of her expectations.

I'm sorry, I type. That's all I can say. There's no excuse for what I did so an apology is all I can offer. I decide to add one more sentence.

I didn't mean to hurt you.

I didn't. It fucking kills me that I made her miserable. I hate myself for it.

I'm sorry too. For making you feel bad. For making you think I regretted what happened between us. I don't. Not at all.

I don't regret it either.

She doesn't answer for a few minutes and fear makes my heart knock against my chest. Outside I hear a dog bark ferociously and a horn honk in the complex parking lot. This place is always noisy no matter what time of day it is. But I bet it's quiet where Reverie is at this time of night. And safe. Even though her parents are being strange and she's nervous, at least she's secure and safe in her home.

I'm always afraid someone's gonna break in in the middle of the night and steal something. Not that I have anything of value here. What the hell could they even want?

But they're out there. Lurking. Watching. I can't offer much but they'll take whatever they can get if they think I'm an easy mark. I can't allow them to see any sort of vulnerability. I can't make any mistakes.

It's exhausting, having to deal with everything in my life. Sometimes I just wish for a fucking break.

I miss you.

I swallow hard at seeing her text and rub my chest. But it doesn't ease the pain in my heart that I'm not with her. That she's not right here in my arms, by my side. Where she belongs.

I miss you too.

Do you really? she asks.

That she doubts me hurts, but I expected it.

Yeah. So bad I'd do just about anything to see you.

Anything?

I don't even hesitate.

Definitely.

Then come see me. Drive out here right now.

Excitement fills me. No way can I do what she's asking, can I?

You're crazy.

I'm serious! Come on.

I want to see you, she adds.

It's too late. And your parents are home. We're taking a huge risk.

I sound like an old man but damn, what she's suggesting is risky. And I think we've taken enough risks these last few days.

They're so distracted they'll never notice. I need to see you, Nick.

When I don't answer right away she sends another quick text.

Please?

I can't resist her. I don't want to resist her. I tell myself I should leave her alone. That it's best we end this now but I can't.

I need to take a shower first.

Ohhh. :)

*I wish I were with you. *blushes**

A smile plays at the corners of my lips. Even in her texts she lets me know she's blushing. My sweet virginal girl is being bad. She's only ever bad for me. Just me.

I wish you were with me too. So we could take a shower together.

I'd like that. A lot.

My body tightens. My mind wanders to what we've shared. How there's so much more I could show her.

I would too.

Hurry Nick. I want to see you.

I'll be there.

Promise?

Promise.

Chapter
THIRTY-TWO

Desire: sexual appetite or sexual urge
One hour later...

I PARKED at least a mile away from Hale House, in a dirt turnout that hopefully no one will pay attention to, specifically the police. If I get a ticket or worse, my truck gets towed, I'll be pissed.

But Reverie's worth it.

It's dark, the outdoor lights at the house are off and I'm making my way to the back door by memory and what little moonlight available that's guiding me. Clouds came in from the west as I drove to the house and I tried my best not to take their sudden appearance as a warning but it was hard to ignore the sign.

The sign that I'm taking a huge risk coming out here in the middle of the night so Reverie can sneak me into her room. We're freaking crazy, doing this.

No lights are on inside the house either, with the exception of a dim glow shining from one of the windows on the second floor. I'm assuming that's Reverie's room. I'm anxious to see her, to hold her in my arms, to whisper in her ear that everything's going to be all right.

"Hey," a feminine voice whispers from the rose garden, making me jump about a foot. I whirl around to find Reverie standing there, wearing a white, lacy nightgown that's both sweetly innocent and outrageously sexy all at once.

Typical Reverie style.

"You scared the hell out of me," I whisper back at her, making her smile as she comes toward me.

"Sorry. I was excited to see you. I wasn't sure if you were coming." She's standing in front of me, looking too beautiful for words and I grab her, haul her in close so her body collides with mine.

Oh, I'll be coming tonight. And so will she. "You shouldn't be out here waiting for me. It's dangerous," I say accusingly, not much force behind my words because damn, she feels good all pressed up against me. Her nightgown is soft and short, the straps are thin and lacy. Lots of skin is exposed, gilded silver by the weak moonlight shining upon us.

"Why? Who's going to attack me? The ground squirrels? They're all sleeping." She smiles, presses her hand against my chest, right over my rapidly beating heart.

"Who knows what sort of creepers are hanging around at night?" I smooth my hand along the curve of her spine, stopping just above her ass. She shivers, her hand going up, curling around my neck, and she tugs my head down to hers.

"Creepers like you?" she murmurs against my lips just before she kisses me.

Ah hell. Her lips are twice as intoxicating as any alcohol I've ever drunk. I lose myself in her kiss, sweeping my tongue into her mouth, tangling with hers. She moans and presses her body full against me, and I can tell she's not wearing a bra.

She's trying to kill me, I swear.

"Baby." I push at her shoulders, needing some distance. "We can't do this out here."

"I missed you so much." She kisses me again and I turn my face away from hers, immediately feeling like crap when I hear the dejection in her voice. "I need you, Nick. Why are you denying me?"

"Because we're gonna get caught out here in the middle of your mom's rose garden and then we're in big trouble." I take Reverie's hand and link our fingers together. "Are we going to your room?"

Time for her to get shy. She nibbles on her lower lip and nods, keeping her head bent. "If that's what you want."

"Wherever you are is what I want." I bring her hand up to my mouth and drop a kiss to the top of it. "Daydream."

She lifts her head and the smile she sends me is heart stopping. "I love it when you call me that."

I say nothing. I wish I could read her thoughts. Does she feel as strongly about me as I feel about her? I can't stop thinking about her. Wanting to be with her. Worrying about her when we're not together. Seeing Reverie again, being with her erases all my worry and makes me forget. Krista's threats no longer matter. Getting caught by her parents doesn't matter. I'll deal with the consequences later.

The only thing that matters is her.

Reverie.

"We're sneaking in through the back door," she tells me as she starts to lead me around the side of the house. "So you'll have to be really quiet, okay?"

"I can do that," I reassure her, letting her lead me. Her hair is twisted into a loose braid that flows down the middle of her back and the thin nightgown she has on hits her about mid thigh. It fits her loosely but the top is made almost completely of lace and the way it looks on her…

It's sexy as hell.

We approach the back French door and she turns to look at me, withdrawing her hand from mine to hold her index finger against her lips. "Sshh," she whispers as she reaches out with her other hand and rests it on the door handle.

I nod my answer and she faces forward, slowly turning the handle and pushing the door open. It doesn't so much as creak, but nothing does in Hale House. Everything's brand new and well maintained. I've only ever been downstairs a couple of times, never really going beyond the kitchen and living room, but the house is unlike anything I've ever seen or been in before. I can almost believe I don't belong here.

I know I don't belong there.

I let Reverie reach around me and shut the door and lock it. She holds her index finger against her mouth again, her eyes sparkling with excitement and I smile at her in return.

This girl is going to get me in so much trouble.

And despite my earlier worry, anger and despair, I know she's worth it.

She leads me through the house and up the sweeping staircase. I keep my gaze focused on Reverie, trying my best not to get distracted by the opulence surrounding me. The place is like a modern museum. All straight, clean lines and blank white walls.

"This is my bedroom," Reverie whispers as she opens the door and pulls me inside. She shuts the door as I stop in the center of the room.

"It's huge," I tell her as she turns to face me. "It's like the size of my entire apartment." I'm not lying. My apartment is tiny and could probably fit inside Reverie's gigantic bedroom. The house is a goddamn palace so I guess I shouldn't be surprised but holy hell.

She lives in a completely different world. One I will never, ever find myself in.

"No way." She shakes her head as she approaches me.

"Hell yes. I'm not kidding." I do a slow turn, taking everything in. On a bedside table a lamp is lit, gently illuminating the room. The walls are a pale blue and the furniture is white. The blue and white printed comforter is thick and looks soft draped across the huge bed. "Is that a king sized bed?"

"I guess so. I don't know." She's standing right next to me and reaches out, taking my hand once more. "Do you like my room?"

"It's freaking amazing." I can't imagine living like this. What irritates more is that I know I will never have the chance to live like this.

So what the fuck am I doing, playing around with Reverie?

"I'm glad you like it." She swings our linked hands between us like we're little kids. Her sweetness soothes me. Makes me forget that we're total opposites. Yeah, maybe I should seriously question what exactly I'm doing with her and why I'm torturing myself when I know this is going to end bad, but when she smiles and looks at me like I'm her everything, I forget all of the bullshit.

"Yeah?" I say because my brain has gone blank, what with the way she's looking at me like she wants to gobble me up.

She nods and bites her lower lip as she tilts her head. "I'm glad you're here with me, Nick. I've missed you." That she's brave enough to admit that fuels me. And reminds me that lately she's the bold one.

And I like it.

We turn toward each other at the same time and I pull her to me, her arms wrapped tight around my neck as she presses her face against my shoulder. "I don't like being away from you," she murmurs. "I was so scared you were mad at me. That you didn't want to see me again."

Sighing, I hold her close and smooth my hand over her head, playing with her braid. "I was never mad at you. It's just…I hate the differences between us. That's all."

"There's nothing wrong with differences, right?"

"We come from different worlds." I pause and swallow hard. "I'm not worthy of you."

She pulls away from me slightly so our gazes meet. Emotion swirls in the blue depths as she glares. "Don't you dare ever say that again," she says firmly, sounding angry. "I hate it when you compare us like that."

"It can't be helped." I sound as helpless as I feel. "It's a cold hard fact you need to face."

"No. I refuse to." She shakes her head and releases her grip on me, only to shove at my shoulders, the back of my knees hitting the edge of the mattress before I fall back on my butt onto the bed. "Tonight, we're going to concentrate on nothing else but each other."

I lay sprawled on the mattress, fascinated when she remains standing at the foot of the bed, right in between my legs. I prop myself up on my elbows so I can see her better and I eat her up with my gaze, how her curves are just a shadow hiding under the billowing fabric of her nighty, those long, sexy legs of hers calling to me. Making me want to grab her and beg her to wrap them around me.

I'm about to encourage her to join me when I hear her whisper my name and I lift my head, my gaze meeting hers. All the oxygen escapes my lungs as she slowly lowers those flimsy little straps off her shoulders, letting them fall to the crook of her elbows before she shrugs completely out of them. The nightgown falls to the ground in a whisper of fabric, revealing her to my gaze.

"Fuck," I whisper hoarsely. I can't look away. Reverie is standing before me in a pair of white panties and that's it. Like she's some sort of gift, a sacrificial offering just for me.

Only for me.

She's trembling. I can see it. "I want you," she says, her voice shaking. "So much."

"Baby…" I let my voice trail off, overwhelmed by the conflicting emotions swirling within me, and what she wants me to do. I want to do it too. So bad it's killing me not to reach out and grab her right now. Push her onto the mattress, pin her beneath me and fuck her until we're both screaming each other's names.

But I can't do that. We've fooled around, but she's still a virgin. I gotta take it slow and make it right. She deserves more than a casual screw. She's worth more than that.

Way more.

"I know we shouldn't be together like this, locked away in my room. I know it's a sin, what I want to do with you." She licks her lips, leaving them damp, and I bite back the groan that wants to escape. "But how can something that feels so good between two people who care for each other be so wrong?"

I have no answer. I'm sure she hears all the time about sin and going against the word of God. She's conflicted and I can sort of understand why. Again her feelings compared to mine reveal just how differently we were raised.

Reverie presses her lips together and briefly closes her eyes, as if searching for strength. She wraps her arms around her front, covering her chest and I wonder if she's embarrassed. Maybe even regretting what she's just done. "I'm falling in love with you, Nicholas," she admits softly. "I know it's probably happening much too soon but I can't help the way I feel."

Ah, damn. Her confession is exactly what I wasn't looking for. Loving her will only end up hurting us both. I know it. She probably knows it too though she'd never admit it.

"Say something," she whispers after a few minutes of silence. She sounds scared.

"I want you too," I immediately answer, sitting up so I can reach for her. My words are a copout but I can't say I love her. Not yet. I feel too raw, too vulnerable yet I'm not the one standing practically naked declaring my feelings for someone like Reverie is.

Christ, I'm such an asshole.

She drops her arms as I grasp her hips and pull her to me, pressing my face against her soft belly. I kiss her there, just above her navel, and her body trembles beneath my lips. I can smell her, feel her, and all I want to do is make her mine.

All mine.

She thrusts her fingers into my hair, holding me to her almost desperately. As if she's afraid I might run away. "You touch me and I want to die. You don't touch me and I want to die. My feelings for you confuse me so much. It...scares me. You scare me in the best way possible."

"You scare me too," I admit. "You walked into my life and turned it completely upside down."

A little laugh escapes her as she relaxes her grip on me and gently combs my hair with her fingers. I close my eyes, reveling in her touch. It feels so good. So fucking right. "You did the same to me you know," she agrees softly.

I'm quiet as I smooth my hands down her back, settling them right above her ass. I want to grab her and pull her on top of me but that she's even standing in my arms with my face pressed against her naked stomach is pretty major. One wrong move and I could have her leaping out of my arms and telling me to stop. I don't want to ruin this moment.

"This probably shouldn't have happened. The two of us," she says, her sweet voice full of such heartache I can feel my own crack heart in two. One half is mine and the other irrevocably belongs to her.

I tighten my hands on her hips, my trembling fingers curling into the flimsy waistband of her panties as I drift my lips across her skin from one sharp hipbone to the other. Her fragrant skin, the unmistakable scent of her is an intoxicating mix I can't resist.

"Maybe we shouldn't have happened but we did," I murmur against her hip before I do what I've been wanting to do for the last five minutes and pull her down on top of me. She's straddling my hips, her knees bent, my body sandwiched between her legs. "There's no going back now, Reverie." I wait for her to protest, to back out, to tell me no. I've been told no more times in my life than I can count. What I want, I rarely get.

But she doesn't say no. She doesn't push me away, slide off me, nothing like that. She's smiling. She's touching me. Her hands feel good on my skin. Her breath is warm and sweet and drifts across my cheek as she speaks.

"I don't want to go back. Not if that means I can't have you in my life." She slowly grinds her body against mine, reminding me that she's almost naked while I'm completely clothed. "I'm falling in love with you," she whispers just before she kisses me. "I know you're probably not ready to say it to me yet but that's okay. I'm patient. I know you'll see that we belong together."

Her words slay me. I want to say those three words back to her so bad but I...can't. I feel like a wimp. I can't man up and tell her how I feel and it's the lamest thing ever. Why am I so scared? Why am I so afraid something shitty will happen between us and that we'll both end up fucked over completely?

If I ever did something to hurt her, I would never be able to forgive myself.

"You're killing me," I whisper against her lips before I devour them in a hungry, never ending kiss. She doesn't even hesitate, just returns my kiss with equal enthusiasm. I'm hard as a rock, my hands are touching her like I have no control of them and as I pull her down on the bed, her body spread over mine, my hands beneath her panties, gripping her ass, my fingers descending between her legs, I know.

I'm done for. The two of us are in this all the way.

All the fucking way.

Chapter
THIRTY-THREE

Dear Diary,

(August 1, 3:12 a.m.) I can't sleep. Nick left the house a half hour ago. I watched him walk across the lawn and down the driveway until I couldn't see him anymore. I made him text me when he got to his truck. I made him text me again when he got home. I called him as soon as I got the text, desperate to hear his voice, needing to tell him I love him.

But I chickened out on the love thing. I told him once already and he didn't say it in return. I'm sort of okay with that. I know he's not ready. Me, on the other hand...I thought my chest was going to burst wide open, I needed to tell him how I felt so badly. I'm glad I said it.

What happened tonight changes everything. My feelings for Nicholas Fairfield are even stronger now. I love him so much. I know every inch of his body and he knows mine. He took my virginity. We're connected now. No one can tear us apart.

No one.

I don't understand why he worries so much about not being

worthy of me. He acts like he's a criminal or something. So he's poor. So what? He works hard and has the kindest heart. He's so thoughtful. It sounds like his mother was a wonderful woman. She must've been, to raise a good boy like Nick. He's also so incredibly beautiful. His face. His hair. His eyes. Those lips. And his hands...I love the way he touches me. How careful he is with me. Almost as if he cherishes me and our time together.

He's perfect for me. Perfect.

But I know my parents won't agree. Daddy and Mama want only the best for me so their expectations are extremely high. It will be hard for any guy to meet their exacting standards, least of all the boy who worked for them all summer. A boy who is unsavory, at least according to Daddy and Mama. I still haven't figured out what exactly makes Nicholas so unsavory. Regardless, my parents won't understand why I like him. Why I want him to be mine.

He's already mine. They might not approve but I'll be eighteen in a year. Then I can do whatever I want. Be with whoever I want.

Maybe once they see how sweet Nick really is, they'll get it. They'll accept him. I can only hope they'll see how good he is to me because he is. He's the best thing to ever happen to me.

Ever.

I keep the little bottle of dreams on my nightstand so I can look at it every night before I go to sleep. I wish for good dreams, where Nick comes to me in them and he does, sometimes. And when I wake up in the morning, that bottle is the first thing I see.

I love what he made me, and what it represents. It's me and him and us together. If we believe enough in the dream, we can make it come true right? I'm a dreamer and so is he.

I'm just trying my best to live up to my name.

Chapter
THIRTY-FOUR

Panic: a sudden overwhelming fear
August 5th

THE shit had to hit the fan sometime right? We couldn't expect to keep on sneaking around and not get caught. It was always in the back of my mind, that her parents would find us kissing behind the stables. Whispering together on the far side of the house. Or worse... wrapped around each other, naked and in her bed in the middle of the night.

Yeah. That's the scenario that scared me the most. She's snuck me up into her room three times in the last five days. My girl is insatiable. She can't get enough and I feel the same because the moment I taste her lips I want more. I see a flash of skin and I want to strip her completely. I'm desperate to hear her tell me she needs me, even more desperate to watch her fall apart because of the way I touch her, kiss her...

I have never, ever felt like this.

Ever.

She wants to be with me all the time too. Not like I can play it cool and resist her. I'm just as eager. I see her and I start smiling. I hear her name and everything inside of me tenses up, anticipating her nearness. I hear her voice and a buzz starts under my skin, ready for her touch.

Not even Krista can ruin my buzz. We had that meeting she wanted the next day. The day after I had sex with Reverie for the first time. I was on such a love high that Krista's threats meant nothing. I told her to go ahead and tell the Hales everything. Hell, I practically dared her. Like they'd believe her. Like she could even figure out a way to get in contact with them. The girl is lazy. She has zero ambition. She yelled and made a big scene on my doorstep when I pushed her out but I shut the door on her. Acted like she didn't even exist.

That seemed to work.

Just because everything seems fine doesn't mean it is. There was an underlying tension bubbling in Hale House that we weren't even aware of at first. Reverie sensed it that one night when her parents came home after being out of town, but after that, she never noticed it again. That's because she was too wrapped up in me.

And I was too wrapped up in her.

"Something is going down and it's not good," Michael says to me in the middle of the afternoon when we're taking a break. We're sitting under a giant tree out on the property, guzzling water and trying to cool down. He'd mowed the lawn and I'd worked the weed eater along the fence line. There's a hell of a lot of lawn and fence line on the property so we were exhausted and hot. Early August is the hottest part of summer and after working out in it, we're drained of energy.

"What do you mean?" I finish off the last of my water and toss the empty bottle back into the open ice chest we like to bring with us.

"The Hales are acting weird. The reverend holes up in his office all day and all night. Valerie refused to get out of bed today. Heather says all she does is cry." Michael shrugs one shoulder. "It's weird."

"Huh. I haven't noticed." Because I'm too focused on my girl to worry about what's going on with anyone else. Michael and I don't see each other as much lately but he doesn't care because he's spending all his free time with Heather.

"Really? Have you talked with your girl Rev? You'd think she'd know what's up with her family quietly freaking out."

My body tenses. I don't like talking about Reverie with Michael even though he knows we're together. It's fairly obvious and I don't bother denying it. I want to trust him but the guy has a big mouth and

Reverie's already been burned by Heather once. He tells his girlfriend one thing too much and she'd probably go straight to Valerie. Then we'd be over. Finished. "She hasn't mentioned anything specific."

"So she feels the tension too."

I guess she did. We tried not to talk about her parents too much. "Yeah, but she has no idea what's going on. They don't tell her anything." I lean against the tree trunk and stare into the distance. What if it's something about us? About me and Reverie? Could they have found out about us sneaking around and seeing each other behind their backs? If that was the case, why haven't they fired my ass yet? Wouldn't that be the first thing they'd want to do, to get me away from their precious and now not-so-innocent daughter?

"I think it has something to do with the reverend's empire. The Flock of the Lambs or whatever they're called. I think the flock is rebelling dude. Or it's bleeding money and they're slowly going broke to the point that there'll be nothing but a bunch of little dead lambs everywhere," Michael says, his voice lowering. I can tell he's joking but his expression is so serious. He lives for this kind of shit though. He loves gossip of any kind. It's why him and Heather go so well together. She feeds him information and he enjoys every second of it.

"You really think they're going broke?" Concern makes me stare hard at that monstrosity known as Hale House in the near distance. It's fucking humongous and worth a fortune. And it's not even their regular home. It's only their vacation home. God knows what their other house is like. I know that they're surrounded by opulence and wealth. Reverie doesn't want for anything and neither does her brother. Valerie Hale is spoiled rotten. Reverend Hale wears a Rolex and a diamond pinky ring, which is cheesy as hell but whatever. These people are rolling in money and they have no problem letting others know it either.

"If his TV show isn't making any money and his other sources of income are drying up, sure. I know his congregation or whatever you want to call them send him donations all the time but that's not considered income. He can't touch any of that money." Michael reaches into the ice chest and pulls out an apple, sinking his teeth into it with a loud crack.

My appetite flees as I think of Reverie. What would she do if her parents lost all their money? She goes to some fancy all-girls high school. I bet the tuition for that place is a fortune. And her brother goes to a private college, drives a ridiculously expensive car and lives in his own place that I can only assume is funded by their parents.

"Good thing the summer season is almost over, right bro?" Michael continues, laughing when I send him a withering stare. "We can bail out of here with our paychecks and not worry too much. Though I'm gonna be pissed if I lose this gig next summer. I was planning for it to be my last one before I graduate for good and never come back here."

I can't even joke right now. All I can think of is Reverie and what she might know, which I'm going to assume is not much. I pull my cell phone out of the back pocket of my jeans and send her a quick text, my heart racing as I tap out every letter.

Are you all right?

I wait impatiently for her reply, thankful Michael isn't eager to get back to work. Considering it's hot as hell, the both of us are completely zapped of energy.

I'm okay. Just had an argument with my mom tho.

Frowning, I answer her.

What's going on? Why did you two argue?

"Texting your lover girl?" Michael asks in a sing song voice. He sounds fucking ridiculous and normally I would laugh but I'm not in the mood.

"Shut the hell up," I mutter as I wait for her answer.

"Sensitive much?" he taunts but I ignore him.

She's been a mess and I don't know why. She gets upset for no reason. She started yelling at me when I said I didn't want to go home early.

My heart drops when I see the last few words she typed.

"They want to leave early," I say out loud.

"Who? The Hales?" When I nod Michael continues. "Well, that's total bullshit. Who told you that?"

"Reverie," I murmur as I answer her text, my heart pounding so loud it causes a roaring in my ears.

Your parents want to go home early? How early?

"Damn it, I was counting on at least two more paychecks coming in. This is utter crap," Michael mutters.

They want to leave in the next few days. :)

Shit, shit, shit.

"Listen bro, I gotta go," I say, pushing up to my feet and brushing off the back of my jeans. I'm covered in dried bits of grass and smudges of dirt. I'm a sweaty mess and I still have two more hours on the clock before I can leave but fuck it.

I need to find Reverie.

"Where are you going? You need to tell me what's up, man." Michael stands as well, concern written all over his expressive face. He's losing something too if the Hales leave early. He counts on this summer job every year to help pay his college tuition. He's not a broke joke like me but his parents are standard middle class, hard working people. And Michael is just trying to do the expected thing and follow in their footsteps.

"I need to go talk to her and find out what's really going on." I turn to face Michael. "Heather's never mentioned anything like this? Not a word on leaving early?"

"No way." Michael shakes his head. "And I would be the first one she would tell too. At least I hope I would be. She's losing something too you know. This job is as important to her as it is to us. She's saving up all her pennies for college."

"It could be all talk. I don't know," I say. "Her parents' way of scaring her into thinking they're leaving?" But why would they do that unless they suspected we have something going on, and if they did suspect, then why not just fire my ass and be done with it?

"Who knows man? As soon as you find something out, will you let me know?" Michael runs a hand through his hair, sending bits of dried grass flying. "Now I'm nervous. I don't want this job to end early. I need every dollar I can make."

"I'll keep you posted, don't worry. Cover for me?" I ask as I start backing away from him.

"You know it. Text me when you find out anything."

"Will do." I say before I turn and break out into a run toward Hale House. My concern isn't about money though. Yeah, I need it. And I definitely didn't plan on having to find another job so soon, but I can suffer through that.

What I can't suffer through is losing Reverie too early. I'd been counting on seeing her through most of August. Spending time with her in her room, out at the beach, at her little clearing among the pine trees. Wherever we can meet, whatever bits of time together we can manage, I wanted. Needed. I just need her.

I'm in love with her. Just the thought of losing Reverie…I don't know what I'll do. This moment was coming, I've known it all along, but I didn't expect it to happen so fast.

Michael's right. Something is definitely going on with the Hales. I just wish I knew what the hell it was.

"Aren't you supposed to be working?" Reverie asks in a teasing voice as soon as she walks into the stables and sees me feeding one of the horses a carrot.

Relief floods me at how normal she's acting, how normal she looks. She's wearing those little denim shorts that turn me on like nothing else and a hot pink T-shirt, her hair in a sloppy bun on top of her head, wisps of blond hair falling around her face.

"I needed to see you." I go to her, draw her into my arms and just hold her close. Breathe her in. I don't try to kiss her. I just want to absorb her for a bit. "I don't want you to leave early," I murmur against her hair.

She clutches at my T-shirt, her face pressed against my chest. "I don't want to leave either. It's the second time Mama has mentioned it to me too. She sounded serious this time though," she says, her voice muffled. "She has a date planned out and everything."

"When?" Nerves eat at me as I anxiously wait for her answer.

"A week from today." She clutches me tighter and I hear her sniff. So help me God if she's crying… "We should've had at least another two weeks together if we were going by the normal schedule. I usually don't start school until the last week in August."

"So what happened? Why are you leaving early?" I ask, impressed I don't sound like a panicked loser because that's exactly how I feel.

"I don't know," she practically wails, shaking her head against my chest. "One day everything's fine and then the next, my mom is talking about shutting down the house and packing everything up. She won't talk to Daddy. They aren't speaking, but he hasn't come out of his office in days so that's no surprise. Something weird is going on. They're being so secretive."

I tug on the ends of her ponytail so she lifts her head, her luminous blue eyes meeting mine. "You don't think it's about us, do you?"

"No." She slowly shakes her head, her eyes going even wider. "I don't think so. Wouldn't they just confront us if they found out what we were doing?"

"Those are my thoughts, too."

A little sigh escapes her. "Evan came to me last night and asked if I knew what was going on. Even he's worried and my brother really doesn't worry about anything."

That is definitely a clue something is up. Evan usually doesn't hang around the house long enough to notice if anything's wrong. "Did he tell you anything that he might know?"

"He mentioned the television station and Daddy's show. I know ratings are down but my dad reassured us a while ago it was normal. But he hasn't been right since they came back from that meeting." She drops her gaze, chewing on her lower lip. "Maybe it's going to get cancelled. That would devastate him. This is his calling."

I've watched him a few times on TV and haven't been impressed. Nervous and kind of scared, most definitely. The man knows how to put the fear of God in a person, that's for sure. He's not that intimidating in real life though. Actually, the guy is pretty pleasant.

What's weird though, is that we rarely speak although I work directly for him. We've exchanged words a handful of times. And once I started messing around with Reverie, I tried to avoid him every chance I got.

"You need to talk to your mom," I suggest as I push her hair away from her face and tuck it behind her ear. "Find out what's really going on. You deserve to know what's happening."

"I know I do. I agree. But what if…" She presses her lips together for a second, like she's unsure she wants to say it. "What if I don't want to know what's going on?"

"You can't be kept in the dark forever," I say gently. "You deserve to know what's going on with your family, even if they want to hide it from you."

"You don't understand." She pulls out of my embrace, frustration and anger written all over her body. "You had this great relationship with your mom and she treated you like an adult. My parents aren't like that. They still treat me like the little girl I used to be. I bet my dad looks at me right now and sees the eight-year-old girl I once was. The one who wore the fancy dresses and always wanted to sing on his TV show. I really doubt he sees the woman I've become."

"Don't get ahead of yourself baby," I tease, but she shoots me a hardened glare.

"I'm being serious, Nick. Maybe I should tell my parents about us." She lifts her chin slightly, looking every inch the dignified princess despite her causal outfit. "What can they do? How can they stop us?"

Oh they can do plenty to stop us. The fact that I haven't told her about my past and the time I spent in jail is weighing on me big time. I'm a liar by omission. And that sucks. My secret is killing me and I need to come clean. I've needed to come clean for weeks. It's just so damn hard to tell her what I've done. What's happened to me and the kind of people I had to spend time with while I was locked up.

It doesn't matter that my friend lied and that's how we ended up in jail. It's the fact that I've been there in the first place that will horrify her. She won't see the injustice it of it all. How time was ripped away from me as I was forced to sit and stew and wait for a judge to decide my fate when I knew it all along.

All she'll see is that I've been arrested and that I spent months in jail. She's so good and sweet and would never do anything wrong. How can I expect her to understand? It's why I've been so afraid to tell her.

"No way can you tell them," I say, my voice stern. "That would be the worst thing ever."

"You know, I really don't think it would. I believe they'd appreciate my honesty." She grabs me and hugs me tight. "I'm sick of pretending we're not together. They won't hate you, Nick. They'll see all of your good qualities just like I do. They'll fall in love with you too."

I reluctantly put my arms around her when I really should be pushing her away and telling her she needs to listen to reason. "Reverie...look. There's something I—"

Michael bursts into the stables, his cheeks glowing red like he just ran a marathon and his expression panicked. "Dude, you need to get out here quick."

Reverie steps out of my embrace so fast it's like she was never there. "What's wrong?"

"Your little neighbor is here. The hot one." Michael waves a hand as he tries to come up with her name. "You know who I'm talking about. Umm...Krista!" He snaps his fingers. "She's outside."

Panic slams into my chest like a punch to my heart. "Krista's here? Where?'

"I found her at the front door, waiting for someone to appear. Thank Christ no one ever answers it. I asked if she was looking for you and she said not really but I somehow convinced her to come with me." He jerks his thumb toward the front door. "She's waiting for you."

My stomach drops like I'm in free fall and I swallow hard. I can hardly look at Reverie but I can feel her anger radiating off her in heavy waves. She doesn't like that Krista's here.

I don't like it either. Because I'm pretty damn sure I know the reason for her sudden appearance.

"I'll be right back." I look at her, see the way she's standing there with her arms crossed in front of her chest in a defensive pose, her back ramrod straight. Her expression is stoic but I see the pain and anger in her eyes.

"Why is she here?"

I glance at Michael who's still waiting for me. "Can you keep Krista occupied for me? Please? I'll be out in less than five, I promise."

"Dude, you better make it two. That chick is chomping at the bit to talk to one of the Hales." He sends me a pointed look before he exits the stables.

I turn back to Reverie, wanting to approach her, to comfort her, but I have a feeling she'd just push me away so I don't move. "I don't know why she's here," I lie, feeling like a complete jackass.

Reverie throws her hands up in the air. "Come on, Nick. Is she wanting to see me? So she can tell me all sorts of sordid little details about your past together?"

"No." I shake my head vehemently. "I think..." Shit. "I'm pretty sure she wants to tell your parents about us."

Reverie's mouth drops open. "How does she even know that we're together? Did you tell her?"

"No. She saw you come out of my apartment. Said she recognized you from when you were on your dad's show a long time ago. She used to watch it and always loved the dresses you wore. Crazy right?" I sound panicked. Maybe because I am panicked. I feel like all my worlds are colliding at once and I can't stop the wreck from happening.

The skeptical look on Reverie's face says it all. She doesn't believe me. "I don't want you talking to her."

"I have to, Reverie. I have to stop her. Do you want her to go to your parents and tell them about us? That you spent the night at my apartment?"

Reverie's eyes fill with horror. "That's why we should've told them in the first place," she whispers. "Then we wouldn't have to worry about this."

I go to her and grab her by the shoulders, pulling her in for a quick hug, but she fights against me. Something she's never done. I release her, my heart cracking at her rejection. "Let me talk to her and get her out of here. I'll come back and then we can talk. Okay?"

She lifts her chin, my stubborn, innocent princess. "I don't want you talking to her, Nick. I mean it."

"I don't have a choice! How else am I going to stop her? You know your parents would flip out if they found out what we've been doing."

We're both quiet for a moment, my mind racing with what I should say to Krista to get her to leave us alone. I'm sure Reverie is mulling over everything I just told her and she doesn't look too thrilled with it. But what can I do? I don't know how I'm going to make this work. How I'm going to keep everyone happy.

"She's just trying to get her claws back into you," Reverie finally says, her voice hushed but fierce. "This is some sort of excuse for her to see you again."

"I don't think so. More like she's doing this to get back at me for dumping her." I have no idea what Krista's intent is. She's pissed. I know that.

"Whatever." Reverie waves a dismissive hand. "I would really *prefer* if you didn't talk to her."

"I don't have a choice."

She sends me a pointed look. "We all have choices, Nick. You talk to her and well, you've made yours."

I'm incredulous. "You're going to break it off if I talk to Krista? I'm doing this to protect you. To protect us!"

"Really? To protect me?" The disappointment in her voice is clear. "Then you do what you feel is the right thing and I guess I'll see what happens." She turns her back to me and I have no choice but to go.

Reverie is leaving it all on me. I want to choose her. There is no other choice. But Krista...she's like playing with fire. You do it too much and you'll get burned.

Problem is Krista wants to set all of us on fire. I'm not her only target. So is Reverie.

And I will do whatever I have to in order to protect her.

Chapter
THIRTY-FIVE

Blackmail: to force or coerce into a particular action
August 5th

"**W**HAT are you doing here?" I grab hold of Krista by her upper arm and steer her around so we're both standing on the side of the stables farthest away from the house. She tries to get closer to me but I let go of her and step away. I'm not about to send her mixed signals. It's bad enough, how much this girl thinks we should still be together.

She sends me a smug smile, looking way too pleased with herself. "I'm making good on my promise. I told you I would come tell the Hales that their sweet, innocent daughter isn't quite as sweet and innocent as they think."

Her promise? More like making good on her threat. "Did you actually talk to them?" I'm worried that she might've. Maybe Michael was wrong and he hadn't caught her in time. Maybe Krista did get a chance to talk to the Hales and now they were looking for us. If that's the case?

Reverie and I are ruined.

"Not yet but I will," she says cheerily as she turns away from me. "I'm going on up to the house now. And you can't stop me either."

Michael had already left and I bet he was halfway to the house by now. It was up to me and me alone to stop her, not that I expected his help. I'm thankful he diverted her for me in the first place. I owe him big for that.

Krista was already headed toward the house, her steps determined though she kept looking over her shoulder, probably checking to see if I was following her.

"Come on, Krista," I plead but she shakes her head, increasing her pace.

Running after her, I grab hold of her arm again, making her stop from walking any further. She shoots imaginary daggers at me with her eyes as she glares at me. She's pissed. So am I. "I won't let you talk to them," I say quietly, trying to keep my temper under control. Last thing I need to do is show her I'm mad and make this worse.

"Who says you can stop me?" She jerks out of my grip with a huff. "I can do whatever the hell I want. I'm sick of you trying to tell me what to do. What do you know about my life? What I do day in and day out? You used me. You fuck me whenever it suits you and then you kick me out of your bed. You won't even kiss me when we do it! I really, really liked you Nick. Not that you cared."

I doubt she liked me. She was using me just like I used her. I refuse to let her make me feel bad for what happened between us. She wronged me first. "You can't tell them, Krista. I mean it. You'll ruin Reverie's life." She'll ruin my life too but this isn't about me. This is about the girl I love. The girl I'm desperate to protect. "Leave them out of this. What did Reverie ever do to you anyway?"

"She stole my boyfriend, that's what! You belonged to *me*, Nick. You and me. It's always been you and me. We're alike. And then this pretty, stuck up little girl has to come along and convince you that you're better than me. Suddenly you don't need me anymore now that you've got her to keep you happy. Well, you're not any better than anyone else. Trust me. You're just like us. Just because you fuck a rich girl doesn't mean you're automatically rich and perfect like her."

Her words sting because they're true. I've known this all along, that me and Krista are alike. That we're probably better suited for each other than Reverie and I could ever be. Reverie and I together don't really make sense.

But maybe that's what makes us work.

"Listen to me. I'll do anything to get you to keep my secret." I grab hold of Krista's shoulders and stare straight into her eyes. She blinks slowly in return, her expression full of shock. "Anything. I mean it. I'll pay you. Whatever you want. Just don't tell the Hales about Reverie and I. I could lose my job. Reverie could lose..." Everything.

Krista goes completely still as my words sink in. "I don't want money," she murmurs, her gaze intent on mine. "I just want you."

Of course. We all want what we can't have right? "I can't give what you want."

"Then I can't give you what *you* want."

I squeeze her shoulders tight, wishing I could shake her. Shake some sense into her crazy head. "What exactly do you want from me?" I ask hoarsely, releasing my hold on her.

"You. One more night with you, Nicky, just the two of us. Please?" She reaches out and scratches her fingernails down the length of my chest, her sharp nails catching on my T-shirt. "I could make it so good for you. You know I can. I know what you like. We're perfect together. You'll see."

"You said the same thing about you and David, that the two of you were perfect together. He told me," I remind her, trying to push down the surge of pain that comes over me every time I think of the two of them together. For all I know she's still fucking around with him. I haven't seen him since that one time he came by my place and that feels like an eternity ago.

I'm over what she did to me. I've moved on. I have Reverie and what I feel for her is a thousand times more than what Krista and I ever had. But it still hurts, the loss of David's friendship.

"David did us both wrong. You know it. He only cares about himself." She takes a step closer to me, her lips curving into a knowing smile. "I'll leave right now if you promise to meet me later tonight at my place. Say yes and I'll walk away from this house and never come back. You won't have to worry about me telling them anything. But you have to promise me that you're mine tonight. All. Mine."

My skin crawls at her words, at the look on her face, at the way she touches me. I don't want this girl. I can hardly stand having her hands on me. I blow out a harsh breath, hoping Reverie can forgive me for what I'm about to do. "What time?" I ask warily.

The smile turns triumphant. "Midnight. I'll come by your place at the witching hour. I'll cast my spell on you and you'll never want to leave me again. You won't need to. I'll keep you perfectly satisfied." She stands up on tiptoe and brushes her mouth against mine but I don't hardly move. I'm tempted to spit in her face, but of course that would ruin everything.

"Fine," I say through gritted teeth, my lips barely moving. I'm disgusted by what I'm doing but I have to protect Reverie. My life is already shit. I don't need to take her down with me.

"Perfect," she practically purrs. "Take me home?"

"How did you get out here?" I practically shove her away from me.

"I drove my dad's car." She shrugs, not even bothered that I pushed her away.

"Then drive it back. I'll see you tonight," I say dismissively.

She pouts. "You promise? Trust me, you don't show up and there will be hell to pay. I'll make up lies about your perfect little girlfriend and let her parents know. Tell them we had a threesome together. That you smacked her around some. Whatever I have to say, I'll say it. I have no shame."

Fuck. Why did I ever get involved with this girl? When did she turn into such a horrible creature? "I said I'll be there."

"Walk me to my dad's car?" She bats her eyelashes.

"You push me too far, Krista," I practically growl, which only makes her laugh.

But at least she leaves. I watch her walk away, my gaze narrowing as her retreating back gets smaller. And smaller. Dread makes me nauseous and I shove my hands in my pockets and hang my head, wondering what I can say to Reverie to make this better. To make her still believe in me.

To gain her forgiveness for what I'm about to do.

"I saw everything, you know."

I turn to find her standing not ten feet away from me, her arms still crossed in front of her chest. "Were you standing there the whole time?" Hell. Then she heard me agree to meet Krista and saw her kiss me.

"No. I was inside the stables. I watched through the window though." She strides toward me, her face determined, her hair flying out behind her. "I can't believe you kissed her!" She shoves me in the shoulder with a firm push of her hand and I go stumbling backwards, almost losing my footing.

"It was nothing," I yell back at her, throwing up my hands in defensive mode. "I swear. It meant absolutely nothing."

"You two certainly looked cozy. How am I supposed to believe you?" The hurt in her voice is unmistakable. I hate that I've done this to her. But I need her on my side, not working against me.

"Maybe you should believe me because you love me and supposedly trust me? But if that's not the case..." I let my voice trail off as I rub at my shoulder. The girl can pack a punch when she wants to. And my chest aches too. This is all falling apart and I don't know how to make it right.

"How can I trust you when you let that stupid slut hang all over you?" Reverie shoves me again but at least I was prepared for it this time and didn't almost fall on my ass. "Why do you let her control you? Who cares if she goes and talks to my parents? If we tell them now then she has nothing to use against us. We can beat her at her own game."

Either way I lose. I don't think Reverie realizes that yet. Or if she ever will. She may have secrets but I have more.

"Your parents won't approve of us, no matter how badly you want to believe they will," I say.

"I can't believe you have such little faith in me or my family." She shakes her head. "But I guess if you're willing to give up that easily, I shouldn't be surprised. I'm leaving in a week anyway. So go ahead. Go be with your slut and make stupid little babies who won't amount to anything. See if I care."

Low fucking blow. She's saying that to hurt me, and it works. "Better than being with a judgmental princess who thinks she's above me," I toss at her as she starts to walk away.

She whirls around to face me once again, her expression indignant, her body rigid. "I never, ever judged you, Nicholas. I fell in *love* with you. And now you're crapping all over it so you can go back to your stupid ex and screw around with her instead, supposedly to protect me? I won't let you use me too."

She's right. I can't argue with her. There's no point. "I fell in love with you too, you know," I admit, my voice so soft I can barely hear it. "Too late now though, huh?"

Again we stare at each other, the both of us seeming at a loss at what to say. I'm trying to come up with something, anything to keep her here with me a little bit longer but my mind is a blank. All I can worry about is her finding out about my jail time. About my best friend the liar. She already knows about my ex the slut. My shitty apartment. My shitty life. My dead mom. She doesn't need to deal with someone like me. She deserves more. Better.

She definitely deserves better than me.

"If you lack that much faith in me, in us, that we can stay together no matter if my parents find out or if the entire world finds out, then forget it. Forget this. Forget us," she finally says, her voice firm yet full of defeat. "I can't believe in this enough for the both of us. It's a team effort but you're not willing to play."

"You'll leave me no matter what," I say, my voice cracking, my heart breaking. "Whether now or later. This can't last. You know it."

She nods once, completely expressionless. I can't read her at all and usually she's an open book. "So you're giving up."

"Do I have a choice?"

"Oh, Nicholas." She sounds so wistful she makes me yearn. Yearn to take her in my arms and never, ever let her go. So we can face the consequences together. "You always have a choice. What's so sad is that you don't even see it." She walks up to me and kisses my cheek, her lips lingering as if she doesn't want to stop.

I close my eyes, savoring her scent, her mouth on my skin, her close proximity to me. I reach out and grip her elbow, holding her close for one last desperate moment, but she gently pulls out of my touch. Until she's over there and I'm over here and it's like she took a piece of me away with her and I'm left broken and alone.

Reverie may be standing in front of me still but I am completely and totally alone.

"I thought you were stronger than that," she whispers before she turns and walks away.

I thought I was stronger too. I guess I wasn't. But she is.

And as she leaves me, she never once looks back.

Chapter
THIRTY-SIX

Dear Diary,

(August 5th, 4:22 p.m.) My heart is breaking. Nicholas left me for his stupid slut girlfriend. I don't understand why. What did I do wrong? How could he go back to her? He's so afraid of my parents finding out we're together. I constantly reassure him that they'll approve of us as a couple. That what we're doing isn't wrong when it feels so right. But he won't listen. He doesn't believe me.

He doesn't believe in us.

I walked away from him before he could walk away from me. I knew I would fall completely apart if I let him walk first so I had to do it. Instead, I made it into my room before I crumpled. I've cried for a solid hour. I'm still crying. My vision is blurry from the tears. My chest hurts from all the sobbing. I have a headache that no medicine can fix. My heart hurts from Nick's rejection.

Is it wrong that I still want to go to him and ask him to change his mind? Is it wrong that I want to sneak out of here and go to his apartment? I don't think so. When the heart knows what it wants, it won't stop until it gets it. And what I want most of all is Nicholas

Fairfield.

Despite his rejection. Despite how easily he gave up on us, I still love him. I still want him. He said he loved me too. That was the first time he ever told me. As our world is falling apart around us, as he lets his ex put her hands all over him and then lets her kiss him, within minutes after that, he's telling me he loved me.

I didn't answer him. How could I? His words both filled my heart with joy and made it shrivel up in pain. I hate that he gave up so easily. I hate that he lets Krista control him that much. Why can't he stand up to her? What sort of control does she hold over him? What does she know that I don't know?

He has a secret. There's really no other reason for him to act like this. I need to find out what his secret is.

I must.

Chapter
THIRTY-SEVEN

Foreboding: to foretell or predict; be an omen of
August 5th (longest day ever)

IT started to rain around seven and it still hasn't let up two hours later. Which is fine really. The late summer rain fits my mood. Angry and relentless, it rages on with a violent wind, the air steamy. I throw open my living room window and listen to the rain fall outside. The occasional crack of thunder, the flash of lightning, I'm taking it all as a sign that everything is going to shit.

Because it is. Everything good in my life is slipping right out of my hands. I let Reverie walk away from me like she was nothing. I let Krista control me like I'm nothing. I agree to do whatever she wants because I'm scared that if my girl finds out the truth of what I've done, what kind of man I really am, she'll run. And I'd rather give in to Krista than face Reverie's parents. My employers.

I'm a coward.

Her words keep coming back to me. That she never judged me, she only fell in love with me. And she's right. She never passed judgment.

From the moment we locked eyes she's shown interest. She's been friendly and sweet. It didn't matter that I worked for her parents. It didn't matter that I'm broke and have nothing and have no plans on going to college and can't take her out in style. Hell, I couldn't even muster up a birthday present for her that was of any value.

But she didn't care. She accepted me openly. So why wouldn't she accept what happened to me openly too?

I don't know. I'll never know because I ruined everything.

Irritated, I go into the kitchen and grab the last beer out of my fridge. Michael brought over a twelve pack a few afternoons ago after we got off work and left the remainders there. I've been slowly drinking them ever since. I wish I had more. I'm desperate to drown my sorrows in this stupid cheap beer. I could probably drink an entire twelve pack and still not be drunk enough to forget what I did.

Cracking open the can, I chug the beer, forgetting my original plan to savor it. I grimace when I swallow, hating the pissy taste of the cheap brand that Michael loves. I glance at the clock on the microwave and see it's only a little after nine. I still have three hours before Krista shows up so she can supposedly seduce me and fuck me silly all night long.

The very last thing I want. I feel sick to my stomach just thinking about it. I don't know how I'm going to make it through this night. And once the night is over, then what? What happens next? Does she blackmail me again? And again and again and again until there's no point to it and we're back together? Co-existing in some warped relationship where she fucks around on the side, I fuck around on the side, but we're never truly free of each other?

Is that what I want for the rest of my life? Hell, I'm almost eighteen. Just imagining being with Krista like that indefinitely feels like some sort of life sentence, worse than jail.

And I have the right to say that since I've done time in one.

I finish the beer way too fast and decide I'm gonna hop in the shower when there's a knock on my door. I'm instantly wary of who it could be. Most likely it's Krista come to give me my torture extra early. Just what I need.

Not.

Without looking through the peephole, I undo the lock with a violent twist of my wrist and throw open the door, a snarl on my face as I prepare to yell at Krista for being too damn early.

But it's not Krista standing on my doorstep.

It's a shivering, soaked-with-rain Reverie.

"What…" I gape at her, hope making my heart light, my head dizzy. "What are you doing here?"

She tilts her head back, the expression on her face nothing short of triumphant. "I know your secret."

I blink at her. She looks crazy. Her hair is dark with rain and her clothes stick to her body, her T-shirt see-through and offering me a glimpse of her lacy, kill-me-now bra. She has on a pair of cotton shorts that cling to her thighs and all I want to do is strip her out of her too-wet clothes and take her into the shower with me. Where I can warm her up.

And show her how much I love her.

"How did you get here?"

"I had Evan drop me off about a mile away. I told him I was going to a friend's house. I didn't tell him who or where." She swipes wet strands of hair away from her face, but a few still stick to her cheeks. "Did you hear me? I know your secret, Nick. I know everything. About your time in jail. About your best friend saying you two killed that guy. How he lied. How you got out of jail and within two months your mom died."

"You walked a mile in the rain in this neighborhood?" Okay, I'm pissed. "You could've got jumped." Or worse. Way worse.

She shrugs. "I w-wanted to s-see you. And tell you that I know what happened to you and I don't care. Well, not that I don't care, because I can't believe you were put in jail for months for a crime you didn't commit. I-I c-can't imagine what your m-mom was th-thinking. How s-scared she m-must've b-been." Her teeth are chattering, she's so cold despite the humidity in the air.

I take her hand and drag her inside the apartment, shutting and locking the door behind her. Her scent fills my head, the dampness and heat from her skin making it even stronger, and without thought I touch her face. Skim my fingers across her cheek, down her nose, tracing her lips. "Why are you here?" I whisper. Despite her drowned appearance she's still the most beautiful girl I've ever seen. My heart feels lighter just having her stand in front of me.

"I already told you." She shoves at my chest but without much force. More like she's clinging to me. And I'm clinging to her. Because I can't believe this is real. That she's in my living room and that my arms are around her and her wet clothes are making me wet too, we're holding each other so close. "I knew you had a secret. Why else would you give Krista so much power? I started doing a few searches on the Internet and found out everything."

Everything. She knows *everything?* I start to register what she said before I yanked her inside…

"Yes. I know." She touches my face, just like I'm touching hers. "Did you really think I would hate you for what happened? You didn't *do* anything. These horrible things were done *to* you. There's a difference. A huge difference."

"I spent months in jail," I whisper. "No one would listen to me when I said I didn't do it. They all laughed at me. I had to defend myself from assholes every single day I was in there. I got into fights more than once." It was the scariest time of my life.

But being here now, knowing there's a chance Reverie could still walk away from me for good, is scarier.

"I don't care. It wasn't your fault, what happened to you. If I can see that, why can't you?" She shakes her head. "I love you, Nick. And I'm willing to fight for you. No matter what."

"Reverie." I bend my head and kiss her because I flat out cannot resist her. It's been hours since I touched her lips but it feels like days. Weeks. Years. "I gotta get you home. You can't be here with me alone."

"No," she says vehemently, shaking her head. "I don't want to go home. I want to stay here with you."

I take her in. The wet clothes, the way her teeth still occasionally chatter. "You should take a shower," I murmur, pushing her wet hair away from her forehead, noticing how chilled her skin is. I want to take care of her. Make sure she's warm and safe and in my arms. "So you can warm up."

"Will you take one with me?" she asks hopefully.

Closing my eyes, I lean into her, pressing my forehead against hers. "What are we doing?" I'm confused. She was so mad at me earlier and I can't blame her. But now she's here. Telling me she knows all about my past and it doesn't matter. I should've trusted her more. I should've had faith that she'd believe in me no matter what. I almost let her get away all because I was too blind to see that she loved me enough to stand by me even though my life is a mess.

I'm an idiot. A lucky-as-hell idiot whose been given another chance.

"We're making up after our second—and much bigger—fight," she murmurs as she nuzzles my cheek with her nose. I close my eyes and pull her in closer, holding her almost desperately. Like I never want to let her go.

Because I don't.

"Do your parents know where you are? That you're even gone?" I ask.

"Like they care. They're too wrapped up in their own problems," she says, making a little noise of disgust. "They know Evan and I left the house. He told them. And I told Evan I would text him when I got to my friend's house. Which I need to do now..."

I let go of her and she pulls her cell out of her shorts' pocket. She types a quick text and then sets her phone on my kitchen counter before she turns to look at me. "Can I take that shower now?"

"Yeah." I swallow hard as I drink her in. She's so pretty. So sweet and accepting and so goddamn perfect for me. Even though she'd deny it and get mad at me if I told her, I'm not worthy of her. Not by a long shot.

But that's fine. I'm not turning her away any longer. She somehow sees the good in me despite my best efforts to convince her otherwise.

"Will you join me?" She flashes me a shy smile.

"You really want me to?"

She rolls her eyes. "Duh. Of course."

Just like that, I know everything is going to be okay.

It has to be.

"I thought Krista was supposed to come see you tonight." Reverie tucks her head in the spot between my neck and my shoulder, her breath wafting across my skin as she lightly scratches my bare chest with her fingers. I'm feeling good. We took a shower together, we rolled around naked in my bed together, and then we talked. A lot. About what happened to me. I told her everything I could, answering her questions and filling in the gaps, confessing my sins so to speak, and I felt cleansed. Whole again. Like I've got nothing left to hide.

But I immediately tense at first mention of Krista's name. Crazy, but I completely forgot about her and our midnight meeting. "Yeah, I was." I glance at the clock. It's already past one in the morning. "She was supposed to be here at midnight."

Reverie pulls away slightly to lift up on one elbow, looking down at me. Her hair has long ago dried and it's extra wavy, flowing over her shoulder like a thick blond curtain. I sink my hand into the silky strands, letting it sift through my fingers and her eyelids lower to half mast. She likes it when I play with her hair. "I never heard a knock."

"I didn't either." Weird. Normally Krista would be making a scene. Kicking and cursing at the door, calling me all sorts of names until I finally answered. "Maybe the rain stopped her from coming over."

"I really doubt a little rain would stop her from seeing you," she says sarcastically. "Check your phone. See if she texted or called."

I do as Reverie suggests, checking my cell but there's nothing. No missed calls, no voicemail, no text messages. Not from anyone. "Nothing."

"Strange," she says softly as I settle back down into bed, pulling my comforter over us. She snuggles up close to me, her head a pleasant weight on my chest as I wrap my arm around her shoulders. "I was fully prepared to fight her for you."

"What?" I chuckle, her fierce words making me smile. "Are you serious?"

"Dead serious." She lifts her gaze to mine. "You belong to me. No way could I allow her to touch you."

I'm so overwhelmed with love for this girl I can hardly speak. "Revi..." I've never called her that before but the way she smiles when I say it, I know I'm going to start using that nickname frequently. Especially if I can earn another smile like the one she's flashing me right now. "You don't have to fight Krista for me. There's nothing to fight for. You already own me. I belong to no one else."

"And you own me," she says solemnly. "Nothing and no one can keep us apart, Nicholas. I mean it. I love you."

"I love you too." I bend my head at the exact moment she tilts hers up and our lips meet in a lingering kiss that turns hot. Deep. "I should probably get you home," I whisper when we break apart.

"No." She shakes her head, her hair catching on the stubble on my jaw. "Evan sent me a text saying he told our parents that we were at his friend's house spending the night. I thanked him for covering me."

"Where's he at really?"

"I don't know but he reassured me that everything's okay. And I believe him." She pauses, her gaze dropping from mine. "He knows about us…sort of."

"He does?" I can hardly believe it. "And he hasn't tried to stop you from seeing me?"

"He says it's my life to live. Evan may act like he doesn't care and fine, most of the time he doesn't, but he's never stopped me from doing what I want. He feels just as stifled by our lifestyle and the image we have to maintain as I do."

"You feel stifled?" I thought she liked being Reverend Hale's daughter.

"Why do you think I'm not on the TV show anymore? Though that was more Evan's doing. He was sick and tired of being paraded around like little perfect dolls. He didn't want to be an example of a good Christian son. He just wanted to live his life, you know?" She's stroking my chest again. I find her touching me incredibly distracting. As in, I'm going to attack her in the next few minutes if she doesn't stop kind of distracting.

"Do you still feel guilty about what we've done? What we've—shared?" I grab hold of her wrist to make her stop touching me but she doesn't. Instead, she curls her hand into mine, somehow interlinking our fingers together.

"No. We may have committed a sin according to the Bible for having sex before marriage but…" She clears her throat. "I love you. And I want to be with you. I don't think that's a sin, to become physical with the one person you care about more than anyone else. It's the purest form of expression if you ask me."

"You make what we've done sound almost poetic," I tease and she lifts her head to glare at me, though I know she's not really angry.

"It is. The way you touch me…what it feels like when you first—um, enter me." She stumbles over the words. "It almost brings tears to my eyes. I know I probably feel too much or whatever but I love it. I love *you.*"

I cup the back of her head and bring her mouth to mine once more. She's a complete romantic. She is the epitome of the fairy princess looking for her one true love coming to rescue her.

And I'm just the lucky son of a bitch she set her sights on. Somehow I'm the one who makes her happy. And that's all I want, for Reverie to be happy.

"I want to try and bring tears to your eyes again," I murmur against her seeking lips, making her smile. "You game?"

"Always," she whispers as I roll her over so she's beneath me. She wraps her legs around my hips, anchoring her body to mine. "Always…"

Chapter
THIRTY-EIGHT

Disaster: a calamitous event
August 6th

I CRACK open my eyes to find flashing lights. Red and blue appear again and again on my bedroom walls, as if going round and round. I squint against the darkness, against the continuous lights, and I know in an instant what it is.

Police cars.

Turning my head, I check out the old alarm clock on my nightstand, the numbers 4:03 glowing red. Reverie is snug against me, sleeping hard, her back to my front, her perfect and very naked butt firmly lodged against my dick. I can still hear the rain since I kept my bedroom window cracked open. It's lessened in intensity though still falling steadily.

And the red and blue lights keep flashing.

I try my best not to disturb her as I crawl out of bed and make my way to my window. Carefully I peel back the frayed curtain and stare at the parking lot. There are a couple of cop cars but only one with its lights on, though no siren blaring, thank Christ. Oh, and an ambulance is there too, its back doors spread open wide and a couple of paramedics pulling a gurney out of the back of it.

Someone's been hurt. I scratch my chest and watch, nearly jump a mile when I feel a gentle hand touch me in between my shoulder blades.

"What's going on?" Reverie asks quietly.

"I don't know," I say, never taking my eyes off the parking lot. "Couple of cop cars out there. And an ambulance. Maybe someone had a heart attack or something. Or they're responding to a domestic violence call." There have been plenty of those around here since we moved in. They're a pretty common occurrence.

"Do they make you nervous? The police?"

I can't lie, especially to her. "Yeah. I always worry they're coming for me," I confess.

She wraps her arms around me from behind, her hands settling low on my stomach. Just like that, everything within me comes alive at her touch. "I wish I could take away your worry," she whispers, kissing my shoulder.

Reverie does. Just being here with me. Holding me and saying all the right things, I feel lighter. More at ease.

Until I see Krista's dad being led to a police car, officers flanking either side of him and his hands behind his back. They must've arrested him. Or they're taking him into custody. But for what?

"That's Kirsta's dad," I say, moving closer to the window so Reverie has no choice but to let me go. "He looks like he's being arrested."

She moves to stand beside me and leans her head against my arm. "I wonder why?"

"I don't know. Maybe something happened between him and…" I don't need to finish what I was going to say. Reverie takes right over.

"Do you think he has something to do with Krista's not showing up here tonight?"

"I don't know." I shrug, unease making me twitchy. I don't like this. It doesn't look good. Where are those paramedics with their gurney? Who are they picking up? What happened? Not like I can bust out there and ask them questions. They'd all tell me to fuck off. Krista's dad would probably point an accusatory finger at me and make up some lie. He's just as bad as his daughter. That's where she learned all her best tricks.

The paramedics come back out pushing the gurney and there's someone on it.

In a fucking black body bag. As in, the person is dead.

I hear Reverie gasp at the same exact time I mumble a curse. I can only imagine what's going on, who that could be in the body bag. Without thought I move away from the window and go to my dresser, yanking out a pair of basketball shorts and putting them on. Reverie's asking me what I'm doing but I don't answer her.

I need to get out there and question them. I gotta know what happened. Because I can feel it in my bones it's not good. I know it.

"Where are you going?" Reverie asks for what feels like the hundredth time as I make my way to the front door. She trails me the entire way.

"I need to get out there and ask what's going on before they leave." The red and blue lights have stopped. No need to keep them going if there's no one to rescue. A dead body doesn't merit a wailing siren and the flashing lights, right? Hell, I have no idea.

"Nick. No." She grabs my hand, stopping me from reaching for the door. I turn to stare at her, looking sexy and tousled and only wearing my T-shirt. The panic on her face is unmistakable though. "You can't go out there. We'll find out what's going on in due time. You run out there and make a scene…you don't want them to suspect you."

"You think they would?" I ask incredulously. "Why, because I've been in jail before? So now I'm always a suspect when something happens around here?"

"No, of course not! If…if that's Krista in that body bag or whatever, then you're connected to her and they'll want to talk to you. She's your ex-girlfriend. An old friend. You make an appearance as they're arresting her father or whatever, and they'll take you away too." She grabs hold of me, hugging me to her like she's never going to let me go. "I'll be so scared if they take you away. Please don't leave me."

I'm torn. I don't want to leave her. But I want to know what happened to Krista. Despite everything, how angry I'd been with her, how much I loathed her in that moment out at the stables when she was trying her best to blackmail me and I caved like an idiot, I still care. I can't help it. I'm scared she's dead and I feel guilty about it.

She was supposed to meet me tonight. If that had happened, would she have been safe? Or is the reason she didn't come over at midnight that she was already hurt? Or…dead?

"Please, Nick," Reverie whispers, her voice pleading. "Stay with me. I'm begging you."

"Okay," I agree, nodding once. "I won't go out there."

Her relief is obvious. "Thank you." She sags against me, her hold tight. "I love you. No matter what just happened, we'll get through this."

My suspicions were true. We went back to bed but I couldn't really sleep. I tossed and turned, pulled Reverie close to me and held her tight. She slept fitfully and I woke her with kisses all over her body. I needed the distraction and only she could make me forget.

But it wasn't enough. I fell asleep afterward and dreamed of death. Of finding Krista on my kitchen floor, her eyes open wide and full of fear, blood everywhere. I woke with a jolt, sitting straight up and panting hard, my body coated with sweat. Reverie was right there next to me, murmuring soothing words, her arms around me, her lips on my skin.

When we finally got out of bed so I could get ready for work, Reverie went to the living room and turned on the local news. The lead breaking story was the suspicious strangling death of a teenage girl and her father being brought in for questioning. She was found on her front doorstep by a neighbor, who called the cops. They didn't name names but they didn't have to. Footage from earlier in the complex parking lot was shown during the news report.

It was Krista. And she was dead.

Gone.

Guilt washes over me, and settles like a heavy cloud. My heart hurts. My head hurts. I hated what she did to me, hated what the two of us had become to each other these last few months, but I sure as hell never once wished death on her. Not even in my darkest moments when I was so pissed at Krista I couldn't see straight.

"I'm so sorry," Reverie says, rubbing my arm as if that could soothe me. I can hardly feel her touch. I'm numb. In shock. "I-I didn't really like her or approve of what she did to you but no one should have to die at such a young age."

I have no answer for Reverie because what she said is true. No one should have to die at such a young age. But Krista did. She was freaking murdered. Someone *strangled* her.

Holy. Shit.

"Do you think her dad could've done that to her?"

"I don't know." I stare at the TV, not really hearing what they're saying. They've already moved on, talking cheerily about the weather. How this storm brought in some much needed rain to the west coast, though it was going to warm up again. An animated sun wearing black sunglasses flashes on the screen as they talk about today's high temperatures and I want to punch my fist in its too-happy face.

Someone fucking died and it's like no big deal. Let's move on. What the hell is wrong with people? Have we become so conditioned that we talk about death and great weather all in the same breath?

"Hey." Reverie's voice brings me out of my thoughts and back down to earth. "You going to take a shower before we leave?"

"I'm fine," I automatically say, though I'm not. Not even close. "I need some coffee."

She exhales loudly. "Me too. Let's leave in a few minutes and pick something up on the way there." She stands, looking determined to make this as normal a morning as possible. Too late. That's so not happening. "I'm going to get dressed." We threw her clothes in the dryer last night after we showered and they were still in there. One of the things Mom loved best about this apartment was that it came with its own washer and dryer…

Sadness bears down on me and I try to shake it off. First Mom and now Krista. In six months' time I lose two people close to me. Why? *Why?*

"Nick." Reverie shakes my shoulders. "I know this is tough. But you need to stay strong and make it through today. Okay?"

"Yeah. Okay," I say with a quick nod. Reverie backs away from me and I stand, going to my room so I can change into my work clothes. I move like a robot, methodically doing the same thing I've done for the last few months but everything's changed. Mom is gone and I've dealt with that. Somewhat. Now Krista is gone too. Reverie is in my house. She spent the night in my bed tangled up with me and we had sex multiple times while sometime out in the parking lot, someone killed Krista.

And now Reverie is riding out to her parents' house with me while I go to work. How we're going to sneak her in, I don't know, but we'll figure something out. We have to. No way am I going to get caught, not now. Though now would probably be the most likely time for us to get caught because I'm so damn distracted I'll likely fuck something up.

I just…I can't even think straight. I am in a serious state of shock. She distracts me though. Reverie. She rides right beside me in my truck and indicates with a wave of her hand that we should pull over at the local coffee place so I do. I wait in the truck while she goes inside and picks up our order, bringing me a giant coffee exactly how I like it, full of creamer and a little bit of sugar. I sip it gratefully, down almost half of it in about five minutes before I fire the truck back up and pull out of the parking lot.

"You okay?" Reverie asks, lacing her fingers with mine and resting our joined hands on my thigh.

"Yeah." Not really but I want to be, especially for Reverie. I can feel the slight tremble in her fingers and I know she's nervous about… everything. What happened to Krista, what's happening with us, what's happening with her family.

As I drive with the windows rolled down, the fresh air blows over us, smelling of last night's rain mixed with the scent of the ocean. The wind sends Reverie's hair scattering, wild strands crossing my face and I bat it away, making her giggle. That rare sound lifts my spirits and I focus on it. Focus on her. The way she fits so perfectly against my side, how good her hand feels in mine. I remember last night, the way she felt moving beneath me, her breath in my ear, my name falling from her lips when I made her come…

I chance a glance at her, overwhelmed at her beauty even though she's wearing yesterday's wrinkled clothes, no makeup on and her hair a mess. She catches me looking at her and she smiles shyly, leans over and drops a quick kiss on my lips. "Give yourself time," she says, her voice soft and full of so much understanding I wonder yet again how I got so damn lucky that this girl is mine. Because she is mine, we've established that and there's no going back. "Death is difficult to deal with. We all process in our own way."

"I feel like I've dealt with a lot of death lately," I say, choking up a little. I clear my throat, getting rid of the lump that formed there. I feel like a baby, wanting to cry. I need to look strong and prove I can take it like a man. It's not that I'm sad for Krista because I was in love with her or anything.

But I've known her for what feels like forever. It's terrible that she's gone. And if her dad had anything to do with it then that's fucked up times a thousand. Fucked up so bad, I can hardly wrap my head around it. I know her dad is an ass and they didn't have the best relationship, but for him to kill her? I just…

Can't imagine.

"You have. But you're strong. I know you can handle it. You've handled a lot already." She smiles at me. "And you have me by your side, so how can you go wrong?"

Her words are sweet, but are they one hundred percent true? Do I have her by my side? If her parents have their way, they'll be gone in less than a week. Back to Southern California while I'm here alone. With no one, not even Krista.

Not that she was a big help but shit. I literally have no one once Reverie leaves, once Michael goes back to college.

Pushing my gloomy thoughts aside, I concentrate on driving and soon we're turning into the Hale's driveway. I slow as we cruise down the graveled driveway, unease slipping down my spine like ice cold fingers. Something's not right. I can sense it. And when I see the police car sitting in the Hale's circular driveway, I know it.

Reverie releases my hand to grip my thigh. "Why are the police here?" Her voice is sharp and high. She sounds scared.

"I don't know," I say grimly, pulling into the little graveled lot and parking the truck before I turn to look at her. "Do you think your parents are looking for you?"

She glances at her cell phone, her thumbs flying as she starts scrolling. "I have no messages or texts. They think I'm with Evan. Remember?"

"Maybe they don't. Maybe they found out the truth, or maybe Evan ratted you out. They probably called the cops if they thought you were missing."

"Evan wouldn't tell on me. I know it," she murmurs as she lifts her head and stares at the house. "I really hope they're not freaking out." She moves away from me and goes to open the passenger side door. "I need to find out what's going on."

She's gone before I can say anything else. Before I can touch her, kiss her, let her know how I feel. I watch as she flies toward the house, her hair streaming out behind her as bright as the sun. My heart aches and I rub my chest, feeling like a lovesick idiot. This moment feels like it's imprinting itself on me. As if I better remember just how Reverie looks because I won't ever see her again.

Worry settles over me, familiar and draining all at once. I take my time locking my truck and walking toward the house. I don't see Michael's car but we're early so he's probably not here yet. I make my way up the driveway, squinting against the sun when I see the two police officers coming out of the house and headed straight toward me.

"You Nicholas Fairfield?" one of them asks.

I stand up straighter, ignoring the prickle of unease that settles between my shoulder blades. "Yes, sir."

The other one approaches, his dark gaze intense as he locks eyes with me. "We need to take you down to the station, son."

"Why?" I look around but don't see Reverie. She must still be in the house. Does this have to do with her not coming home last night? Am I gonna get charged with kidnapping or something? That's a federal offense. I could do serious time if the charges hold up.

Would her parents really do that to me?

"We want to ask you a few questions," the other cop says, his voice a little softer, his demeanor much more relaxed. I get what they're doing. I've been through this before. I know the local police are real big on the good cop versus bad cop tactic when they question people.

"About what?" I ask as the meaner one comes to grasp hold of my arm. I tear out of his hold and back away. "Am I being arrested?"

"No, no. Nothing like that." The good cop smiles. "We just need to talk to you. Find out where you were last night."

"I was at home." The minute the words leave me I regret them. I need to keep my lips shut. I learned that long ago.

"Uh huh. Well, you can tell us all about it when we get to the station." The mean one grabs my arm again and steers me towards the police car.

"What's this all about?" I ask again, hating how my voice shakes the slightest bit. I can't help it. Cops make me nervous. "And my truck's here. Can't I just follow you?"

"I'm sure the Hales won't mind if you leave your truck here," the nice cop says, all easygoing like nothing's wrong. But he's a liar. Something is definitely wrong.

"I didn't take her from here," I blurt out, unable to control my rising panic. My heart is beating so hard I feel like it's going to explode out of my chest. "She showed up at my place last night. She wanted to be with me."

"Who you talking about son?" The nice cop squints at me, his expression eager.

"Reverie Hale." I'm pointing out the obvious. Who else would I be talking about?

"This has nothing to do with Reverie Hale." The nice one frowns and glances at his partner, looking confused.

I'm confused too. "Then what is this about?" I ask. It dawns on me as soon as I ask the question and the mean-as-hell cop confirms my suspicions.

"It's about Krista Benson's murder. You know, your precious little girlfriend? She's *dead.*" The bad cop spits the words out like bullets and each one is a direct hit to my chest.

I rub at my chest again. My lungs are tight. I feel like I can't take a deep breath. They think I had something to do with her murder. Holy. Shit. "I didn't see her last night," I offer up weakly.

"You were supposed to meet her." They both have a hold on me now, each of them gripping my arms and walking me over to the police car. One of them opens the back door and shoves me inside and I sit sideways on the narrow seat, thankful at least they didn't put the cuffs on me.

"I didn't. I swear. You can ask..." My voice drifts and I glance out the tinted window of the backseat of the car. I don't see Reverie anywhere and relief floods me. She doesn't need to get drawn into this mess. I need to talk to her but I don't want to ruin her cover with her parents. If they knew she was with me last night there would be hell to pay.

But she's my only alibi.

"Who can we ask what? Were you with someone else last night? Now is the time to tell us."

I clamp my lips shut and blow out a frustrated exhale through my nose. I'm screwed. Fucked. This feels too familiar. I remember when the cops showed up at my apartment long ago, Mom ushering them in quick for fear the neighbors would see. Her fear is almost comical to remember now when I think of how they escorted me out of the apartment in handcuffs for everyone to see. And everyone did see.

My poor mom. It still hurts to think of the pain I must've put her through.

The detectives seemed to get some sort of sick thrill when they delivered the news to me so matter of fact. I sat facing them across a giant table, the room cold and nondescript, the grim glee in their voices when they spoke to me.

You killed a man with your best friend, Nick. Now tell us the truth.
Give us your side of the story. We know you did it.

They'd been wrong then. Just like they're wrong now.

"You not going to talk?" The kind one asks as he slips into the driver's seat, his gaze meeting mine in the rearview mirror.

Slowly I shake my head, keeping my lips shut.

"Fine. We'll talk at the station," the mean one states as the other starts up the car. "And let me just give you a warning. It's not looking so good for you, Fairfield. Your ex lying dead in front of her door the same night she was supposed to meet with you. We know you two were having problems and fighting all the time. Her dad gave us all the dirty details. Said you two were together."

I just bet he did. Made up a few lies too I'm sure. I swallow hard and turn my head to the side, watching as the car backs up close to the garage before the cop puts the car into drive and starts down the driveway.

Once again I'm going to pay for someone else's sins. And if it comes down to it, I *will* pay only to protect her. I'm not letting Reverie get involved in this. Someone killed Krista and it sure as hell wasn't me. Reverie could be in danger. Whatever happened, I need to put myself as far away from Reverie as possible. I'm doing this because I love her, not that she'd understand.

I'm toxic. Bad luck. No good. Just like I told her, time and again.

Getting arrested may be the only way I'll be able to stay away from her. She'll leave town soon with her family and go back to her normal life. She'll escape this mess untouched. I don't want her involved. I'll find another alibi. The cops have zero evidence. They can't prove I did it because I didn't.

And then I'll go on with my life. Without her.

No matter how much it hurts.

No matter how badly I'll miss her.

My everything.

My Reverie.

WANT TO KNOW WHAT HAPPENS TO NICK AND REVERIE?

Find out in the sequel
HER DESTINY
coming August 25th, 2014

Dear Reader,

Thank you so much for reading HIS REVERIE. I hope you enjoyed this first installment of Nick and Reverie's story as much as I enjoyed writing it. I've wanted to write a book that was mostly in the boy's point of view for a long time and I loved being in Nick's head.

If you have the time, I'd really appreciate it if you left a review on Amazon, Barnes & Noble, iBooks or Goodreads. Or you can send me an email to missmonicamurphy@gmail.com - I always do my best to answer all email and I love hearing from readers.

And don't fear (I know, I know, you probably want to smack me for that cliffhanger ending) - HIS DESTINY, the conclusion to Nick and Reverie's story, will be out August 25th!

Hugs,

Monica Murphy

Other Books by Monica Murphy

One Week Girlfriend Quartet
One Week Girlfriend (Book 1)
Second Chance Boyfriend (Book 2)
Three Broken Promises (Book 3)
Drew + Fable Forever (Book 3.5)
Four Years Later (Book 4)

Billionaire Bachelors Club
Crave (Book 1)
Torn (Book 2)
Savor (Book 3)
Intoxicated (Book 3.5)

Indulgent Pleasures
Owning Violet (Coming Soon)

About the Author

Monica Murphy is the New York Times and USA Today bestselling author of the One Week Girlfriend series. She writes new adult and contemporary romance for Bantam and Avon. She also writes romance as USA Today bestselling author Karen Erickson. A native Californian, she lives in the foothills below Yosemite.

Website: www.monicamurphyauthor.com
Facebook: www.facebook.com/MonicaMurphyAuthor
Twitter: www.twitter.com/MsMonicaMurphy
Email: missmonicamurphy@gmail.com

This paperback interior was designed and formatted by

www.emtippettsbookdesigns.com

Artisan interiors for discerning authors and publishers.